VOL. 4 2017

LUCKY NUMBER ELEVEN

ADRIANA LOCKE

Cover Design:
Kari March Designs

Photograph:
Adobe Stock

Editing:
Adept Edits

Interior Design & Formatting:
Type A Formatting

BOOKS BY
ADRIANA LOCKE

The Exception Series
The Exception
The Connection, a novella
The Perception
The Exception Series Box Set

The Landry Family Series
Sway
Swing
Switch
Swear
Swink

The Gibson Boys Series
Coming Soon!

Standalone Novels
Sacrifice
Wherever It Leads
Written in the Scars
Battle of the Sexes
Lucky Number Eleven
More Than I Could (coming 2017)

To Layla James. You're so incredibly loved.

And to Carleen. You're the best.

Exposé Top Story:
BEST MAKING HEADLINES

THE TEMPERATURE SKYROCKETED in Chicago this week and it had nothing to do with the weather. Our two favorite ballers went head-to-head (or should we say helmet-to-helmet?) on the practice field and there's video to prove it.

Sources tell us the (sweaty, aggressive, hot-as-hell) fight that got Branch "Lucky" Best, Finn Miller, and visiting Columbus quarterback Callum Worthington ejected from practice (you must see this video!) was not over a fumbled play. It was over nothing less than Layla James Miller, Finn's younger sister.

Does Layla's name sound familiar? It should. Until about five minutes ago, you could find her on Callum's well-formed arm . . . until he gave us whiplash showing up in Tahiti with the face of Ares Cosmetics, Carly Mathewson. But Callum and Layla aren't dating anymore, so where's the beef?

Give us a sec.

Layla James is now *scoring* with Blranch. Yeah. We'll give that a minute to sink in.

Word has it Finn isn't all that hyped about his sister *playing ball* with his (former?) best friend. Branch's playboy image is well-known and even better documented. A keyword search of his name on our site alone brings up thousands of hits of him with women and rarely are two the same.

The question remains: why does Callum care?

We'll have to wait and see. In the meantime, we'll be crying in our Rosé and hoping our favorite bromance gets back on track. (And, seriously, go watch that video!)

ONE
BRANCH

"THIS IS WHY YOU'RE HOT."

"Really?" I sit back, lifting a water bottle to my lips and smirk. My eyes don't leave hers. "I had no idea."

That's a lie. This look, the one that's currently melting her panties straight off her teeny little waist, has worked in my favor since I discovered it at the ripe old age of fourteen. Should it have worked on my math teacher? Probably not. But it did make acing algebra about a hundred times easier. I could use it then without even really knowing what I was doing. Now, with fifteen years of experience under my belt, I can play this look like a fiddle.

Fanning her face with a stack of index cards outlining the questions she's supposed to ask me for *Exposé Magazine*—something I don't even think she realizes she's doing—she blinks rapidly. "Tell me something no one knows about you."

I place the bottle on the little table beside me and shift in my seat. Her last question is the only question that is asked in every single interview I've ever done. Every last one. And they all think it's so original.

I used to humor reporters and give them something to print, but in the last couple of years, I've thought better of it. Maybe my self-promotion has gotten better. Maybe there's less to tell (since they already know so damn much). Or maybe I'm simply a little more cynical than I used to be. Either way, I loathe this question. It's like just because I'm a public figure they're entitled to every detail of my life.

"Branch," she gulps, her cheeks turning a shade of crimson, "my notes from this interview aren't going to be very . . . helpful."

"And why is that?"

She refuses to look at me.

"Let me see your notes," I say, reaching for the index cards.

"Um, no."

"Oh, come on," I tease. "What's on there?"

"Just . . . I need something substantial so I don't get fired." The slightly pouty lips, dipped chin is a look women give me all the time.

"Nice tactic."

"Tactic?"

"Yeah. You're appealing to my emotions."

"I don't know what else to appeal to."

Roaming my eyes down her face to the low-cut blouse that showcases a nice set of B-cups, I let them linger for a long couple of seconds before bringing them back to her eyes. I lift a brow. "I'm sure you have no idea other than appealing to my . . . *emotions*."

"Well . . ." Her gaze drops to the paper on her lap as she turns an even deeper shade of red.

"How many interviews have you done?"

"Total? Or sports?"

"Total."

"Five," she admits with a sigh. "I only got this one because the sports writer got meningitis."

"So you're here by default?" I ask, leaning forward. My arms resting on my knees, I clasp my hands in front of me.

"No. I'm here because I begged for the opportunity."

"To interview me?" I nudge.

"Something like that."

"Do you beg often?"

Her tongue darts across her lips, leaving a trail of wetness. "Only when necessary."

She tucks a strand of hair behind her ear. There's something about the gesture, a tinge of normalcy behind the overt sexiness, that makes me reconsider. As I try to talk myself out of giving in, I also wrack my brain for some fun fact that can help her save her job just in case she's not feeding me a load of shit like I suspect she is.

"I hate dogs."

Her eyes light up like a scoreboard. "You hate dogs?"

"I know, I know—this is a complete asshole thing to say. I get it. But the Blaney's Doberman left a lasting mark on more things than the back of my right thigh. For some people, it's clowns. For me, it's four-legged beasts. To each their own."

Her pen flurries across a legal pad, the sound reminiscent of Coach's dry erase marker on the whiteboard at practice. "What else do you hate?"

"Oh, no. I gave you one thing," I say, not falling into her trap.

"What do you love then?"

"My mama."

The door leading into the makeshift interview room opens. Finn Miller struts in, yanking a pair of sunglasses off his face. "Ready, Party Boy?" he grins.

"Yeah, I think we're done here." I look back at the reporter as she gulps. "Got what you need?"

"More or less," she says slowly, innuendo thick in her tone.

Finn chuckles beside me as I slide off the leather chair.

"Thank you, Branch. For everything," she says, her voice all breathy.

"Dear Lord, what did you give this one?" Finn asks.

"An exclusive," I joke, shoving my Legends hat backwards on my blond hair.

"Oh, that's what we're calling it these days?"

The reporter, whose name I didn't catch, clutches her notes to her chest. "Maybe we can all three do something together one day."

"That's called a threesome and I'm in," Finn deadpans.

Her mouth drops open. "I meant an interview!"

"Sure you did," he chuckles, holding the door open for me. "Let's go, Branch. Time's a-wastin'."

"Good luck with your column." Giving her a nod, I follow Finn into the deserted hallway.

There's a spring in his step that worries me a little as we make our way towards the elevators. Why I agreed to accompany him on a weekend getaway without actually getting details is beyond me. The last time I did this we ended up ice fishing in Michigan. Who does that?

"Where are we going again?" I ask, hoping he'll forget he didn't tell me and just spill it.

No such luck.

He punches the down button for the elevator and leans against the wall. "You'll love it. I promise."

By the cheesy grin on his face, I have doubts.

Two
Layla

"HOW YA DOING OVER THERE?" Poppy Quinn wrinkles her perfect button nose at me from the driver's seat. "That face isn't my favorite on you."

"Um, I only have one face."

"That would be incorrect," she says matter-of-factly, turning her gaze back to the winding road ahead. "You have a bunch of faces and that one, the one you're making right now, makes me feel like downing a shot of tequila."

"Everything makes you feel like downing a shot of tequila."

The scenery turned green at some point over the last hour, the grey-scale of Chicago washing away with the vividness of lush grasses and dense forests as we head south. I've taken this trek countless times to the little cabin my parents purchased on Lake Michigan when I was a baby. My older brother, Finn, and I spent every summer up here until we moved out and went to college.

Glancing at Poppy's furrowed brow, I sigh. "I'm fine. I promise."

"It was the song on the radio, wasn't it? You were fine until it came on."

"I *am* fine," I insist, sitting up a little taller in my seat. "I'm on my way to my favorite place in the world with my favorite person in the world," I say, laughing as she dramatically places a hand on her heart.

"That's so touching. Hits me right in the feels."

"What's there to be upset about?" I forge on. "Just that my ex-boyfriend is on a vacation to Tahiti, one that I was supposed to be on with him, that I *planned*, mind you. Instead, he's with Carly Mathewson, the model he's probably been cheating on me with. No biggie."

Fists clenched at my sides, I imagine Callum Worthington with that blonde bimbo in the perfect over-the-water bungalow that I picked out.

My feelings about him are all over the place. I had myself convinced I was in love with him, but I'm too *not* upset about not being with him anymore to have really loved him. My anger isn't even from losing him. It's from feeling like I was a little placeholder in his bed until he was ready to move a new body into my place.

The fact that she's a freaking model is just icing on the cake.

My mom says mistakes aren't mistakes unless you fail to learn from them. I definitely learned from this Callum ordeal—most of all that I'd be capable of setting my morality aside if the situation were right. I'd have no qualms about going all *Misery* on him if I could get away with it. My conscience is eased by the fact he'd probably like the attention. Second of all, I learned to trust my gut.

I was at a football game with a friend that interviewed players for a pseudo-sports blog. Callum and I started talking while she was finishing up with the coach, and when I looked up, it was a year later and he was telling me he didn't want to see me anymore.

My gut told me that day to stay away from him. I was turned off by how much he talked about himself and found some of the simplest things annoying. Still, his charm could be turned on and his gestures grand when he wanted them to be and it was enough for me to consider I was just being picky.

I should've been pickier.

"You know," I say, "I just wish I knew why."

"Why what?"

"Why he bothered to lead me along if I didn't matter . . . and I obviously didn't matter. Did he love me? Did he cheat on me with *everyone* I suspected?" Looking at Poppy over my shoulder, I shrug. "It just hurts my feelings."

"I'm going to try super hard to remember that I have to validate your feelings, even when they're stupid—"

"Really?"

"*Yes, really,*" she insists. "It's been three months and who the hell cares why he told you to leave? Just be glad he did."

"Yeah . . ."

"You can't seriously miss the dick."

"Oh, I do miss the dick," I say, tongue-in-cheek.

Her laugh floats through the car, her long, dark locks shining in the summer sunlight. "So he could deliver more than a well-timed pass, huh?"

"He was decent. Not the best, not the worst. I think he thought just being Callum Worthington gave him another couple of inches."

"I told you not to trust a quarterback," she reminds me. "You should listen to me more. I know things."

"And you knew he was no good just because he's a quarterback?"

"Yup. Think about it. Quarterbacks only release the ball. In the grand scheme of things, it's telling about their make-up."

"Oh, smart one, please tell me more."

"Let's backtrack," she says, making a circle pattern in the air with her finger. "You dated a kicker before Callum, right?"

"Yes."

"And you had to constantly bolster his confidence, right?"

"*Yes.*"

"That's because kickers have all the pressure. Ever heard of 'icing the kicker'?"

"How does this have to do with Callum?" I laugh.

"Quarterbacks don't take hits well and if they don't perform, they're traded for something better. *Plus,*" she continues, "they pass the ball. They don't hold on to it for long. It's a clear sign of commitment issues. Once they're in the pocket for too long, if you feel me, or feel too much pressure, they down the ball. Throw that thing at the ground if they have to."

"You're crazy," I giggle.

"I'm a thinker," she says, tapping her temple. "On that note, I don't think you should date more football players."

"You and Finn both."

"Me and Finn. I like the sound of that," she winks. Before I can reply, she hustles on. "If you're all *not* heartbroken, why are you hauling my city

ass to the country for the weekend? You know I don't do things like . . . *this*,"
she says with a wave towards the cornfields lining both sides of the road.

"I'm not heartbroken, but that doesn't mean I want to sit around
and think about being traded for a model. That bruises the 'ol ego a little,
you know?"

"Just tell Finn to put a bounty on him when they play Columbus."

"I think that's already done," I laugh. "He had a moving company
come get my stuff back to Chicago and the one guy told me my brother
said he had their bail money plus a bonus if they could get a fist in Callum's face."

"I love your brother."

I give her a look.

Poppy and my brother have definitely hooked up in the past. It's
usually for just a night, sometimes two, in the midst of a celebration.
They're both fun, kind of goofy, and two of the biggest flirts I know.
They're also two of my favorite people in the world. I think they could
be great for each other, with some work. While loyalty may be a strong
trait of both, monogamy is not.

"I don't like that face either," she grins. "It's judgey."

"Weren't you just telling me a minute ago how bad football players
are for my health?"

"No, I was telling you how bad kickers and quarterbacks are. I didn't
say a word about tight ends, and I think Finn Miller has one hell of a tight
end."

"Ew," I say, making a face. "That's my brother."

"That's one heck of a fine specimen whether he's your brother or
not—"

"There!" I spot the rusted blue gate that indicates the start of our
property and almost jump up and down in my seat. "Ooh! This is it!"

"Don't have a heart attack on me."

The gravel cracks under the weight of the SUV as we slip through
the gates and follow a narrow track up the hill.

"You'll love it up here," I gush, taking in the familiar surroundings.
"The lake is beautiful, and there are no neighbors for a mile or so any
direction. There's a little town not too far away where you can get the

best lemon cake ice cream anywhere."

"Sounds rad," she mutters.

"It *is* rad," I sigh happily. "I haven't been up here since Callum tossed me to the curb so he could move Carly in or whatever the hell he's doing, so just pretend to love it so I can be happy."

"That's what I'm here for. To make you happy."

"This is why I love you," I say, patting her on the shoulder.

With each roll of the tires, my problems drift a little further away and memories of my childhood roll in. Summers filled with flip-flops, hamburgers grilled on the back porch, s'mores, and lightning bugs come flittering back, making my cheeks ache.

The windows go down as butterflies scatter from the tall grass lining the driveway and the glistening water appears in front of us. It's the color of the sky before a storm—a deep, dark blue. Waves splash happily against the shoreline, and I close my eyes and just revel in being here.

Poppy pilots the car to the front of the house and shuts off the ignition. "Oh, this is gorgeous."

"It so is," I sigh, opening my eyes and pointing towards the lake. "Look at how peaceful the water is today."

"Uh, I was talking about *that . . .*"

THREE
LAYLA

"YOU'RE RIGHT, LAYLA. I'M GOING to *love* it here."

"Shut up," I hiss, trying desperately to take my eyes off the chiseled, sweaty man standing in the middle of my lawn next to my brother. "Who the hell is that?"

"That would be your hottie brother. And, damn, girl, he looks even better in the off-season when he's not quite so leaned out. That ass . . ."

"Not Finn," I groan, leaning forward to get a better glimpse as Mystery Man moves, the sun ricocheting off his drenched body. "Who is with him?"

"I don't know his name, but he looks like a damn good time."

They look our way and I slump back in my seat. "These windows are tinted, right?"

"If not, I'm fairly certain we aren't making a great impression," she laughs. "I'm assuming Finn isn't expecting us?"

My head bobs side-to-side as I watch Finn's friend. A pair of bright blue mesh shorts riding low on his hips, his thick, muscled body widening as my gaze travels up to his shoulders.

Finn says something to him that makes him throw the football he's holding towards my brother. He laughs, and although I can't hear the sound, it makes me smile too.

"You're fucked."

"Yes, please." Clearing my throat, I try to thrust my way back to reality. "Okay. Enough. We are all adults here."

"Which is why we need to stop gawking at their ridiculous bodies and imagining what their sweat tastes like and—"

"Really, Poppy?"

She laughs, picking her sunglasses up from the middle console. "You were thinking it."

"Here's the thing," I say, feeling some sense come back to me, "whoever that is was brought here by my brother. Between that and the way his body screams *athlete*, that means one thing."

"That his sex appeal is off the charts? Because I concur. If that man wants to give me babies, I'll take them."

I flip her a look. "It means that he's trouble. A football player. The kind of guy you just told me I need to stay away from."

"You do. Doesn't mean I do," she says, putting on her glasses and stepping out of the car.

"Damn you, Poppy." Heaving a deep breath, I open my door and step into the warm afternoon air. "Hey, Finn!"

My voice is a little wobblier than I'd prefer and my gaze a little too weighted on my sibling, but I can't look past him. My peripheral vision is catching enough movement to keep me feeling like I'm being swamped by the waves of Lake Michigan.

"What are you doing here?" Finn comes my way, his grin stretched ear-to-ear as he tosses the ball back to his friend. "I didn't know you were coming up."

"Last-minute decision," I say, tucking a strand of my sandy blonde hair behind my ear. "Didn't know you were headed this way either."

"Branch and I thought we'd get away for a few days before the pre-season starts." He looks away from me and his features darken just a bit. "Hey, Poppy Quinn."

"Hey, Finn Miller," she flirts. "Good to see you."

"I don't know how it gets any better than seeing you."

"Always a charmer," she smiles. "So, this is Branch Best, huh?"

"That's me."

His voice is more Southern than I expected, which only adds another cinder block to my already sinking mental capacity. The honeyed twang that's just barely detectable is enough to make my knees threaten to give out.

His eyes fall on mine, the pools of blue twinkling in the light. The corners of his lips tug up into a sexy, playful grin. One thickly-veined arm extends in front of Finn as he reaches towards me. "I'm Branch Best. And you are?"

"My sister," Finn warns, knocking his hand away. "No touching, Best."

"It's a handshake!"

"It starts with a handshake with you," Finn explains. "Or a spilled drink. Or an exchange of insurance information . . ."

"She ran into me."

"Maybe to start. But I'm pretty sure I walked in on you running right into her."

Poppy and I laugh as Branch sticks a football in Finn's stomach, making him bend over long enough for Branch to extend a hand to me again and flip me the most adorable smile I've ever seen. "Branch Best. It's a pleasure to meet you."

Before I can think twice, I slip my palm into his. On contact, I jump and instinctively pull away, but he clasps down onto my hand with his large, calloused fingers. He grins again. "Do you have a name, Finn's sister?"

"Layla. Layla James," I say. Gulping a breath to steady myself from the warmth radiating off him, I get a lungful of . . . *sex*. Or that's what it screams at Defcon One to my brain, anyway. It's a scent that pulls me towards him, makes me want to climb his slippery, impressive body like a tree. "Nice to meet you," I say, still sorting the heated, spiced scent through my senses.

He does me a giant favor and releases my hand. "Are you guys staying here this weekend?"

"We were going to," I say, looking at Finn. "Are you?"

"Yeah."

"It'll be one giant sleepover," Branch winks, getting an elbow in the side from my brother.

"One question," Poppy interjects, looking at Branch. "What position are you?"

"I typically like the bottom so I can watch—oomph," he says, getting another elbow from Finn. "Wide receiver. Why?"

Looking at Poppy, I can't help but laugh as her eyes light up.

"You got a problem with wide receivers?" Branch asks.

"You do," Finn interjects, giving me a narrowed glare. "They aren't any better than quarterbacks."

Branch looks from me, to Finn, and back to me. "Why do we not like quarterbacks?"

"My sister was dating Callum Worthington."

"No shit?" His face puckers like he just bit into a lemon. "How in the hell did that cocksucker end up with you?"

"He didn't. We're not together anymore."

Branch's eyes heat, the look causing my pulse to quicken. "I'm not a bit sorry to hear that."

"You better forget you heard any of that," Finn warns. "This is my sister, Branch. Not a cheerleader or reporter or some chick from a dating app. Got it?"

"Finn, relax," I say, shoving a swallow past the lump in my throat. "I appreciate the big brother spiel, but I can handle myself."

"I know you can," he says, pulling his gaze away from Branch. "But you can't handle him."

FOUR
BRANCH

"HEY, YOU ABOUT READY TO head into town and raise some hell?" Finn asks from the doorway. "There's a little bar downtown or a bigger one a few miles the other way. Your call."

Pulling my gaze from the window, I look at my friend. "Small town girls are more fun. Let's start there and work our way through."

Finn laughs and disappears around the corner. "Give me twenty. Just going to jump in the shower."

Swiping the cross necklace my grandmother gave me when I graduated high school, I put it on. It rested in a shoe box up until a couple of years ago when I found it looking for something else. It's made up of these little wooden beads with red shiny ones sprinkled in, and more days than not, it hangs around my neck.

It's an odd choice for me. My only adornments typically include a gold watch—the first expensive thing I purchased after I signed my contract, the smirk I got from my dad that both gets me in and out of trouble, and a tattoo that spells my last name running down my right forearm. Jewelry really isn't my thing, yet this little trinket has somehow become some sort of security blanket. I just feel better, more grounded, more *me*, when I have it on.

Twisting the beads between my fingers, the house is quiet as I head down the hallway towards the kitchen for a glass of lemonade. Wooden beams loom overhead, the staircase flooded with the final rays of sun filtering through the stained glass window. I hit the landing and turn the corner and stop just short of my target.

Layla stands at the kitchen counter in a pair of grey cotton shorts and a white tank top. I haven't seen her since the little meet-and-greet in the front yard a couple of hours ago. She and her friend disappeared to the lake while Finn corralled me back to the house for a game of pool and away from any shot at seeing his sister.

She tucks a piece of hair that's fallen from her ponytail behind her ear as she examines a slew of things that appear to have spilled from a bag sitting askew on the black marble worktop. I can't take my eyes off her. It was hard enough to act normal earlier today with Finn standing by my side, but now he's not here.

I stand in the doorway like a fucking stalker and gawk at this woman who's made me feel like a damn bloodhound since she stepped out of the car.

She's positively gorgeous in the most unassuming way and has an energy that just makes me want to be near her. I find myself wanting to hear her voice, searching for her laugh, looking to see where she is . . . and it's so annoying.

Her brows tug together, a cascade of lines forming across her creamy skin. My fingers itch to run along the ridges, smoothing them out, feeling the softness of her skin beneath mine.

Instead, they go to my cock and attempt, in vain, to smooth *it* out. The movement catches her attention and she shoots upright.

"Branch!" she exclaims, a hand going to the base of her throat. "I didn't hear you come in."

"How do you think I got the Most Valuable Player title last year?" I wink. "I'm quick."

A smile plays coyly on her lips. "Noted."

Our gazes lock together somewhere over the marble island separating us as her innuendo becomes apparent. It's all I can do not to think about her body beneath mine, my palms memorizing the curve of her hip, the bow of the small of her back.

"I'm also very good with my hands," I add.

"So I see." She tries to hide her grin as she brushes her line of sight down my body and to my hand resting on my now throbbing cock, then back to my face.

A smile tugs at my lips as she laughs, a soft, unpretentious giggle. "That's not helping anything, Sunshine."

I stride across the kitchen, looking around as discreetly as I can and am relieved that I don't see Poppy. A little one-on-one with this girl is the perfect way to kick start a weekend to remember.

Taking a seat across the island from Layla, every effort is made not to pant at the sight of her ample tits filling out her skintight shirt.

"Sunshine?" she asks, leaning against the counter.

"Your hair," I say, working on a whim. "It reminds me of the sun."

"My hair is a dirty dishwater blonde. Not so sunny."

"But there are blonder streaks," I say, feeling my cheeks heat. "Anyway, what are you doing? You have a little bit of everything here."

Sorting through the various items, I hope my attempt at distraction works. "Sunglasses, lip stuff, medicine, a tampon," I say, holding up the slender package.

She rips it out of my hands. "Give me that."

"Words every man wants to hear," I crack, watching the apples of her cheeks turn a couple of shades red. "I've had two interactions with you so far and you've been feisty in both. I'm guessing this is a thing with you."

"Apparently."

"I like it."

She flips her gaze back to me. This time it's softer, a bit of hesitation in her golden eyes. "It's gotten me in trouble a time or two in my life."

"Trouble's not a bad thing, you know."

"Said from the man who won Best Baller Bad Boy from *Exposé Magazine* a couple of months ago," she laughs.

"Ah, so you do know who I am," I tease. "I was afraid there for a minute."

"I bet you were terrified." She lifts a wallet off the counter and plucks up a small, circular tin. "Found it!"

"What is it?"

"It's lip balm, but not just any lip balm," she says, opening the lid. "It's the best honey-based balm in the universe and I thought I'd lost it."

She slides a finger along the top of the container, and then, like a vixen I didn't quite have her pegged to be, rolls it along her bottom lip.

"That's not helping either," I groan, my hand going to my lap. "I tell you what—your brother has you all wrong."

Smacking her lips together, the sound echoing around the room, she tosses the tin down again. "How's that?"

"What? Your lips? They're fucking amazing."

"No," she laughs. "How does my brother have me all wrong?"

"He talks about you like you're this harmless, helpless little thing. I'd venture to say you're neither."

"I'd venture to say you're right."

I sift through the mess in front of me again, wondering what else there is to know about Ms. Layla James Miller. Spotting a business card propped against a hairbrush, I pick it up.

"Give me that," she says, reaching for it.

There's a level of panic in her voice that only makes me more curious. Leaning back in the seat, I bring the off-white card to my face. "Logan Curie, Sex Therapist."

I almost drop the damn card.

"Give me that, Branch."

I don't. I look at it again. The words have not changed.

There's a streak of alarm hidden just below the surface of her lit-up eyes and high cheekbones that prickles something in my chest. There are a million questions on the tip of my tongue and a million-plus-one offers I'm willing to make to cure whatever ails may have her seeing a sex therapist. But there's something in the horror she's trying to hide that keeps me from it.

I hand her the card.

"Go ahead," she says, refusing to look at me as she shuffles the discarded items back into an oversized yellow bag. "Ask."

"I have nothing to ask."

"Yes, you do," she snorts. "Just do it so we can move on."

"You don't have to tell me anything," I say, grabbing a couple of almonds out of a dish in front of me and popping them into my mouth.

A hefty sigh passes those lips I want to lick as she hangs her head. "We're going to be here all weekend. I don't want to look at you and see the questions in your eyes every time, okay? Just ask me and let's get this over with."

Contemplating if she'd actually answer as to why she has a sex ther-apist's card in her purse and if I really want to put her on the spot, I toss another almond into my mouth and grin. "Fine. You're right. Layla, do you need help getting off?"

I bite the inside of my cheek to keep from laughing as I watch her head snap up. Her eyes widen as her mouth hangs open.

"Fuck you," she says on a laugh.

"Yes, please." Pausing to give her a moment to recoup, I lean back in my chair. "I'm kidding. Wait. No, I'm not. I'd totally bend you over this counter in a half a second if I thought that's what you wanted and Finn wouldn't walk in and castrate me. But, being that I'm only ninety-eight percent sure that's what you want and a solid hundred-percent sure Finn would remove my balls, I am only playing."

"Ninety-eight, huh?"

"Fine. Ninety-nine," I grin.

"You're all the same," she scoffs, placing both hands on the counter. "You think I'm a guaranteed thing because people wear your name on the back of their jerseys."

"Ah, come on, Layla. You know you want me," I tease. "It's okay to admit it."

"You flirted. I smiled. That's hardly asking you to put your cock in me."

Those words shoot fire through my veins, a charge that lands be-tween my legs. If it fazes her, she doesn't let on. She stands all sweet and innocent, taking in my reaction.

My equilibrium is thrown off, my head spinning a little faster than I care to admit—much faster than I care for her to know.

"You think that was flirting? You ain't seen nothing yet."

"So that wasn't flirting? What was it then?"

"I was just trying to do you a favor," I say with a shrug.

She laughs. "Oh, you were, were you?"

"You were what?" Finn's voice rings from the doorway, announcing his arrival.

My shoulders slump, irritation scratching my nerves as I sense him coming up next to me. "I was offering to help your sister with a few things this weekend."

"You're not helping her with shit, you jack hole."

"I'm an expert in the field she needs help with," I goad, looking at Layla out of the corner of my eye. "Just trying to be a nice guy."

"There's nothing nice about you," Finn jokes. "Now come on. There are plenty of women down at Crave who would love for you to show them your expertise tonight."

Standing up, I keep one eye on Layla. Her brother's comments have washed away some of the playfulness from her features and I'd give my left nut to get it back somehow. Opening my mouth, I close it again when Finn begins to talk.

"Heading down to the bar for a few," Finn tells his sister. "Call me if you need anything."

"Be careful. Don't do anything stupid."

"It's Linton," he laughs. "If I do, I'll call the Sherriff. The last time it just took two autographed pictures and a couple of passes to a game."

She looks at me. Her eyes are electric, moving with so many things I'd like to ask her about, but can't. Not right now. "Have fun," she says, throwing her bag over her shoulder. "I'm going to find Poppy and take a nap."

Finn heads to the door and I follow. Before I turn the corner, I stop. "Offer stands, Sunshine."

With a wink that brings back some of the lightness to her beautiful face, I follow her brother out the door.

FIVE
BRANCH

"SHE'S *SO* GROSS." THE GIRL on my lap points at a female with her tongue down Finn's throat a table away. Despite the dim lighting of Crave and the packed house, Finn's current entertainment is putting on a performance for the ages. "You can see her ass cheeks out the bottom of her skirt."

"You can't sell it if you don't advertise." I take another slug of the beer I've been nursing for the last hour. Setting the bottle down, I take in her lifted, colored-in brow. "She shows ass. You show tits. What's the difference?"

"The difference is I'm not a whore," she says with a hint of superiority that irks me.

"You might want to be careful with that."

She twists her lips together, considering if I am insinuating that her following me into the john, locking the door, dropping to her knees, and giving me head like a porn star—all without even giving me her name—constitutes a whore in my book. I let her ponder that.

"I only offered that because it was you, Branch Best."

"And maybe she's only tongue-fucking him because he's Finn Miller," I volley back, watching my best friend almost fall out of his chair. "A very, very drunk Finn Miller. Up you go."

We get to our feet, and I turn to the group of people that have congregated around Finn and I. They're all pretty much sloshed, thanks to Finn's open tab, friendly spirit, and recent signing bonus for a contract extension.

LUCKY NUMBER ELEVEN 23

"See y'all next time I'm in town," I tell them. "Don't burn the place down."

"Can I get one more picture?" Peck, a guy I've taken a handful of photos with tonight stands, his cell phone in hand.

"No more pictures," the bartender says, coming around the end of the bar. He gives me a knowing look. "Peck, watch the bar for me for a minute, will ya?"

Peck nods and meanders to the backside of the counter, giving me a nod of his hat as he takes an order.

"You're trusting him back there?" I laugh.

"He's harmless. Known him since I was a baby." He extends a hand and we shake. "Name's Machlan Gibson. Nice to meet ya."

"Thanks for letting us crash your bar," I laugh, watching Finn straight hit the floor. The crowd around us bursts into laughter. "I gotta get him out of here before this shit ends up online."

"Hey!" Machlan booms. Instantly, the crowd quiets down. "Nobody's gonna be posting any of this online or you're banned for life and I'll tell your mama all the sordid things I know about you. Got it?" Once he's made eye contact with half his patrons, he turns back to me. "Now let's get him out of here before Peck gets heavy-handed with the whiskey and all hell breaks loose."

It takes the two of us to get Finn's six-seven ass to his feet and strapped into the passenger's side of my black Rover. The crowd surprises me by staying inside on Machlan's command and giving us some room.

"Hey, thanks again, Machlan," I say as the window rolls down and I get settled into the driver's seat. "Shit. I forgot to pay the tab."

"Don't worry about it. Finn will get even with me."

"You do realize he probably owes you a few hundred, right?"

"He'll be in and settle up. I've known the Millers most of my life." He shakes my hand again and turns back to the bar. "Thanks for coming in tonight."

Flicking on the ignition, the lights come to life. I pull down the small road with the town's only two streetlights to the stop sign at the "T" at the end of the road.

Finn snores beside me, drool coming out of the side of his mouth.

Laughing, I swing a left, and within seconds, it's nothing but unlit countryside.

"What are you laughing at, asshole?" Finn mutters, not bothering to open his eyes.

"You have slobber all over your cheek."

"It's a part of the process. It's how you still know you're alive. You can feel the spit." One eye fights to open. "You're sober, right?"

"I'm driving, aren't I?"

He lets his lid drop closed as he snuggles into the leather seat. "I like it here."

"You're more than welcome to sleep in my car, but don't get your spit all over the place. I have limits, man."

"I mean, here. In Linton. At the cabin."

"You just liked the way that girl fondled you," I chuckle.

"I did. Not gonna lie. But I also like just being with normal people for a change."

"Maybe you're just drunk as hell."

Maybe not, too. There's a feeling up here that I can't quite put my finger on. It reminds me of being home, back in Tennessee, a place I haven't visited in a long damn time. The quiet, the way the night actually gets so dark the stars look like little silver lights in the sky, the way the people shake your hand and ask you how you are and then actually wait for your response. They're all things I'd almost forgotten about. I'd stopped expecting them and now that I've witnessed them after all these years, I realize how much I like them.

"Do you ever miss just being a normal person?" Finn asks, as if he's reading my mind.

"I've always been exceptional, so I have no idea what you're talking about."

He acts like he didn't hear me. "I'm not saying I don't enjoy an easy lay, because God knows I do. But do you remember a point when it wasn't just laid out there for you because you're on the starting line-up for the Legends? You know, when you had to actually work for it?"

"Yeah," I say, forcing a swallow that burns all the way down. "The ones smart enough to make you work for it are smart enough to stay the hell away."

"If I ever settle down, I want to be sure she's with me because she wants a life with me. Not because the first ten choices didn't."

Finn moans on, blubbering in his drunken stupor while my mind twists with a few things it's been toying with lately. Like, how I am nearing thirty and have an excessively large bank account, but little else to show for myself.

When I was drafted, I thought the contract and endorsements and money were everything. I didn't see the shady side of things, the parts that are downright disturbing. Despite my college coach's advice to "find balance," I didn't and now I live this life I've started to feel is very lopsided, and I have no idea how to find the happy medium of fame and normalcy.

Finn laughs as I pull the car next to Poppy's. Turning off the headlights, I spy a candle flickering on the screened-in porch. My pulse quickens as I wonder if Layla's out there.

"All of this is the alcohol talking," Finn chuckles. "I kinda wax poetic when I drink whiskey."

"Yeah, I know. It's a fucking truth serum for you."

"I need a serum that will magically plant me in my bed," he groans.

"Can you walk? You're a big motherfucker to carry in by myself."

"I'd pay to see that," he says, struggling to sit up. "Can I do it without puking? That's the real question."

Climbing out of the car, I make my way around the front and help him out of his seat. He makes it to the house okay, but stops at the front door to vomit in the hedges.

"You are one nasty motherfucker," I laugh, opening the door as he walks in. "How much did you drink?"

"Too much." He grips the handrail leading upstairs and wobbles his way to the landing. "Did you pay Mach?"

"Nope. You'll need to settle that tomorrow."

"I don't even want to know what that looks like." He stumbles into his room at the end of the hall and falls face-first into the blankets. He's snoring before his dangling feet stop moving.

Turning to go, I stop in my tracks at the sight before me. Layla is standing just inches away. Her straight hair hangs loose over her narrow shoulders, her body's curves on full display in the clingy white one-piece shorts and tee-shirt thing she has on.

"I can smell the liquor from here," she says, waving her hand back and forth in front of her face as she peers around the corner at Finn. "He's in one piece. I'll call Machlan and let him know."

A niggle of jealousy fires away. "You know Machlan?"

"Of course." She pulls the door closed and then stands with her hands on her hips. "Crave is our favorite place. They have great hamburgers and sometimes, if Peck is in a good mood, the best steaks you've ever had."

"I make a good steak. How do you like it?"

"Well done." She walks by me, the scent of pineapples trailing behind her. She doesn't look over her shoulder to see if I follow, and while I'm sure I seem like a lost puppy, I do, indeed follow.

"Well done isn't even steak anymore," I contend, a couple of steps behind her. "It's overpriced hamburger at that point."

"So you probably don't agree with dipping it in ketchup either?"

I just look at her, making her laugh. She flips on the lights in the kitchen and retrieves a bottle of red wine from the fridge.

"I did a whole piece on dipping sauces on my blog," she says, bottle in hand. "I tried a Chimichurri, an ancho-chile-almond sauce, this fruit one that had plums and cherries that was supposed to be out of this world." She wrinkles her nose. "Turns out, I just like ketchup."

"I just like that you've thought so much about it," I chuckle.

"I'm not a normal girl. You hear men complain all the time about their girlfriend not knowing what they want for dinner. Look, I knew what I wanted for dinner at lunchtime because I've been thinking about it since then."

Her face has been stripped of makeup, a set of diamond stud earrings shine from her earlobes. She looks fresh, clean, so natural. My chest tingles like I've just taken a shot of Jager, and I haven't had any damn Jager all night.

She bends over and picks up a napkin off the floor. Her cleavage is on full display, her shirt scooping so low it's obvious there's no bra on those babies.

She lifts a glass from the counter and pours a glass half-full with wine. "Want some?"

"I definitely want some," I croak, licking my lips.

She rolls her eyes. "Wine, Best. Do you want some wine?"

"I better not," I say. "Have any lemonade in there?"

"I do." She sets down the wine glass and grabs a clean one from the cabinet. "I'll pour some and head to the porch. Why don't you go wash Crave off yourself."

"How about I pour the lemonade and you wash me?"

"I can't deal with you," she laughs and leaves the room.

I watch her go, her ass swaying to the beat of a song I can't hear. Leaping off the stool, I head to the shower. She's right—I gotta get something off, but it isn't Crave.

Six
Layla

THE LIGHTNING BUGS FLICKER AWAY on the other side of the screens that separate the porch from the outdoors. Warm, summery air whispers through the little room off the living area as the ceiling fan whirls overhead.

It's a perfect summertime night at the lake house, the water gently brushing the shore just a few yards away.

My laptop sits untouched on the loveseat beside me, discarded after a couple of hours of my brain's refusal to think about anything other than Branch Best. Once Poppy went to sleep—claiming this place is the most relaxing place she's ever been, I tried to work on a couple of blog posts for next week. I got nothing except a complete description of Branch in the text box which looked a whole lot more like a sex box by the time I wrote "The End."

The depiction, although thorough and glowing and including a prediction of what the rest of him might look like, does nothing to accurately sum up the way he looks standing in the doorway in nothing but a pair of steely grey shorts and a smirk that takes my breath away.

"Hey," he says finally, shoving off the doorframe. His biceps flex, his stomach muscles rippling as he makes his way towards me. "I'm not interrupting anything, am I?"

"I wish you were," I sigh. "I can't get anything done."

"I've heard that." He slides into the wicker seat across from me and pops his bare feet up on the coffee table that separates us.

"You've heard what? That I'm lazy today?" I say, trying to ignore the way the air in the room just shifted like it's accommodating his presence.

"No. That I'm distracting."

"You say that like it's a badge of honor."

"It is."

"Maybe they mean you're annoying."

He grins, knowing damn good and well that's not what anyone means. Settling into the cinnamon-hued cushions, he changes topics. "So, why can't you work?"

"I don't know. I thought coming up here would sort of decompress my mind and I could get back into the flow of things. But I've just sat here all night and looked at the water and struggled to find any inspiration at all."

"What is it you do again?"

"I have a lifestyle blog."

He furrows a brow. "So you're a reporter?"

"Uh, no. Not at all. I just write about things I love, things I think other women like me might like. Food, fashion, a little home décor stuff which is funny since I'm living out of boxes right now."

"I moved into my house before the start of last season and I still have boxes to unpack," he shrugs. "I figure maybe one day I'll just toss everything. I mean, if I haven't used it in almost a year, what are the odds I really need it?"

"That gives me heart palpitations. You can't just throw stuff away. You have to look at it first. It could be important!"

"If I look at it, I'll want to keep it which means I'll have to put it away. It's easier to chuck it."

Tucking my legs under me, a lightness in my chest that I haven't been able to find in a few weeks trickles over me. "Just pay someone to do it."

"And find something online for sale in a few weeks? Come on," he cracks. "I can see the headline now: 'Branch Best's underwear up for auction. Starting price one dollar.' It would be a disaster."

Laughing, I reach forward and pick up his lemonade. He reaches for it, our fingers brushing along the cool, damp glass as he takes it from me.

"Where's Poppy?" he asks, getting comfortable again. "I haven't seen her since this morning."

"Asleep. Although she downplays herself, she's kind of a big deal at her job. She works tons of hours and until the middle of the night a lot of times. I think she just realized she could sleep and no one would bother her."

"Except Finn," Branch winks.

"She'd love that."

"The two of them ever have a thing?"

"You really have to ask me that?" I ask, taking a sip of my wine. "I don't know how often they see each other, I just know they have. There's not enough time in the day for that kind of information overload."

Branch laughs, his eyes dancing. "He kind of goes through the women, doesn't he?"

"Don't you all? I've seen enough stories about you to know you're no saint."

"You know how the media gets," he grins. "They make a lot of shit up. Exaggerate stuff all to hell, although I'll admit I'm no saint. It's so much more fun being a sinner."

My cheeks heat and I pray to God he doesn't have x-ray vision and can see through my closed computer and read all the various sinner-y things I sex-box'd out earlier.

"It's a part of the job," he says easily. "You dated Callum. You know how it works."

At the sound of his name, it's like I'm doused with a bucket of ice water. Callum's cocky face next to Carly's on a jet ski that surfaced this morning on every entertainment website I dared to check flashes before my eyes.

"Sorry," Branch says, his tone lowered. "I shouldn't have brought him up."

"No, it's fine," I lie. "I just have to stop feeling like my head is on fire when his name is mentioned."

"The break-up went well, I take it."

I glare at him, causing him to crack a smile. "You know what? Let's keep talking about him so I'll end up hating him so much I won't do this again. For the fourth time."

"So, this is a habit of yours?"

"Two football players and a hockey guy. I'm done. Habit broken."

"Well, I've officially dated a model and an actress and I'm done too."

"With models or actresses?" I ask.

"Dating," he laughs. "It's just not for me."

"I read a book once," I say, stretching my legs out in front of me, "that said you're supposed to date people that share your values. Like, if you're super religious, find your guy at church. If you love to read, go to a bookstore. Blah, blah, blah. That's my new angle."

"I think I'll just have to be single. Finn doesn't do it for me."

Not expecting that comeback, I can't help but laugh. "Good, because Poppy would be tough competition for you this weekend. She's just getting started."

"Well, so am I . . ."

My gaze flips to his, and he snatches it like a flytrap. His pupils are dilated, his bottom lip combing between his teeth, as he rakes my libido over hot coals.

"Why are you guys so anti-monogamous?" I ask, clearing my throat to try to break the hold Branch has on me. "Brick layers can be monogamous. So can electricians and teachers—"

"You had me until teachers," he says, leaning up. "Have you seen what teachers look like these days? Shit, man. Some days, I consider admitting I cheated my way through high school and asking to be re-enrolled."

"You're an ass," I chuckle.

Refusing to look his way, I keep my eyes on the water. His gaze is heavy despite the fact I won't return it. It's too deep, too hot, too *everything*.

"You should consider yourself lucky," he says finally. There's enough grit in his tone to make me look at him again.

"What's that supposed to mean?"

"We aren't the guys you keep around."

"I've noticed," I grimace.

He strokes his chin, watching me with a furrowed brow. "Guys come into this league off these huge college careers. They're courted for everything and have shit thrown at them from all avenues—money, women, even men, if they want it. You get cars and clothes and your mom's light bill paid if that's what needs to happen. And then things get even worse. More money. More conniving women. Bigger egos. It fucks us up."

"Are you fucked up?" I ask, the wind seeming to chill just a bit as it rustles across my skin.

"Probably." He sits back in his chair and releases a sigh. "When I came to Chicago, I met this girl pretty quick. She wanted to be a photographer, but had this purity about her. Just salt of the Earth, if that makes sense."

"I love that description."

He smiles sadly. "Within a year, she'd changed completely. She was taking modeling jobs, being really hard on herself. She was in the spotlight so much with me that I think it got to her. We fought constantly over everything. She became really self-conscious. I looked at her at one point and didn't even know who she was anymore or if she wanted me because she loved me or if she loved the money and opportunities," he sighs. "It became so convoluted and she became a really nasty person."

"What happened to her?"

"I don't know," he sighs. "She had a meltdown, rightfully so, over some shit she saw in a magazine. Packed her bags and left and that was that."

"You didn't call her? Go after her?" I ask. "At least check on her?"

"A part of me figured she was better off. Another part thought it would end at some point anyway. But," he says, leaning forward, "what gets me now is that I probably did that to her. I was off doing rookie shit. Partying. Enjoying this newfound fame and money and being the guy everyone wanted to be around. It was a crazy, crazy time in my life. Hers probably got sacrificed as a part of that."

I'm not sure what to say. It almost feels like a confession, like he's telling me some truth I'm supposed to pay attention to. It's nothing I don't know, yet I feel sorry for him. This weighs on him, there's no doubt. And whether his theory is right or wrong, it's sad either way.

"I have checked on her on social media," he admits, sitting back. "She seems to be doing okay."

"Well, that's good."

"Yeah. I just wonder what would've happened to her had she not known me. She had the world at her feet, capable of so much. It was a rude awakening to both of us, I think."

"A rude awakening to what?"

"To the reality, at least in my world. This is a culture, not just a team.

There's a reason some guys make it in the league and other guys don't. You ever wonder why a certain guy with great stats coming out of college doesn't get drafted or why he gets cut loose early? Coaches know he can't take the culture. It's that different. Don't get me wrong," he says, lifting his lemonade again. "I love my life. I wouldn't trade who I am or what I do with anyone in the world. But I'm smart enough to know it for what it is and not fuck someone else up with it."

"Such a hero," I wink, bringing my glass to my lips as he does the same.

"Hardly. My point is you should feel lucky you saw the light in time."

We sit quietly, the waves washing away most of the heaviness of our conversation. A few small glances are traded, a couple of hesitant smiles, as we relax in each other's company.

After I've downed a lot of the wine and Branch's glass is nearly empty, I don't realize I laugh out loud until he calls me out on it.

"What are you laughing at?" he asks.

"Just . . . it doesn't feel like I'm sitting with *the* Branch Best," I tease.

"Did you have expectations, Sunshine?"

"I didn't realize it, but I guess I did."

"In what way? I never leave a woman unfulfilled. It's a thing with me."

I take in his tanned face and thick, wide shoulders and almost shiver. The wine is making its way through my veins, pumping me full of the buzz that's just barely enough to distort my judgment.

As I open my mouth with every intention of telling him I need to go to bed, he shoots me the smirk that has a straight shot to the apex of my thighs.

Words, ones I shouldn't be uttering, come toppling past my lips.

"I guess I expected . . . *more*," I tease, lifting my shoulders just a touch for effect.

"You want more? I have so much *more* you'd be screaming for less."

The gravel in his tone roughs over my skin, sending a cascade of goosebumps rippling across me. The confidence in his dark, hooded eyes nearly elicits a moan from my parted lips.

It takes every bit of effort I have to keep my head about me. As I fight the wine, I'm wise enough to know I have to get away from him or be a complete hypocrite and just start shedding my clothes.

"That's what they all say," I chime as smoothly as I can. I lift my eyes to his as I stand.

Big. Mistake.

Without a movement, with not so much as a flick of his thickly roped muscles, he does everything he's hinted at. He undresses me, kisses my skin, draws a line from my temple, down my chest, over my belly, and down my legs using nothing more than his gorgeous, azure eyes.

I stand in front of him, pinned to the spot by nothing more than a gaze so hot I almost blister.

"I'm heading upstairs," I tell him, squeezing the computer to my chest. "Can you make sure the doors are locked before you turn in?"

"Sure."

He waits for me to say something else, but I don't. I walk by, the side of my thigh brushing against him, and take the stairs two at a time.

Once I'm in my room, I lean against the closed door and heave a breath of non-Branch air.

"At least you're not thinking of Callum," I whisper out loud. Padding across the hardwood floor, I climb into bed to the sound of lapping waves outside my window.

SEVEN
LAYLA

"WAKEY, WAKEY!" POPPY'S HEAD POKES around the corner. "You up yet?"

"Does it look like it?" I groan, pulling the comforter over my head. The sunlight is streaming through the windows thanks to my mistake of not pulling the blinds last night. One of the many perils of red wine. "What time is it?"

"Almost noon. Get your ass up, my friend."

"I don't wanna."

The mattress sinks with her weight as she takes a seat on the edge. "Too much wine last night?"

"Not really. Just tired."

The blanket is jerked away and her perky face is peering down at me. "What did you do when I went to bed? Anything you want to tell me?" She presses my cheek with the tip of her finger. "You don't look like you got laid."

"Because I didn't," I laugh. "Get off me."

"I can see why with that mindset."

I swat at her until she stands, unable to control my laughter as I see her attire. Cut-off jean shorts, a strapless red tube top with a white bikini beneath that squeezes her boobs together into one huge cleavage show, and gold hoop earrings paint quite a picture, one I'm confident was created for my brother's benefit.

"What?" she says, fingering a hoop. "Are these too much?"

"*You* are too much," I laugh, scooting up against the padded headboard.

"Why are you up already?"

"Because I went to bed too early. *And* because Finn and Branch have been up doing push-ups and wind-sprints across the front lawn for the last hour and I wasn't about to miss that. *And* because I wanted to make my super morning smoothie for Finn."

"You made my brother a smoothie?" I deadpan.

"And he slurped it all up," she says, wiggling her eyebrows. "Okay. Enough distraction. Tell me."

"Tell you what?"

"Tell me why your cheeks just turned pink. What happened, Lay?" Her voice turns sassy as a hand falls on her hip. "Spit it out. Or did you swallow?"

"Stop it," I laugh. "Nothing happened. Branch brought Finn home pretty late and I happened to be up working on my blog. We sat on the porch and I had some wine and he had some lemonade and that was it."

"No touching?"

"No touching. I promise. I'd tell you." Closing my eyes, the lines of his chiseled torso greet me.

"Let's put on our bikinis and head to the lake. That should help your cause."

"First of all, it's not my cause. He's worse than Callum!"

"He's *hotter* than Callum."

"Second," I insist, shooting her a look, "weren't you just telling me yesterday to stay away from guys like him?"

"I said nothing about wide receivers. That's a whole different game." She looks at me like I'm crazy for not following along. "Think about it. Their job is to hold on to the ball at all costs. They'll take a hit, get pushed out of bounds, but what do they not do? They don't fumble. They score, and baby, when he scores, you better give me every little detail."

"Oh, my God," I groan, swinging my legs out of bed. "It's way, way too early for this."

"But," she sing-songs, "you're out of bed. That's a win."

"You better have coffee made."

After a pit stop in the bathroom, I make my way into the kitchen. Branch is sitting at the island, laughing at something Finn said. My brother is standing in the kitchen next to Poppy, coffee mugs in all of their hands.

"Well, good morning," Finn says. "I was starting to think you were avoiding us."

"I was up late working," I say, pointedly not looking at Branch while I make a cup of coffee for myself.

"How's the blog?" Finn asks.

"Good, more or less. I'm a little behind from being sick last week, but once I get these last couple of posts made, I'll be caught up. I was hoping to sit on the beach today and see if I can bang them out."

Branch begins to choke, causing us all to jump. When I turn around, he's sitting at the table, his eyes wide, trying to get himself composed. "Sorry," he coughs. "Too much creamer." He glances at me, a shit-eating grin on his face.

"You have a problem with me completing my tasks today?" I ask, pressing my lips together to keep from smiling.

"Nope. I hope you *bang them all out*."

Poppy's laugh beside me catches my attention and makes me realize she and Finn weren't paying a bit of attention to Branch's comment. With a shake of my head, I turn to my brother.

"What are you guys doing today?" I ask. "I thought you and Branch might take the boat out or something."

"We might. But I need to run in and pay my bill at Crave first, and unless Machlan's machine is running which you know it's probably not, I'll have to head to the ATM and get cash."

"Can you take that much cash from an ATM? Isn't there a limit?" Branch jokes.

"Fuck off," Finn says, turning his attention to Poppy. "Hey, uh, didn't you say you needed something from town?"

"Oh, uh, yes," she says, thinking on the fly. "I do. A lot of things."

I look at my friend. "What could you possibly need from town?"

"Oh, just some things I couldn't fit in my suitcase. Essentials, you know."

"Such as . . ." I goad.

"Diet Coke," she offers. "Sunscreen. A fucking phone charger, okay? Does it matter?"

Branch and I die laughing as her cheeks turn red.

"You are so full of shit," I say, catching my breath as she struts out of the room.

"I'd ask you to go," my brother says to Branch, "but, you know . . ."

"No worries. I'll stay here and . . . behave."

"I'm gonna trust you fear me enough to do just that," Finn says, clasping him on the shoulder. "You good, sis?"

"I'm good. Tell Machlan I said hi. And if Peck's there, tell that bastard he owes me. He'll know what for."

"Peck?" Poppy asks, sticking her head around the corner. "Is that someone's real name?"

"It's a nickname," Finn laughs, guiding her towards the door. "We'll let you figure out what for."

———

MY TOES WIGGLE INTO THE soft, golden sand as I close my notebook. The sun is warm, but not too hot as I sit on the beach and finally get some work done.

The words came fast and easy today. That doesn't happen often. The ideas I had for blog posts came to life and I mapped out an entire fall series in the last hour.

My chin lifts to the sun and I close my eyes and revel in the satisfaction of feeling my life get back on track. Since my break-up, I've spent the last three months in chaos. Moving from Columbus, getting settled, and finding more freelance writing work to support my new digs in Chicago left me exhausted and uninspired.

A new idea pops into my mind and when I open my eyes, I scream. Branch laughs, dropping onto the sand beside me.

"How did you not hear me?" he asks. "I even stepped on some kind of burr back there and shouted some pretty ungentlemanly things."

"I don't think anyone has ever accused you of being a gentleman."

"You don't know that. My grandma happens to think I'm the sweetest boy she's ever known."

"She had how many daughters?"

He laughs, putting his arms back into the sand and stretching his long, lean body out in the sun. Wearing only a pair of white and green swim trunks and a necklace of some sort, he sits only inches away. My eyes refuse to look anywhere but at the lines cut into his abs.

"You're a smartass, you know that?" he asks.

"It's been said." Sitting up, I brush the sand off my hands. "What does your grandma think about her grandson being a football star?"

"I don't know. She wears my jersey to her card games on Thursday nights and asks me to send her signed pictures for her friends and members of her church. I guess you could say she's a fan."

"I bet she is."

"Hell, to be honest, she'd probably be just as much of a fan if I dug ditches for a living. I'm the only grandson she has from the three daughters she gave birth to," he says, rolling his eyes that my joke was actually right. "I'm kind of the favorite."

"And you struggle with accepting that, I see," I giggle.

"It's a lot of pressure! I can't let Gram down."

We laugh softly, the breeze coming off just cool enough to keep the sweat away. Boats float around, their flags waving brightly against the bright blue sky.

"So, tell me about you," he says.

"You know Finn and you've met my parents."

"How do you know I've met your parents?"

"Let's just say Mom was impressed," I shrug.

"Ah. That's why she sends me baskets of those peanut butter chip brownies when she sends Finn his monthly care packages."

"She sends you those?" I bark, dropping my jaw. "Those are my favorite and she never sends them to me."

He looks adorably amused as he strokes a hand down the center of his stomach. "You don't have the goods, Sunshine."

Scooping up a handful of sand, I toss it on his legs. "I officially loathe you."

"Just for that?" he laughs. "It usually takes at least one date before they loathe me."

The necklace bounces against his chest as he laughs, the little beads sparkling in the light. I reach over and pick up the end, turning it over in my palm. "What's this?"

"That's from Gram. It was a graduation gift from high school. My grandfather had one like it, only his beads were yellow and mine are red."

He watches me examine the intricately carved wooden beads and the shiny red ones. They're the color of rubies and heavier than I expect.

"This is beautiful, Branch."

"Thanks. I kind of like it." His head turns to mine and the soft smile deepens into a smirk. "I kind of like you in that bikini too."

The necklace drops to his chest as I squirm away from him. "I thought we were having a moment."

"Sunshine, I'll give you as many moments as you want."

"I don't want any of those moments with you," I say, picking up my notepad again. "It would just amp up that ego that's already out of control."

"I beg to differ," he gasps. "My ego is totally in control, thank you very much. I can't help it I just say what I think and what you want to hear, even if you won't admit it."

Finding my pen half-covered with sand, I scribble out a few things that have been lingering in my head. When I look at Branch, he's grinning.

"What?" I ask.

"I want to ask you a question."

"Okay."

"Will you play catch with me?"

"What?" I laugh. "Are you serious?"

"Finn's not here and I have no one to play with."

"Branch," I say, holding up my hands, "football is not my thing."

"It doesn't have to be your thing. You just have to catch the ball and then throw it back to me."

Plopping my stuff back down on the sand, I shake my head. "I know how to play catch. That's not the point."

"Then you have no excuse," he says, hopping to his feet. "Come on."

He reaches down, extending a large, rough hand. His fingers have obviously been broken a number of times, different digits extruding different ways. It's kind of gross and kind of sexy, but before I can think about it too much, my hand is in his and he's yanking me to my feet.

Jogging down the beach, he stops and faces me. I'm half afraid I'm going to stand here and gawk at him and get hit upside the head like in a cheesy romantic comedy. I see how that happens now. It's a real thing.

He brings his arm to his side, the cuts in his arm muscles on full display as he brings the ball to his ear and launches it my way. It's fast and hard and I catch it like the professional's little sister that I am.

"Hell, yeah!" he says, beaming. "You can catch a ball too?"

"Did you forget who I am?" I place my fingers on the laces like Finn taught me when I was ten. Pulling it back to the side of my head, I let it sail back with a flick of my wrist.

I've never thrown a more perfect spiral than this pass. Branch stands, arms to his sides, as he watches it spin through the air. Just before it almost hits him in the chest, he swipes it out of the air.

"Color me impressed." He tucks the ball at his side. "Did Finn teach you that?"

"Of course. Who else?"

He winds the ball back and throws it to me again. "Maybe Callum?"

"Callum didn't teach me anything," I say, snapping the ball out of the air. "He was too busy doing other things. And other people."

I toss it back to him.

"Now you don't know that," he jokes. "He might've been meeting friends for coffee."

"Are you trying to piss me off?" I catch his pass. "Because if so, you're doing a damn good job."

"Don't be pissed at me. I'm not the asshole who cheated on you."

"But you would, wouldn't you? I mean, don't you all?"

He snags the pigskin and stands still. "I'm offended you'd lump us all together like that."

"You are not."

"Yeah, you're right," he chuckles, passing the ball to me again. "I'm not. But, no, I don't think everyone cheats. A large percentage, probably. But I don't cheat because I don't make commitments. See? Problem solved."

I'm about to tell him what a bullshit answer that is . . . until I think about it.

"You know what? I think you're right," I tell him.

"I am?"

"Yeah, I'm as amazed as you."

He narrows his eyes, but a smile plays on his lips. "It saves you so much time and pain. If they do something stupid, not your problem. If you don't want to go to the movie to see some crazy shit, who cares? If you want to have your cock sucked by a stripper on the Strip, so be it."

The ball hits the sand at my feet. I don't blink, just raise a brow. "For one, that was the shittiest pass I've ever seen. For two, I don't have to worry about getting my cock sucked."

"Thank God," he says, jogging towards me. He lifts the ball. "If you have a cock, my weekend plans are fucked."

"Ha." I head towards my towel, feeling his gaze burn into my bottoms. "If that's your plan, you need a backup."

"That sounds like a challenge."

"Of course it does," I say, putting my notepad in my bag. "Isn't that all you really want? A challenge? A game to conquer?"

He scoffs, but I can tell I'm right. Looking up from my kneeling position, the longest, most confident look crosses his handsome face. "I don't know what I really want."

With that line, he surprises me. Leaving me sitting on the sand, ball tucked to his side, he walks back to the cabin.

EIGHT
BRANCH

"THEN HE COMES DOWN THE stairs with his—"

"Stop!" Layla shouts, covering her ears. "I can't hear any more of this."

"I wasn't even to the good part," I laugh, setting down my bottle of beer. "Come on. Just let me finish."

"No," she laughs. "No. No more. I can't."

Poppy wipes tears from her eyes from laughing so hard at my tale from the locker room. Finn stands next to her, watching me tell the story. He knows half of what I've just said isn't one hundred percent true, but it was good enough to entertain the girls. And him. He was laughing too.

Music plays on the overhead system as we shoot the shit. Finn brought back beer and steaks for the grill from his earlier trip to Linton. While the girls made some dips for chips and some vegetables Poppy apparently insisted on that almost caused bloodshed in the grocery, Finn and I worked the grill. It's been one of the best, most relaxing afternoons I've had in a long time.

"Tell them the story about the direct message with the donkey nuts," Finn requests.

"Okay, so this girl—"

"Answer me this," Layla cuts me off. "Do you ever get normal messages? I mean, these stories are insane. Is your inbox full of crazies?"

"It was until those pictures of the commissioner's daughter got leaked last year," I grimace, thinking back on the mess I had on my hands from that little episode. "After that, Coach made us all shut off our inboxes on social media."

"I thought that was a lie!" Poppy exclaims. "Seriously? Those pics of her were real?"

I grin. "The pictures were real. But her tits weren't."

"Good to know," Layla flinches, swirling wine around in her glass."

"Nah, it wasn't that good," I say, the look on her face making my stomach ache. "I wish I hadn't fucked around with her at all, to tell you the truth. Caused a lot of headaches."

Poppy stands in front of Finn and leans back, her back against his chest. He catches my eye over her head and shoots me a wink.

"Hey, Branch," Poppy says. "Why do they call you Lucky?"

"Because he's lucky someone hasn't killed him by now," Finn cracks.

"So funny," I say with a poker face. "The year Finn and I started in the league, we played our division rivals the very first game thanks to a mistake by the people who set the schedules. That game usually doesn't happen until later in the season. Anyway, two of our wide receivers were out with injuries, so I was in. We were down by a touchdown and time was ticking."

I think back to that moment, my skin breaking out with goosebumps. "So, a pass was made that got deflected. The ball shot up in the air, maybe ten yards downfield from where I was. Somehow I get under it, but only as it was almost hitting the ground. The defense started making the 'incomplete pass' sign, just trying to sway the refs, you know? And I jumped up, demanding I caught it."

"You were running around screaming it, if I recall," Finn snorts. "He was pointing at the screens overhead, forcing everyone to watch the replay."

"I wasn't letting them *not* see it. I caught that thing."

"Did they give you the catch?" Layla asks.

"Yeah, after a review. Everyone kept saying it was the luckiest catch ever and the name kind of stuck."

"Do you think you're lucky?" Layla's voice is quiet, almost thoughtful, against the music and Poppy's giggling at whatever Finn is whispering in her ear.

I sink into a chair beside her. Setting my beer on the table, I peel at the label. "I don't know that I believe in luck, really."

"Why not?"

"I think luck is just being ready when an opportunity presents itself. There are a lot of people that could be lucky if they spent more time preparing and less time moping or bitching or being scared." Taking a deep breath, I stop fucking with the bottle and look into her gorgeous eyes. "Does that make any sense at all?"

The way she looks at me makes me want to come undone. It's like she cracks open my outer shell and watches me bleed in front of her, something I don't do for anyone.

People can't handle that level of truth, that vision of what you look like or say that isn't what they think it'll be. When you're a public figure, everyone thinks they know you and you better live up to that or they'll call your ass out. It's a burden to keep that façade up, but I always have to.

"It does make sense," she agrees. "It's easy to call people lucky because it doesn't give them anything. Like, it doesn't acknowledge anything about them—their work ethic, or decision making skills, or sacrifice. It's just they're lucky. I've always thought it was kind of bullshit."

"You and me both," I whisper.

Before things can get any deeper, her phone buzzes on the table. "Oh, shit."

"Who is it?" I ask.

"Callum."

She almost spits his name, her eyes narrowed as she watches it glow. Finn and Poppy are too busy in their own world to notice the way Layla just tensed up.

"He called earlier and I told him not to call me back. I mean, he's in fucking Tahiti with another woman. Why would he even want to call me?"

"For this reason right here," I say, spinning the phone around on the table. "It keeps you talking about him."

"I don't want to talk about him. I want him to die." She looks at me. "Not really. I don't need that karma on my head. I just . . . I wouldn't be sad if something really bad happened to his knee, okay?"

Laughing, I pick up the phone with a crazy idea. "Let me answer it."

"What?" she squawks. "Why would I do that?"

"Because it would be fun."

"I don't know . . ."

"Oh, come on," I say. "You aren't dating him, right? What do you have to lose?"

"What do I have to gain?" she counters.

"A little amusement."

She gives in, unlocks the phone, and swipes the call. Handing me the phone, she tilts her head like she's second-guessing her decision. I grab it before she changes her mind.

Callum is a complete dick. His reputation around the league sucks, stories float around about him every year in regards to the way he treats his team. I've seen him at clubs throughout the years and watched him interact with different people. It's a wonder someone hasn't rung him up.

A little shot of adrenaline hits me as I bring it to my ear. "Hello?"

I keep the phone pulled slightly away so he doesn't hear my breathing. There's no reason to distract him from the fact a man just answered her phone. Let that sink in a little.

"Who is this?" he says finally.

"Who is this?"

"I asked first."

"True, but you called me," I remind him, winking at Layla whose hands are folded together and hovering near her mouth. "Seems to me you should introduce yourself."

"Where the hell is Layla?"

"She's . . . preoccupied," I say, getting entirely too much enjoyment out of his irritation. "Can I help you with something?"

His breathing rackets through the line like a linebacker watching you across the field, ready to take you out. "Put her on the phone."

"She's really not in a position to talk right now. Can I give her a message?"

"Who the fuck is this?" he snaps.

"Branch Best."

The stunned silence gives me all I was after, a little shock to the cocksucker. If anything, it'll make him realize he's not God. If anything more, maybe he'll leave Layla alone.

"What the hell is she doing with you?"

"Oh, just the usual . . ."

"Just the usual, huh?" he jeers.

"Well, usual for me. Not sure what usual is for you. How are you doing, anyway? We haven't talked for a while. We should totally hang out more . . ."

I think it's the friendliness in my voice that he knows I don't mean that causes something to break on his end. The sound of glass shattering in the distance shouldn't make me laugh, but it does.

"Bad day, Callum?"

"Fuck you, Best. Fuck. You."

"So hateful."

The line goes dead.

"Was he pissed?" Layla asks.

Finn and Poppy are watching, having caught on to what was happening. Finn shoots me a look and I know he and I will discuss this later.

In the meantime, I turn back to Layla. "Do you think he was pissed? He's an angry boy."

"Ugh," she groans, taking the phone from me. "Maybe he'll stop calling me now."

"Tell him to call me," Finn demands. "He's just trying to keep you on the hook, Lay. Just cut all ties with him."

"I'm trying. I didn't answer earlier or text him back yesterday. I'm over it."

Finn's right, but I want to chime in and tell her the exact game he's playing. Hell, I've played it before. He's going to string her along until he's ready to dip his stick in her again.

She sits next to me, tucking a strand of hair behind her ear. Her forehead is pinched as she turns her phone completely off and I find myself wishing I could do something to make him stop bothering her. But I can't. It's not my place.

Poppy's face breaks into a smile as she looks at Layla. "Glad to hear it. Come on," she says, heading towards her and offering her a hand. "Finn, turn this music up."

Finn does as instructed and a new hit song floats through the house. Layla gets to her feet and joins Poppy in dancing through the kitchen, shaking their asses and laughing their heads off.

I grab a beer and sit down and watch Finn join them, dirty dancing with Poppy as Layla pours another glass of wine. The laughter is a constant here, as is the comfortable, homey mood. I wonder what Christmas would be like here with a giant tree in the living room, one so tall it hits the ten-foot high rafters. I consider being snowed in with a fire in the stone fireplace or watching fireworks over the water on the Fourth.

"What the fuck is wrong with you?" I chuckle, bringing the beer back to my lips. "Get your ass in check, Best."

NINE
LAYLA

"I LIKE THAT ONE."

My computer almost flies off my lap as I jump at the sound of the voice behind me. "Damn it, Branch!"

Falling back against the lounge chair, I press one hand against my chest. My heart is pounding against my rib cage at an alarming rate. At first, it's because I didn't hear Branch come onto the patio. Then I see him. And smell him. And hear his sexy chuckle as he takes a seat on the chair beside me and then I know the tempo has nothing to do with being scared and everything to do with being *Branched*.

The more time I spend with him, the more I see that he's not just the player I see in the media. I went to bed thinking about how he talked to Callum last night and what Callum must be thinking and the way Branch looked at me the rest of the night.

We had fun afterwards, staying up entirely too late talking and playing gin rummy. Through the laughter and jokes, Branch and I had a weird vibe between us, almost like we were both afraid to get quite too close to the other.

"I like the first one," he says, touching my computer screen. His forearm extends above me, *this close* to hitting my breast but not quite. "I mean, if you're wanting an opinion. You've wavered back and forth between the two images for ten minutes now."

"How long exactly have you been standing there?"

"Long enough," he grins, stretching back again. "If you don't mind me asking, how do you make money doing that?"

I select the image he prefers, the one I was leaning towards anyway, hit save and then close my computer. Before I answer him, I take him in.

He's stretched out beside me in a pair of purple shorts. His hair is wet like he just got out of the shower, the dark blond strands sticking together and up every which way. There's a dose of stubble dotting his cheeks and chin that gives him a touch of scoundrel that appeals to every sexual organ in my body and most of the others.

Clenching my thighs together, I watch *him* watch *me*. He seems unhurried, like he has nowhere to go and the genuine curiosity laced in his question makes me give in.

"I get paid in different ways," I admit. "There's ad space on my blog and I have a newsletter that works the same way. I also write pieces for magazines and a few affiliates." He still seems interested, so I continue. "I've also just started to sell online training courses about decorating, makeup, and blogging. You'd be surprised how many options are out there if you aren't scared to work."

"Maybe that's what I can do when I retire. Do online training courses about actual training."

"You could. Teach younger athletes how to work out like a champion."

"That would be one course. I hear the big money is in porn."

"I think that's true, but only if you have the goods," I sigh. "Big goods, big money. Little goods, little money."

"By goods, do you mean cock?"

Laughing, I nod my head. "Yes. Sorry that wasn't clear."

"So I could just quit football now and work in porn? I don't know what the concussion risk is like, but I'm guessing a lot lower."

"I would think so. Does everything go back to sex with you?" I ask, lifting a brow.

"Babe," he grins, "if a guy ever tells you they don't think about sex at least twenty times a day, they're lying."

"I just assume every time a guy opens their mouth they're lying."

His laugh makes me laugh, and before I know it, I'm completely lost in his grin. And eyes. And the start of a dimple in his right cheek that lends a slight adorableness to his overall charm.

"You were right," he says finally, rubbing a hand down his thigh.

I try not to follow the movement and stay focused on language. "About what?"

"Every time I look at you or think about you I'm wondering why you had a sex therapy card in your purse."

"Branch . . ." It's more of a whine than I care to acknowledge, but a whine nonetheless.

For a split second, I wish Poppy and Finn hadn't gone into Linton for lunch so I could excuse myself to see what they were doing. There's no way out of this conversation.

I place my computer on the table next to my drink. "Can't you just forget you saw that?"

"What on earth would a woman like you be doing at a sex therapy class? What even is that? Is it kinky? Should I sign up? Is it like a giant orgy? If you're into that—"

"No, I'm not into orgies," I chuckle, rolling my eyes.

"Such a shame."

"A lot of thought went into that," I note. "Does this mean you've thinking about me, Branch Best?"

"A hell of a lot more than I should be, Layla James Miller."

A large lump takes residence in my throat as I try to play off his comeback as the trait of a player and not for face value. That would get me in trouble I know better than to get into.

"While we're on the topic," he continues, "is James your middle name or some kind of holdover from a previous marriage?"

"Holdover. I was married when I was eighteen to this world-renowned rock star that visited Chicago. When we divorced, right after he left me with our triplets, I decided to keep his last name as a middle name."

His jaw drops.

"Of course it's a middle name," I laugh. "It was my mom's maiden name."

"I was wracking my brain for rock stars with the last name James," he teases. "Okay. We can move on now."

"No, no way. Now I want to know why your name is Branch. There must be story behind that."

He shrugs. "Not really. My great-grandfather was a Baptist minister.

When his wife had my grandfather, they named him Branch because he
was a 'branch,'" he says, using air quotes, "that would spread the word
of God to the rest of the world."

"That's . . . fun," I offer.

"Sure it is. I'm sure they're super proud of their great-grandson who
has only spread the word 'God' mid-orgasm."

Bursting into laughter, I lean my head back to the perfectly clear
sky. "You could always trade in your pads for one of those black outfits
with the white collar," I say, wiping tears away from my eyes. "I can only
imagine those sermons."

"I bet every seat would be taken."

"Oh, I bet you're right," I agree. "I'd fight someone for a seat."

"As long as I have a face, you have a seat."

Oh.

My.

God.

His smile straddles the line between mischief and debauchery the
way my legs want to be straddled over his face. It's a wicked, taunting
kind of gesture that puddles me.

"What has gotten into you today?" I ask.

"Sometimes I wake up a little spirited."

"Spirited. Got it," I say, settling into my chair.

"Sex therapy. Go," he commands.

"I haven't gone," I say, unable to look away from him. "Poppy has
a friend that goes because her husband had an affair and she wanted to
feel sexy again."

"So why did she give *you* the card?"

My cheeks burn, the sweat breaking out along the top of my breasts
more from Branch's scrutiny than the summer sun. "A joke?"

"Why did she give *you* the card?" he asks again, not buying my excuse.

When I don't answer, his legs swing towards me and he sits upright.
Elbows on knees, strong shoulders angled slightly my way, his brows tug
together as he awaits my response.

I know he asked me a question, but I can't remember what it is. There
are too many stimuli to process to think of such trivial things. The way

his body wash floats on the warm summer breeze, the way little beads of sweat form against his smooth, tanned skin. The way his teeth are so straight and white and his nose angled and that damn dimple that dips into his cheek as he watches my irises widen when he lays his palm on my bare thigh.

My body clenches at the contact, something I know he notices because his fingers lightly press into my skin a little harder. My lips fall apart as I drag oxygen into my lungs to help clear the fog.

"There's no way you need a sex therapist. No way in hell."

"Maybe I do. You don't know me."

"I know you're sexy as *fuck*," he says, the last syllable so enunciated that it feels like it bounces off me. "I also know you're well-spoken and intelligent and you make me laugh every time I'm with you."

"Which has been like four times in our lives, so it's not like I'm setting records here."

He smiles, but I think the fact that he does annoys him.

"You are seriously bothered by this, aren't you?" I kid. "You aren't going to let this go."

Like a petulant child, he fires back immediately. "No, I'm not."

"Tell me why it bothers you first and then I'll tell you why I have it."

"It bothers me," he says, not missing a beat, "because I can't imagine a woman like you not having complete confidence in herself. And if it was a man that you were talking to, it also makes me think I went into the wrong profession."

"Oh, like you don't have enough women to talk about sex with."

"I don't want to talk about sex," he clarifies. "I want *you* to tell me all your sexual secrets."

Despite the heat, a chill rips across my body. I actually shiver. His eyes train on my lips as my tongue brushes against them in an attempt to bring some moisture back to my mouth.

"Tell me something, Sunshine."

"You think you can call me some cute nickname and have me open up with all my dirty secrets? Does this work with other women?" I ask, cocking my head to the side.

"I haven't tried it with other women."

"Why?"

"Quite frankly, I don't have to. Now, back to the dirty secrets you were getting ready to tell me."

Emboldened by the ease of our banter, I lift my legs off the side of the chair and face him. Leaning forward, I whisper, "I wasn't about to tell you anything."

His nostrils flair at the proximity of our bodies, his legs capturing mine between them and holding them in place like a clamp. "Would you rather show me?"

"You aren't a sex therapist."

"Trust me—there are plenty of testimonials I could gather that would say sex with me is wholly therapeutic."

Laughing, I try to sit back but his legs lock me in place. "I'm sorry to disappoint, but I honestly have no dirty secrets. I was going to see the doctor on the card for some confidence boosting, if you must know. That's the shameful reason. Now, if you'll excuse me . . ."

"No."

"No?"

"I'm not excusing you," he says. "If you get up and walk away, I'll feel sad." He sticks his bottom lip out.

Looking at the unmistakable bump in the crotch of his shorts, I lift a brow. "I think the word you're after is *blue*."

"Well played." He widens his stance so I can get up if I choose, but he doesn't get out of my way. Not in the slightest. "If you don't feel self-assured sexually, then you've never had great sex."

"I've had plenty of great sex," I counter. "I just feel a little . . . unsure about myself. That happens sometimes to regular people that don't have the entire population throwing themselves at your feet."

"If you've been having great sex, you wouldn't be unsure about yourself," he contends. "Great sex makes you feel good about yourself. It gives you way more than an orgasm. It gives you . . . pride. Confidence. It builds you up mentally as much as physically."

"This is getting deep," I laugh.

He rests his head against the cushion and looks at me. "You can't have mind-blowing sex without involving the mind. It seems whoever you've been fucking doesn't know the first thing about that."

"I haven't been fucking anyone."

"Since Callum?"

"Since Callum," I confirm.

"How long ago was that?"

"Why do you care?"

"Just making conversation."

"Seems like you're prying, Mr. Best."

———

BRANCH

I *AM* PRYING. I'M PRYING so damn hard it hurts.

Tugging my bottom lip between my teeth, I grab onto the slice of self-control I have left. It's waning, dangling on a spinning string that gets more difficult to hold on to with every flutter of her long eyelashes.

"What's wrong with a little getting-to-know-you?" I ask.

"Nothing . . . if you ask the right questions."

It's not the answer she gives, but the way she gives it that makes me want to scoop her up and carry her inside and lock ourselves in a bedroom for the rest of the afternoon. She's sweet as honey and as sinful as the day is long.

Narrowing my eyes, I drag a fingertip across the top of her thigh. "Are you turned on right now?"

"I'm not answering that," she breathes.

"You don't have to. I already know the answer."

"Oh, you do, do you?"

"It seems," I say, trailing my finger up her torso, across her pebbled nipple, and up the side of her throat, "that your body is a little more honest than you are."

"I didn't say yes or no. I said I wasn't answering."

"Okay, you want to do a visual representation. I can do that. It's like instead of discussing the formation of the play, we're going to do a walk-through."

She laughs, but lets me take her hand and pull her to her feet. We stand inches from one another, her head coming up right beneath my chin, as she looks up at me with her bright golden eyes sparkling.

"The question was," I say, letting my hands go to her hips, "are you turned on right now?"

"I thought you already knew the answer?" She does that eyelash flutter thing again and I feel like I'm going to explode. "My turn."

"For what?" I say as I lift the edges of her shirt up just enough so my hands can wrap around her waist. Her body is soft, her skin warm, and the way she moves under my touch has me breathing much harder than necessary.

"For me to ask the questions."

The little vixen wrapped in an angel's façade takes her hand and touches the side of my face. The back of her hand runs down my jawline, the scraping sound from my unshaven face zipping through the air.

Her eyes don't leave mine as she traces a line down my throat, over my shoulder, and across my pecs before dropping down the ridges of my abs.

"Are *you* turned on?" she asks.

"I've been turned on since you stepped out of the car yesterday."

She grins as I run my hands up her sides, feeling the soft, round curve of her body.

"What do you propose we do about this state we're in?" she asks.

"I think we have a couple of options. One, we can take ten giant steps back and then you go inside and I'll go down by the lake and we stay apart until your brother gets home."

"I don't think that'll work," she says. "I'll just watch you from my window while I touch myself and I—"

My mouth captures hers before she can finish her sentence. Her lips part, her hands go to my hair, not at all fazed by my sudden ferocity. I can't take it. There's no way I can handle tiptoeing around this woman that makes me crazy any longer.

I cup her face in both hands, holding her face still so I can kiss the hell out of her. She tastes of tea and summertime, of heat and arousal, and the longer our mouths move against each other, the more I want—of her kisses, of her body, of her.

Fuck. Me.

Stroking her cheeks with the pads of my thumbs, I plant my lips in the center of hers and then pull away.

Holding my breath, unsure of what I'm going to see in her eyes, I relax when she smiles.

"Now that," she says, a little breathless, "is a little more what I expected you to be like."

"Is that so?"

"I mean, not one hundred percent, but closer."

Taking her hand, I pull her to the foot of the chaise lounge. Positioning her so she's facing me, I lift the hem of her shirt and drag the cotton material off her body. She's braless, her tear-drop breasts, heavy with the weight of the C-cups, hanging perfectly off her frame.

"I'm about to get you nine inches closer if you don't tell me no," I growl.

"Let me think about it," she says, tapping her pursed lips.

"Can you think about it while we get you out of these shorts?" I hook my thumbs in the elastic waistband and drag them down her toned legs. She shivers as my palms hit the back of her thighs, skimming her smooth skin as I reach her ankles.

Stepping out of the shorts, she looks up at me and grins. "My turn."

With a sway of her hips, she reaches for me. I don't have to be told twice. I cut the distance between us with a step and hold my breath as her hands dip below the top of my shorts. Instead of just yanking them down, she runs her hands from the front around to the side, letting the backs of her hands run along my skin.

My blood sings in my veins, my cock throbbing so damn hard I think I might pass out. As she finally drops my shorts, the mesh fabric not needing any direction once it's over my hips, she steps back and stares at just how much I want her.

"Damn," she mutters, her eyes widening.

Although her reaction is something I'd love to watch over and over again, my need for physical action is much stronger.

I reach for her and she surprises me by taking my hand and allowing me to pull her naked body against mine. Her tits smash against my chest, her back arching as I place a hand in the curve just above her bubbled ass. The other cradles the back of her head as I move my mouth to the shell of her ear. "You. Are. Gorgeous."

Crashing my lips to hers again, I draw the hand twisted in her hair down her back and around her side. As my tongue enters her mouth and she moans into mine, my palm cups her breast and savors the weight and the feel of her in my hand.

Her head falls back and I guide her body closer to mine again. My senses are filled with everything Layla and the more I get, the more I want. Need. *Crave.*

An urge overtakes me, one I haven't felt in a long damn time. It's a desire to not just get off, something that usually finds me about now when I'm with a woman, but a wish to *enjoy it.*

Twisting a beaded nipple in between two fingers, I roll it around and feel her muscles loosen against me. She pants against my mouth, pressing her pussy against my thick, more-than-ready cock. The friction is almost too much to bear.

In a move she's not expecting—and without breaking our kiss—I sweep her up in my arms and lay her on the chaise lounge a few steps away. Her eyes are open, watching me, teasing me, in a way, as I straddle her in the chair.

Pulling away, we're both breathless, panting in a desperate attempt to get precious oxygen into our bodies. She grips my shoulders, her dainty hands not close to covering the width of my arms.

"I want you, Best. Now."

"It's a good thing I'm ready to give it to you. Now."

Moving so my body is on one side of the chair, I dip my head and draw in her peaked nipple. She lifts off the chair, her head pressed into the cushion, as I lick and suck the globes of her breasts.

Reaching down between her legs, I glide two fingers between her legs. Her slit is so wet, so hot, I think my cock is going to go off from the imagery alone.

She bends her knees and lets them splay to the sides, giving me more access to her pussy. I take what's offered.

Moving around to the bottom of the chair, I nestle against the cushions between her legs. Looking at her from this vantage point—eyes wild, hair mussed, lips parted and swollen from my kisses—I grin. Keeping my eyes on hers, I insert one finger, then two, feeling her muscles tighten around me as I work them slowly back and forth.

"Branch," she moans, reaching for me.

Dipping my head, I use the pad of my tongue to lick a long, thick streak up her pussy. She pulls her legs back farther, burying her hands in my hair, shoving my face farther into her body.

She bucks against my fingers, working herself against what I'm willing to give her at the moment. Her lashes, the ones she bats my way, are lying flat against her rosy cheeks as I swirl my tongue around her swollen bud.

My body aches, every sound she makes pulling my libido another rung higher. I suck her flesh, lap up the juices she's releasing for me, feeling her flex and push against me.

It's goddamn heaven.

I press a kiss to her clit before pulling back. Stretching her tight hole open with three fingers, I bury them inside her before removing them altogether, a move that gets me a dirty look. I laugh.

"What's that look for?" I say, wiping my face with the back of my hand. I shuffle my body so I'm hovered over her, the tip of my cock sitting at the opening of her body. "You look pissed."

Her hands find my ass and press down, urging me to fill her. "Stop playing, Branch."

"And you weren't sure you were turned on."

"No, I was sure," she says through gritted teeth. "I wasn't sure if you were."

"Oh, right," I chuckle.

Swirling my hips so my head teases her opening, I press barely—just barely—so the tip begins to part her. She gasps, locking her heels around my waist, her thighs tensing as she waits for me to move.

Eyes locked on hers, I slip against her. She's so slick, so warm, I groan like a teenage boy ready to fire the entire fucking thing because I have no control.

Her hips tilt, and whether I mean to or not, I slide so easily into her tight channel, and with every inch I go, I want to go another. And another. And another until I'm hitting the back of her pussy and watching her eyes roll to the back of her head. She sucks in a breath at the same time I do, my cock throbbing against the tensing muscles of her vagina.

I still as her eyes fly open and we both realize our error.

"I need to get a condom," I whisper.

"Ugh," she whines, her legs dropping to the side. "I mean, yeah, you do, but . . ." She lifts her hips with me still buried balls-deep inside her. "But this feels too good."

"I have one in the pocket of my shorts," I say, summoning every bit of adult I can find to do the right thing. The only thing. "It'll take ten seconds."

"Which is nine too long."

"I think you'll like nine just fine."

"Asshole," she laughs. "You seriously have one in your pocket? Were you that sure of yourself?"

"No," I say, pushing away before I say fuck it. "But a man can hope, can't he?"

My length glistens, coated with her wetness, a pool of pre-cum dotting the tip. I find my shorts, rip open the condom, and roll it down my shaft in record time.

I hover over her in a half push-up and feel her fingers lightly draw a line across my clavicle. "There are boaters on the lake," she whispers. "Think they can see us?"

"Maybe."

"Should we go in?"

Knowing she's already ready for me, I rest the head of my cock against her and thrust until I'm fully seated inside her body. She moans my name, her nails digging into my shoulder blades.

"You want to stop and go in?" I ask, retracting until I'm almost out before laying it to her again.

"Branch!" she calls, sweat glazing her skin as she gives her entire body to me.

"Was that a stop?"

"No," she whimpers, skimming her hands to my hips. "Don't you dare fucking stop."

Watching her full tits bounce with every slam of my body against hers, I chuckle. "If you say so."

TEN
LAYLA

"COME IN." I WATCH THE doorway to see who is on the other side. My heart starts to race as I hope it might be Branch coming in for round three.

Round one, on the patio, was the most voyeuristic sexcapade I've ever had. Round two, almost an hour later, was a quickie with my hands against the refrigerator door. It was an impromptu bang session that resulted from him coming down in a pair of boxers and me bent over picking up a piece of ice off the floor.

Although my body aches, and my neck apparently kinked at some point and is beginning to scream in discomfort much the same way I was screaming his name just a little while ago, I would totally, absolutely, with no hesitation say yes to round three. And four. And five.

The thought of Branch's hands touching my skin makes me shiver as I await the opening of the door. I love the way they feel rough, almost like a fine sandpaper, against me and the way his stubble scratches along my skin.

Poppy trounces in, a wide, jovial smile parting her pinked cheeks, ruining my daydream.

"There you are!" she says, almost skipping to the side of the bed where I sit. "I've been looking everywhere for you."

"Did you guys just get back?" I ask, glancing at the clock. "You were gone forever."

"I didn't think you'd mind. Besides, you can get lost on backroads, you know."

Even if she wasn't my best friend, I'd know that look in her eye.

"Don't even tell me. He's my brother," I gag.

"Who else am I supposed to talk about it with? You're my bestie."

"You're out of luck on this one. There's not a detail in the world I want to know about Finn," I flinch. "Just the thought makes me ill."

"If he weren't your brother, the things I'd—"

"But. He. Is."

She giggles, her happiness contagious, as she sits on the bed beside me. "Tell me what you were doing while we were off back-roading."

"I got some work done. Made a few calls . . ."

"Got in a fight with a cat and it clawed the top of your boobs . . ."

"What?" I look down to see red marks from Branch's fingers and lips marking my chest. "Shit."

"And, just like that, the Illinois Legends lose a wide receiver at the hands of a very tight end."

"Shut up," I laugh. "I'll just put on another shirt. Finn will never know."

"He will never know what, exactly?" she asks, tapping her chin with a fingernail.

"That Branch just made me come five times in the span of less than two hours while telling me how beautiful I am and how much he loves my body and . . ." My face heats and I look away. "Best afternoon of my life, pun intended."

In a very un-Poppy-like way, she says nothing. After a long pause, I turn to look at her. She's watching me agape.

"What?" I ask.

"Five times? Are you fucking serious?"

"Oh, the fucking was serious all right, and yes, five times. I mean, a couple of them sort of ran together so that's not a scientific number or anything."

"But *five times*. Damn."

"I was hoping you were him," I sigh.

"I have never been happier that I let you talk me into something I didn't want to do before. Coming up here was the best decision we ever made."

Our laughter blends together as I stand and change out my shirt.

"So, you and Branch are actively fucking now?" she asks.

"No. I don't think so. I mean . . . No. We're not."

She wrinkles her nose.

"Maybe for the weekend, but that's it," I say, dropping back on the bed. "He's this crazy confusion of dangerous and wonderful. I've never laughed so much with a man, Pop. He's terribly funny and has the stupidest sense of humor. And buried under all that brawn is a nice guy, I think."

Remembering back to his stories about his Grandma and the way he gives me room to breathe when he senses I'm a little overwhelmed, a softness eases through me.

"He can be sweet. Then he's so filthy I get whiplash." Wrapping my hand around the back of my neck, I work it back and forth. "Literally."

"So? This seems like a good thing."

"It's not," I sigh. "I tried to trust my gut with this one, but now I'm thinking maybe it was more my vagina than my stomach. It's tricky."

"Seems pretty cut and dried to me. You came five times. What's there to overthink?"

"That it's me, not you, Pop. I don't keep doing the same thing over and over and over again."

"I do if it's worth it," she laughs.

Standing, I walk to the desk my dad bought at a flea market when I was twelve. It's inexpensive and we painted it white one summer and left it in the sun to dry. It ended up raining that night and the paint was technically ruined, but I loved the splatter marks, the little indentions in the surface and begged them to let me keep it as-is. They did.

Running my finger over the bumps, I listen to Finn and Branch's voices trickling up from downstairs.

"It's not worth it to me," I admit. "I think the sex was so good because we both know where we stand. This is a weekend fluke, a romp in the final days of summer before we go back to reality and assume our real lives."

"You don't think you'll see him once this weekend is over?"

I look at her. "I don't want to see him once this weekend is over." Dropping my hand from the desk, I shrug. "I want to get serious about things. I've done enough gambling with my happiness over the last few years to know I don't win. Dating athletes is the biggest blackjack hand ever and the House doesn't lose."

"I can't handle all this philosophy stuff," she says, scrambling to her feet. "Subject change: Peck said to tell you he's happy to get even but you have to show up."

Poppy leads me downstairs, telling me about how much she loved Machlan and Crave and the backroads of Linton County.

I listen to her stories, even admire the way she seems to have taken up with my friends, but in reality, I'm tuning her out. Searching for the sound of Branch's voice is almost impossible over the roar of white noise through my ears coupled with her rambling.

My hand trembles as it glides down the banister as we descend the staircase.

I haven't seen him since he pinned me to the refrigerator and fucked me so hard it knocked the little basket off the top my mom keeps receipts in and I'm nervous to see him now with Poppy and Finn around. It reminds me of being a teenager and having a major crush on a boy and having to interact with him in front of your friends. You know one little slip can make you the laughingstock of the school.

As we round the corner and my sight lands on him sitting at the island, his easy smile melts away any apprehension I had.

"I got burgers to go from Crave," Finn says as the microwave blares behind him. "I had to heat them up."

"Really? From what I heard, the entire car was pretty hot on the way home," I say, trying not to smile.

Branch, however, doesn't bother stifling his as he stops the microwave and takes out a burger. "Poppy, you little rascal."

"You—" she starts, then realizes her misstep and stops. With a quick glance at me, she starts again. "*You* are an asshole."

Branch hands me a burger, his fingers brushing mine as I accept the sandwich. We sit at the table, on opposite ends, and start to eat before I realize my brother and Poppy aren't.

"Aren't you guys eating?" I ask.

"I already ate," Finn smirks. "No, really, Machlan is having a party at the lake tonight. He invited us to come out."

Not wanting to be the first to respond, I look at Branch over my burger. He searches my eyes before turning his attention to Finn.

"You two wanting to go?"

"Yes," Poppy giggles. "Those people are crazy. Seriously, who knew rednecks could be so much fun?"

"I love the Gibson boys," I say, ignoring a strange look from Branch. "But I don't really feel like one of their parties tonight. It gets loud and the last time we were there, Peck let out the neighbor's cows and we spent all night trying to herd them back into the pen without the owner knowing it."

"I'll stay with her," Branch says, his offer sounding amazingly innocent. Still, Finn raises his brow. "My agent sent me some contracts for endorsements that I've had for a couple of days. I'm happy to stay and get that shit done."

"That's all you're getting done, right?" Finn asks.

"I don't know what you're referring to." Branch winks, tossing his paper plate in the trash, and carries his burger with him as he disappears out of the kitchen.

Poppy follows him. "I'm going to grab a sweatshirt in case it gets chilly tonight. Be right back."

I almost feel guilty that Branch wasn't warned that Poppy's behind him. She's not going for a sweatshirt. She's going up there to interrogate him in a way only she can.

Maybe it'll be good for him. There's no doubt no one has ever put him in his place like Poppy Quinn is about to.

I'm chuckling under my breath when I look at Finn. "What?" I ask, taking in his puzzled face.

"Heard from Callum?"

"No. Why? Should I have?"

He shrugs. "Not really. You just seem really chipper this afternoon."

"Can't a girl just be happy?"

"Sure. Just wondering why."

"Because my big brother is such a respectful, loving guy that stays out of my business," I say, standing up and walking around the island. I kiss him on the cheek. "Now go play with Poppy and be happy yourself."

He stills, his eyes turning a deep shade of emerald like our father's. "I'm not kidding, Lay. Don't fuck with Branch."

"He's nice."

"Yeah. He's nice. But his people skills aren't what I'm worried about."

"Finn, seriously, stop it."

"I work with these guys. I'm Branch's friend. I see things you don't see, know things you don't know. I'm sick and tired of watching you hook up with guys like this and then get your heart broken."

"My heart is not broken, thank you very much," I glower, placing my hands on my hips. "My heart was a little tender for a minute because that's a normal thing in a break up with anyone except heartless assholes that just jump from one bed to another."

He shoots me a warning, but I ignore it. "I love you, Finn. I do. And I appreciate your looking out for me. I have no plans to get tied up with Branch in any way. I'm not an idiot, okay?"

He pulls me into a quick hug and smiles. "Good. That makes me feel better."

"What does?" Branch asks, walking back in the room.

"Nothing. See you two later." Finn tosses me a final look before nodding to Branch as he walks out. The front door opens and closes, and immediately, the air shifts and pulls.

Branch sits back down at the table, having changed into a pair of soft, faded jeans and a plain white t-shirt. "So, what's the plan tonight?"

"Don't you have contracts?" I ask, sitting down and pulling the newspaper up in front of me.

"No. I just told him that so he would leave. I got them done days ago, before I ever came up here." He flicks the paper, making it pop. "They still have printed papers up here?"

"Yes. Isn't it sweet? A man brings it to the end of the driveway every afternoon. Finn must've brought it up."

I scan the front page, the headlines all centering around the Linton County Water Festival. Pictures of carnival rides, horseshoes, food trucks, and bands performing on the bed of a semi-truck span the entire first three pages.

Suddenly, I get an idea.

Setting the paper down, I look at Branch. "When was the last time you went to a carnival?"

"A what?"

"You know, with rides and elephant ears and lemon shake-ups?"

"High school?" he guesses. "Maybe? Maybe middle school. I don't know. Why?"

I scoot my chair back and grin. "Get ready. We're going to the Linton County Water Festival."

"We are not."

"Yes, we are," I giggle.

"Why?" he groans. "Those things are for kids, not adults."

"Okay," I tease. "When did you become an adult?"

He dips his chin and looks at me through his lashes. "Really, Sunshine?"

"Oh, come on. Stop being difficult," I say, taking his hand and pulling him to his feet. "Go get a hat and whatever else you need and let's go."

He tries to have a standoff with me, but it doesn't last long. Before I'm even close to giving up, he stomps up the stairs. "God, you're infuriating."

"Just get your stuff and get back down here and no one will get hurt."

BRANCH

"YOU HAVE THAT ALL OVER your face." I brush a spattering of cinnamon and sugar off her chin. "If we weren't in public, I'd just lick this off you."

"Good thing we're in public then," she says, bringing the plate to her lips. She tears off a huge piece of cooked dough and shoves it into her mouth. "You're good, but not this good."

"If you weren't so pretty, watching you would be disgusting," I laugh.

She shrugs, not giving a fuck what I think.

We stroll through the park, where the Water Festival is in full-force. White Christmas lights are strung over the street that's been shut down for the occasion. Vendors hawking trinkets line the right side, food stands fill the left. On ahead is a bank of games and carnival rides and one very loud cover band that's doing a shitty job of covering class country. It's kind of amazing.

The air smells of fried food and is filled with laughter and music. It reminds me of being a kid and the music festivals in Tennessee. I'd start begging to go right after school, and if I was lucky, we'd trek down there on Friday night for a few hours of running amok.

Layla takes a few steps off the road and dumps the remaining elephant ear into the trash can. She pauses to help a little boy get a red balloon out of a tree, the string a touch too high for the kid to retrieve. She stands on her tip-toes, halfway hopping into the air until she comes down with the end and holds it triumphantly out to the boy.

Watching her interact so easily with the child, just as easily as she did with the veteran that welcomed us into the festival, is a sight to behold. She talks to them like they're old friends, and by the time they're through, they probably are.

She saunters back my way, dressed in a pale purple summer dress that hits just above her knee. She could fit right into this little town as another PTA member or woman working the table for the local church. She could fit right in, but she'd stick out. She's the most beautiful woman here.

Before I can really do much damage with my imagination, she reaches me. "You having fun yet?"

"Oh, I'm having a ball," I sigh.

"You love it. You know you do."

"Yeah, maybe I don't hate it." Glancing down, she's looking up at me with a knowing smirk. "Fine. It's fun. All right? You happy?"

"Yup."

"Good because—"

"Lemon shake-ups," she breathes, her eyes twinkling. "Come on, Branch. I need one."

"You do not. You just ate a pound of dough smothered in sugar. If you have any more, you'll go into diabetic shock."

She stops in her tracks and very carefully lifts her chin. "Tell me again I don't need one."

The lights dangling overhead appear to make her glow. Her blonde hair shines like a halo . . . then you get to the look on her face. That's different. That begs you to push her because she's willing to throw back.

Not many girls are like this. Most would ask to go to a fancy restaurant or to have box seats at a concert. Lots of the women I know would have on killer heels and a face full of make-up and do whatever I said and half of what I didn't. Not this one. I'm not one hundred percent sure she brushed her hair today. She's an enigma, one I can't wrap my head around quite yet.

"Get me one too," I say finally.

"That's what I thought." Winking, she trots off to the stand. I stay back, hovering near a telephone pole, and watch her order two drinks. The man shaking the white plastic cups is obviously enchanted with her. He smiles too wide, leans in too close, and I'm not even sure he takes her money. But by the time she's back to me, all I can think about is the grin she's wearing and the way her eyes are lit up like a carnival ride.

"Here," she says, thrusting a cup at me. "These are amazing."

The cold, sweet, and slightly bitter drink hits my taste buds. "Wow. This takes me back."

"This is my 'must get' thing at festivals," she admits, leading me down the street. "My mom got me hooked on these as a kid. She always made my dad buy her one, even if the line took forever."

"That was me with candy apples. I used to love the shit out of those."

"We're going to get you one."

"No, we aren't," I laugh. "The season is getting ready to start. I can't be eating total crap."

As if I haven't said a damn word, she sidles up to another stand with a green awning. "One candy apple please."

"Sure thing, madam."

We watch the guy pluck a cherry red apple from a tray and wrap it in plastic wrap. He hands it to Layla while I pay. She gives it to me as we walk away.

"You'll thank me later," she promises.

"The way your legs look in that dress, I hope so."

"Ha. Ha. Ha."

We walk slowly through the streets, stopping for a brief minute to listen to the band and watch couples dance to the music. Everyone from little kids to old people in wheelchairs are clapping their hands, some are whistling, others are talking with the people around them.

I stand next to her and take it all in. There's something so pure and relaxed about this that I can't quite make it out. People don't act this way anymore. Places don't have this feeling of camaraderie. It's amazing this even exists.

Then I look at her, dancing with an old man in a pair of bib overalls to an old Waylon Jennings song. She's chatting him up as he does his best to lead her in a little circle. There's no doubt he's having the time of his life.

The band plays the final few notes and Layla kisses her partner on the cheek. Catching me watching, her cheeks turn the faintest shade of pink.

"Sorry," she says. "That's Peck's uncle. He's like a million years old and the sweetest old thing in the world."

"Don't be sorry. That was nice of you."

"I love it here," she sighs, looking around. "Doesn't being here just make you feel nice?"

"That's the sugar talking," I joke as we start towards the games.

"It is not."

"No, you're right. It is nice here. I'm actually having a good time." I bump her with my shoulder. "Thanks for bringing me."

She looks at me out of the corner of her eye. "Thanks for coming."

"Like you gave me a choice."

"True, I didn't. But I had a suspicion you'd like this."

"Really? Do I come across as the guy who likes kiddie rides?" I whistle through my teeth. "I need to work on my reputation."

It's her that bumps me this time. "No, asshole. But you do come across as a guy who needs to be reminded every now and then that it's okay to just chill out."

"I chill out all the time."

"I think you misunderstand the term 'chill out,'" she says.

"It's an easily understood term. I don't think you can misunderstand it."

She side-eyes me. "It doesn't just mean relax or not work out for a day. It means to have fun, take it easy, you know? To kick back and enjoy yourself."

"Well, I 'chilled out' a lot lately then," I grin. "I'd like to 'chill out' like that again."

"I bet you would . . ."

Stopping in the middle of the street, I shake my head. "And?"

"And what?" she giggles, turning to face me.

"And you wouldn't?"

"I didn't say that. I just didn't reply."

"And . . ."

"And, yes, Branch. Once you play me in a game of Skee Ball, I'd love nothing more than to 'chill out' with you."

"Skee Ball? Are you fucking serious?"

"Dude," she says, pointing a few yards over. "It's the best game of all time. Except maybe Plinko. But I've never actually gotten to play that."

She takes off without me and I just follow along, shaking my head.

"Where in the hell do you get this stuff?" I ask, wrapping an arm around her neck and pulling her close to me. "Plinko?"

"I watched *The Price is Right* every day growing up. My mom would record it on our VCR because it was on right before her soap operas. I wanted to put that chip down the ramp and watch it bounce."

"Sounds kinky," I shrug.

"You can put your chip down my ramp and watch me bounce when we get home."

"Damn it, woman. I'm going to be Skee Balling with a hard-on now," I say, letting her go.

She laughs, her voice catching the attention of the game attendant. He takes my money and gives us tickets and we find two booths side-by-side.

"This is serious," she says, rubbing her hands together. "No talking. No bumping. No interfering with the other person's game whatsoever or you're disqualified and your chip remains in its slot the rest of the night. Got it?"

It's my turn to laugh as my balls come crashing down the ramp. "You're a woman after my own heart."

"No, I'm a woman who wants no part of your heart," she deadpans. "I want your blood right now and your cock later. Keep your heart."

"I think I just fell in love."

She rolls her eyes and counts us down and we begin the most epic game of Skee Ball Linton has ever seen.

Eleven
Layla

POPPY'S GIGGLE FROM THE ROOM next door filters through the thin walls of my bedroom. Watching Branch do pull-ups from a low-hanging limb off a tree in the yard, I have half a notion to get dressed and go down there with him.

Last night at the festival turned out to be more than I even expected. It took Branch a while to really loosen up and let his guard down, something that I don't think he really does all that much. But when he dropped it, he really dropped it. So much so, in fact, that I waited for almost an hour while he showed a group of high school boys how to throw a football and catch a pass on the tennis courts.

I've never seen him quite like that. Invigorated. Energized. Talking a mile-a-minute and jumping from one thing to another. I think that little side track was his favorite part of the night, although he insists it was his victory over me in Skee Ball.

My bed still smells like him, sticky, red candy smeared on my sheets from our romp when we got back. I showered after and again now when I woke up and still feel the tackiness on my thighs and breasts. So worth it.

He catches me watching him and drops to the ground and busts out a number of push-ups, all the while maintaining eye contact. I laugh, give him a thumbs up, and then walk away from the window.

I have to. He's a glorious sight all shirtless and golden from the afternoon sun, but this little fest will come to an end when we go home tomorrow and I need to start applying the brakes now.

By the time I get dressed and stretch out a little, my muscles aching,

Poppy and Finn are already in the kitchen. They're whispering back and forth as I enter.

"Secrets are lies," I say, plucking a strawberry out of a bowl.

Poppy turns around and smirks. "No, I know what a lie is and it's not a secret. Or, maybe it is. Is it?"

I toss her a look and mouth, "Stop it" while Finn's back is to me. "How was the party at Machlan's?"

"Those boys are nuts," Poppy giggles. "I kind of love them."

"What happened?" I ask, looking at Finn.

"Just the normal shit. Peck had bottle rockets so I'll let you determine how that fared."

"Oh no," I laugh.

"Pretty much. What did you do last night?" he asks.

"Branch and I went to the Water Festival, actually. I ate way too much."

"She did." His voice slides into the room from the doorway.

Looking over my shoulder, I see him standing there, leaning against the frame. His eyes are on me, but they're filled with something I haven't seen in them before and can't even begin to figure out.

"You can't take Layla to a festival and not drop one hundred dollars on food," Finn laughs. "Let me guess: lemon shake-ups."

"And elephant ears," Branch adds. "And candy apples."

"That explains that," Poppy says, her eyes twinkling.

"That explains what?" Finn asks.

"Um, the stick on the counter this morning," she fumbles. "I was like, 'Damn, that looks like a candy apple stick.' Guess it was."

My head goes to my hands as she continues with her makeshift story. She can't tell him she asked me about the red smears on my sheets earlier. Finn would go crazy.

"I'm going to take my strawberries," I say, grabbing the bowl as I stand, "and go sit on the porch."

"We'll be right out," Poppy says, turning back to Finn.

I brush past Branch on my way. He slides his hand to the side and lets his fingertips dance along my thigh. It's such a simple touch that I can't look at him. I just keep walking.

My skin tickles where he touched me for minutes after. As I get situated on the wicker love seat and think about him in the other room, I smile like a loon. I know it. I can't help it.

Even on my best days with Callum, it was work—work I thought would pay off in the end. I wrote off the stress between us as spillover from practice or the last game or decided his irritability must be from the things he took to stay fit. With Branch, there's none of that. It's so *easy*.

Their laughter comes around the corner before I see them and I watch the doorway for Branch. His eyes find mine right away, softness mixed with mischief in those blues.

Everyone grabs a seat like we've done this a hundred times. We eat fresh fruit and coffee that Poppy made and laugh and talk about our jobs and tell stories from summers past. They let me snap some pictures of their plates for my blog and I mentally put together the post as Poppy takes our dishes to the kitchen.

A wind chime tinkles in the corner, the warm afternoon breeze gently nudging it back and forth as we sit, stomachs full, and relax. Branch sits across from me, his feet up on the table again, his hands on his belly and eyes closed. Finn stretches out on a chaise beside him, a binder of football-related stuff on his lap. Poppy comes back from the kitchen and sits next to me.

A contented sigh passes my lips as I feel my body, although sore from my romps with Branch, give in. It's one of those moments I've experienced only a few times in my life. It's a calm in the center of my core, a contentedness that I wish I could channel every day.

My computer sits beside me where I left it at some point. As Poppy checks her email on her phone, I attach my phone to my laptop and download the pictures I just took for the blog. Wanting to get the vision I have for the Summer Fun post I can see so clearly, I click open my browser. There are tabs lining the top and I start to click on each one and close them.

Then I stop.

My eyes dart from the screen, over the rim of the computer to Branch, and back to the screen again.

I gulp.

I hit refresh.

Exposé's website is front and center, a tab open from when I was checking on Callum when we first got here.

Now, on the main page, is a picture of *Branch* in Crave. He's wearing the same shirt he came in that night smelling like the bar. The letters hanging above his head, in all bold caps, reads: "Best Having the Best Time."

A lump sits in my throat, my cheeks hot like I'm going to get caught doing something wrong. When I glance up at Branch, he hasn't moved.

I don't need to peruse the article to know what it's going to say. The picture of the girl in shorts so short you can almost see her hoohah sitting on Branch's lap is pretty much a spoiler. Still, I'm a glutton for punishment, so I read on.

EXPOSÉ TOP STORY:
BEST HAVING THE BEST TIME

SEEMS LIKE OUR *favorite bromance hit up local favorite, Crave, in tiny Linton, Illinois this week. Our sources tell us Miller was seen buying shots and playing pool while our honey-haired honey Best went missing in action with the "lucky" lady on his lap.*

These two are in town on a quick retreat before the pre-season starts and should be reporting for training in just a few short days. Anyone else awaiting those pictures and stories? Just us? Didn't think so.

PS: Lucky Lady—we're so jealous.

FORCING A SWALLOW AND TRYING to manage the feelings screeching through my head, I close the computer and stand. Poppy looks at me with a quirked brow.

"Gotta pee," I mumble and make a quick exit from the porch.

Taking the steps two at a time, I'm in my bedroom in ten seconds flat. My computer goes skidding across the comforter.

I don't sit. I pace. Back and forth I go in front of the window that overlooks the lake. The pale pink curtains that have hung in this room since I picked them out when I was seven years old flutter in the wind from the open window.

Before I can make sense of anything, the door flies open. I whirl around to see Poppy standing in the doorway.

"You did *not* have to pee," she says flatly. "What's wrong?"

"Nothing is wrong."

"What did you see? Don't tell me you were looking up Callum's vacation," she sighs. "Damn it, Layla."

"I wasn't looking up Callum or his fucking vacation. Here," I say, thrusting the computer at her. "Open it. Passcode is 'milkshake' with a one instead of the i."

"Chocolate or vanilla?"

"Just look," I sigh, rolling my eyes.

The exact moment she gets to the "honey-haired" piece is obvious because her eyes bug out. "Ooohhh . . ."

"I'm not mad," I say, more to myself than to her. "It's not that at all. It's expected. It's the natural order of things. I just stupidly forgot that and thought he was all about me this weekend, which, I guess, is a part of his charm and I'm totally capable of understand that because I'm an adult," I say, throwing my hand through the air and knocking a candle off my dresser. It shatters on the floor and breaks into a handful of pieces. "Starting now."

Poppy puts the computer carefully on the bed. "You can be mad."

"I'm not mad!"

"You're not mad," she says, trying to not show her amusement. "You're . . . irritated."

"I'm not irritated either. I'm . . . I'm . . . I'm going home."

Now she laughs. "Because we're adults, right?"

"Yes," I say, stomping to the closet and pulling out the few things I bothered to hang up. "I'm an adult and I can go home so I don't have to look at his smug face for the next couple of days."

"Maybe he's not smug."

"Maybe not," I say simply, shoving my things into my suitcase. "But if you want the truth, I'm a little embarrassed."

"At what?"

I fall onto the bed, the adrenaline from the last few minutes catching up with me. Looking at my best friend, I feel the fight wane. "I'm embarrassed at myself."

My friend sits beside me. "Why would you be? It got you to stop thinking about Dickface and got you off—how many times? Five?"

"Five that time. I haven't told you the rest," I sigh. "But that's not the point."

"No, the point is there's nothing for you to be embarrassed about."

"I know that. *I do.* I'm a grown woman and he's most definitely a man," I whimper. "But maybe it would've been nice to think about this two weeks from now and not wonder who came before me and who came after."

"You mean that figuratively, right?"

"Shut up," I whine. "Was that girl texting him while we were at the Festival? Did he see her there? Will he see her when we leave?"

"So what if he does?"

Reality settles in atop the embarrassment and twinge of self-pity. He will see other women. I'll see other men. But still.

"Maybe it would've been nice not to feel like I was a point on the scoreboard," I sigh.

"You don't know that's what it is."

"Oh, I do. At least number two." My head hangs, my chin almost touching my chest. The position makes my neck pain rear its ugly head again, the twinge making me grimace. "I just don't want to look at him, Pop. I don't want to look at him and know I was 'Saturday and Sunday,' you know? I need a little dignity."

She pulls me into a quick hug and then stands. "We go home." Marching to the door, she stops before she pulls it open. "And I know you don't want details, but your brother promised to take me on the boat tonight and do very, very wicked things to me. You are the only person I'd leave that invitation for, but I might never forgive you. Just so you know."

"I owe you."

"Ha," she says, pulling the door open. "You owe me twenty."

—

BRANCH

SETTLED.

What a terrifying fucking word.

It's not a bad feeling, though, as I stretch out. My muscles are relaxed, my cock satisfied, which is a miracle in and of itself.

I haven't ever felt this relaxed—not even on vacation in the Dominican Republic last year with a model whose name started with an L.

There's something about this place that just digs into your bones and takes over everything . . . and there's something about that girl that has taken over my brain.

I don't know what it is, exactly. Sure, she's beautiful. Her sense of humor is spot on. She's intelligent and classy and has a mouth that I would love to discipline with my tongue every time she breaks from sophistication and says something dirty. She's a conundrum, a riddle, a seemingly hot ass chick that has something underneath that I want to explore and I plan on doing just that tonight if I can figure out a way to get Poppy to get Finn out of here.

Everything inside me yells to be careful, tread lightly, because this one is a hazard. Layla isn't dangerous like most women with their plots and plans. She's a risk because she doesn't have either. There's something incredibly sweet and attractive about that. My only saving grace is that she's Finn's sister and the weekend will be ending soon enough. We should be safe and enjoy this while it lasts.

A vision of her legs around my neck, the pink of her pussy bared just for me has my cock going rock hard and my brain working overtime on how to take care of that as quickly as possible.

"What?" Finn asks, making me jump.

"What, what?"

"What are you thinking about?" he laughs. "You just had the weirdest look on your face."

"Ah, nothing."

"No, it was something . . ."

"How are the new plays?" I ask, motioning to the playbook in hopes he'll be easily redirected. "Anything too crazy?"

"Just variations on what we ran last year. We'll see how Chauncey does in the other slot. Some of this shit is going to make him or break him."

"I—" I stop talking at the sound of something banging behind us. Finn flashes me a curious look as we get to our feet and head into the greater part of the house.

Layla and Poppy are coming down the stairs, dragging their suitcases behind them. Everything I've heard Layla say about leaving replays in my mind and nothing I can find makes me think her plan was to leave today.

My gaze sears into her and she feels it. I can tell by the way she refuses to look my way. My jaw sets, my arms crossing over with I know is a tell-tale sign I'm irritated, but I can't make myself uncross them either.

"What the fuck?" Finn looks at the girls. Only Poppy will look at him back. "Where are you going?"

"We're heading out," Poppy says too happily.

"I didn't think you had to leave until tomorrow," Finn bounces back, clearly as irritated as I am that they're leaving. "We had plans, remember?"

Layla gets to the bottom of the stairs and tucks a strand of hair behind her ear. "I have some work to do and I just can't work here," she lies. "I've gotten crap done since we arrived and you know me and work ethic."

"You seem to have been pretty productive to me," I point out, goading her into looking my way. She doesn't.

"Did Branch piss you off?" Finn asks. "I knew I shouldn't have left you alone with him."

If he only knew.

"No, Finn," she says, forcing a swallow. The motion causes a little gold chain to move against the hollow of her throat. "Nothing like that. I just really need to get back. There are a couple of promotion contracts on my desk and I need to unpack. I had no business coming up here this weekend. Work, then play, and Lord knows I've not earned the play part yet."

"Fine. Let us help you with your bags," Finn says, reaching for Poppy's floral piece when his phone rings in his pocket. He pulls it out and looks at the screen. "Hey, I need to get this. It's Machlan. Can you wait a second?"

"Sure."

"Hey, Machlan," Finn says, disappearing into the kitchen.

The awkwardness is tangible as the three of us stand in the foyer. Poppy clears her throat and touches Layla gently on the shoulder. "I'm going to take my things outside."

Layla nods, gripping her necklace, and watches Poppy cart her bag out the door.

"What's going on?" I ask before the door even shuts.

"Nothing. Why?"

"I didn't know you were planning on leaving today."

"Plans change," she shrugs.

Nodding, I try to stay loose. "They do. But that was quick. I had your pussy in my mouth—"

"Branch!"

"What? It's the truth."

"And it's also not public information," she hisses, looking towards the kitchen. "Look, if you don't mind keeping this our little secret, I'd appreciate it."

My brows pull together. "I get you don't want Finn to know. But why are you acting all weird about it?"

"I'm not," she says, tucking another strand of hair out of her face. "I just, you know, am more of a private person than a lot of people and I'd rather not land on a magazine."

She gulps, like she misspoke, and I can't help but lift a brow. She looks away and plays it off.

"For what it's worth, it was a fun weekend," she says.

"I agree. The best one in a long time."

We share a smile, one that stings my chest. Making a move to help her with her bag, I'm stopped when she stops.

"I got this, Branch."

"Let me be a gentleman and help."

She laughs, the sound pulling my lips up too. "You erased any gentlemanly behavior already today."

A hundred things race to my lips, a host of things I want to say are on the tip of my tongue, but I don't. Something in her eye stops me.

"Good luck this season, Branch," she says quietly.

"Thanks." I dig for pockets to stick my hands into, but my shorts don't have any. "Maybe we'll run into each other sometime."

"I don't think that would be good for either of us." She re-grips the handle of her luggage. "Fantasy Land is over and we're back to reality."

"What's that supposed to mean?"

"It means . . ." She looks around the room before settling her eyes on me. "It means this weekend was great. See ya."

I can't even form a response to that. I stand in the doorway like a chump and watch her walk to her car. A part of me wants to chase her and ask her to stay and another part of me remembers why I don't chase women. Even her. Finn's footsteps are what finally breaks my haze.

"Hey," I say. "They went on out. I'm gonna get a drink."

Blowing by him, he tosses me a curious glance but doesn't say a word. I pour a glass of lemonade, smiling at the remnants of the candy apple in the trashcan beside the refrigerator.

She felt so good wrapped around me. The way she teased me, taunted me, slightly mocked me and had me laughing was something I haven't really experienced before. Sex is usually one of a few things: a power struggle, an interview, the means to an end, a physical need. With Layla this weekend, it was . . . different.

The door shutting rings through the open-aired house and Finn's shoes squeak against the wood floors. He comes in, scratching his head. "That fucked up my plans for the night."

Mine, too.

"You think Layla really had to work?" I ask.

"Hell, no. That was a lie."

"Why would she lie?" I take a drink to keep from making any sort of face that would give Finn a clue as to why I'm so curious.

"I don't know," he says, grabbing a beer from the fridge. "My guess is it's something to do with Callum."

"That motherfucker," I grumble.

He shakes his head. "He might've called her or texted her or some shit and she just didn't say anything. I didn't tell her this, but he called me a couple of nights ago too."

"For what?"

"Manipulation." He twists the top off his beer and tosses it into the trash. "Told me how worried he is about her, how she's not taking the break-up very well and he hopes I'll keep an eye on her. What he means is he's afraid she'll move on and wants me to keep her busy so she doesn't meet anyone else."

"Piece of fucking shit."

Finn downs most of his beer in one gulp as I try to sort this out in my head. He twists the bottle between two fingers.

"Machlan said to apologize to you," Finn says.

"For what?"

"Apparently there is a story running on *Exposé* today about you and some chick from Crave."

The glass slips from my hand and hits the floor with a loud, ominous crack. "Shit," I mutter, scooping up the large shards with my bare hands.

"He said he knows who yapped to the magazine and he's banned them from the bar. Some new girl in town but not the one you fucked that night."

I look at him with a seriousness I rarely do. "I didn't fuck anyone that night."

"Sure you didn't," he laughs. "Anyway, he said to tell you he's sorry and he hopes you'll come back in sometime. Now I'm gonna grab a shower and figure out what the hell to do tonight."

He walks out and I stand in the center of the kitchen, broken glass in my hand, but with a newfound clarity. Dumping the pieces in the trash, I bust ass to the screened in porch to see a vacant spot next to my car.

I'm tempted to figure out her phone number, even if it means stealing Finn's phone, and call her to tell her I didn't fuck anyone . . . then logic sets in.

It doesn't matter.

It doesn't fucking matter.

TWELVE
LAYLA

EXPOSÉ TOP STORY:
BRANCHING OUT?

B RANCH BEST AND *Finn Miller were spotted out and about this weekend at a grand opening for new hotspot Grandiose on Osborne. Owner Selma Puress looked quite cozy nestled between the two, but don't think we haven't zoomed in on the location of her right hand a time or sixteen million.*

Thanks to songstress GiGi last summer (and her sneaky camera skills), we know Branch is seriously packing. Did he "pack" Selma on Saturday? If so, she's not telling. Yet. They always do, and we'll keep you posted when it happens.

GETTING INTO "THE FLOW," THE state of being so engulfed in something you block out everything else, is easy when you have something to avoid. That "something" toys with my daydreams and heats up my nights. Knowing, for my own good, I can't focus on his cocky smirk, heated gaze, or those sweet, simple touches he did in an almost absentminded way—like it was natural—I've poured myself into work since arriving back home.

What's most bothersome about the whole thing is it's just as much the non-sexual moments that resurface as the sexy ones. If it was just the fucking that I couldn't forget, I could just grab a vibrator and get rid of that urge. But it's not.

I find myself thinking just as much about the joy in his face when he was playing catch with the kids at the fair. The levity in his laugh when he beat me at Skee Ball. The way his fingers pressed against the small of my back as we walked along the beach and the feel of his breath against my cheek when he told me I was beautiful under the moon.

It's those things that I fight to ignore, those little moments that make me wonder "what if?" It's Callum and his texts over the last three weeks since I've been home that remind me of what the other side of 'what if' looks like. The headlines Branch has been making help that vision be a little clearer too.

Seeing him with Selma Puress was a little harder than I thought. I've analyzed that image more times than I should've and ended up more confused than anything.

Is that smile real? It doesn't quite seem to be, yet his hand rests against her skinny waist like she's more than an old friend.

Rolling my desk chair back, I stand and stretch. The knot that started at the base of my neck has expanded down the middle of my back. It's a contributing factor to my extreme efficiency since I can't sleep. It hurts too bad.

The traffic below my apartment on Gilmore Avenue is bustling in the early afternoon. It usually doesn't get too bad until the lunch rush, but the horns from frustrated motorists drift up the twenty-six stories to my ears.

The colorful paintings bring splashes of life to the whitewashed walls that were here when I moved in a few months ago. I envision the living room a dove grey but haven't had time to do it, and I've always wanted a strawberry red wall in my kitchen but Callum thought it was ridiculous.

"Hey," Poppy's voice sings from the doorway, dangling a key in her hand. "You're going to be sorry you gave me this."

"Just be glad you aren't ten minutes later or I'd be naked."

"Hey, if I swung that way . . ."

"Shut up," I laugh, carrying my coffee cup to the sink. "What are you doing?"

"Not much. On lunch break now but I'm thinking of calling off the rest of the afternoon."

"Why?"

"Because . . ." she says, snarling. "It's work. There's nothing to do there. I mean, there's stuff to do," she corrects, "but nothing I *want* to do. What are you doing today?"

Yawning, I lean against the cabinets. "I've worked all morning. I'm so far ahead I don't even know who I am anymore."

"Wanna get some lunch?"

"If we can go get a hot ham and cheese from Yusi's."

"Random."

"I saw a commercial for them last night and I need a hot ham and cheese. *Need*, Poppy. I can't stop thinking about it."

She presses her lips together. "What else have you been thinking about?"

"No," I sigh. "Branch hasn't called. He won't, and despite what you think, I don't want him to."

"I'm calling bullshit."

"He's on *Exposé* again this morning," I tell her, using the headline to make my point. "With Finn. Did you see it?"

"Yeah, I saw it. Finn told me he was going, so I'm not worried about it. We aren't exclusive, anyway."

"I think my brother could be exclusive. Branch? Not so much. And that's exactly why I don't want him to call. I can't deal with this. I can barely deal with it and it's not even my problem. The only thing I need right now is a ham and cheese sandwich."

"I'm not taking you anywhere looking like that."

Heading down the hall, I enter my bedroom. I leave the door open so I can talk to my friend. "What'd you do this week? Anything fun?"

"Oh, I've had fun this week, but not the kind you wanna know about."

"Are you still messing with my brother?"

"Putting it lightly."

Throwing on a pair of black yoga pants and a white and black striped top, I look in the mirror. The top is wrinkled and makes my frame look wide, so I jerk it off and replace it with a pretty teal-colored t-shirt. My hair in a bun, flats on my feet, I'm back in the living room as Poppy's wraps up the PG-version of her latest tryst with Finn.

"You didn't hear any of that, did you?" she laughs as I grab my purse.

"I tried not to."

She squares her shoulders to me, her purple-y lipstick shining as she presses her lips together. "Branch asked me about you a couple of days ago."

My heart flutters in my chest, even though I try to mentally shoot it down. "Where did you see him?"

"At Finn's. He was really cute about it, Layla. He asked how you were and if you got your work done. And for what it's worth, he knows you didn't need to get any work done."

"Fuck him."

"You already did that."

Sighing, I drop my purse back on the sofa. "It was amazing. I won't lie. But I mean it too when I say I wish I hadn't done it."

"Spreader's remorse?"

"What the hell is that?" I laugh.

"You have remorse you spread your legs. It is what it sounds like," she says matter-of-factly. "Granted, most women have it because they wake up and the guy is married or not nearly as good-looking as he was with a couple of shots in ya, not because he's the catch every woman wants to make."

"He's the catch you make right before you get blindsided."

"Nice football analogy!"

"Whatever," I sigh. "Call it whatever lame term you want, but I do wish I hadn't done it." I walk to the window and look down at the traffic. My emotions are still a little bruised and hearing him ask about me only feels like another knock right where it hurts. "I think it was too soon after Callum."

"What makes you say that?"

"I don't know. I've had one-night stands before. You know that."

"Remember the singer from the karaoke bar on the south side?" she giggles.

"Worst one-night stand ever," we say in unison before falling into a fit of giggles at the guy who asked me to fetch him a toothbrush the next morning.

"I have no problem with detachment," I point out. "I can get on for the sake of getting off, but I have such a weak spot for athletes and Branch is . . ."

"The best of the best?" she snickers.

"So cheesy," I laugh. "But, yes, more or less. He's off hanging out with models and I'm in my pajamas until noon eating Nutella off a spoon. It makes me feel sad and I want my girl power back."

"I hear you. Your feels are fair."

"Ooohhh," I tease. "Are you validating my stupid feelings?"

"I suppose I am," she grins. "But I'm still standing firm on wide receivers and tight ends being okay for future reference."

"Nope."

She looks scared to ask why I responded so quickly, so firmly to her stance. Taking a couple of steps back, doing this back-and-forth thing with her torso, she smacks her lips together. "Nope," she reiterates.

"I'm done with football players. You and Finn are right," I say, feeling the bitterness of the words as they launch into the world. "It's an ugly, predictable cycle and I'm a moron for signing up for this self-inflicted abuse. I need to find a cute accountant and an aloe vera plant and some cooking magazines and start over again fresh."

"I veto the accountant and think you should go more blue-collar because they're good with their hands, but I'll buy you your first aloe vera plant. Speaking of gifts, are you going to Tiffany's party?"

A vague memory of being asked to attend a friend's dirty thirty party tickles my brain. "Do I have to?"

"No, but you should," she says. "It'll be fun. It's Tiffany, for crying out loud. God knows what she's set up."

"Fine," I huff. "They'll probably have good appetizers there."

"What is it with you and food?" she laughs.

"I'm starving from doing posts about picnics and romantic getaways and sensual foods. You'll never believe what I read that you can do with grapes."

"I don't even want to know."

"Oh, but you do, but you have to read it yourself. Look it up sometime."

Lifting my purse back on my shoulder, I wince. One hand shoots to the back of my neck as I hold pressure on the spot that aches so bad it throbs.

"What's wrong?" she asks.

"Spreader's remorse."

"Did that sexy bastard give you a sex injury?"

"It was a parting present. Get it?" I joke, wincing again as another shot of pain shoots down my back. "Damn it. It hurts."

She watches me, gauging how much discomfort I must really be in. "I have an appointment tomorrow with my acupuncturist. Want to take it?"

"No."

"She's really good. I've seen her for years and she's terrible to get into. Just take my appointment. You can't keep living with the pain and I know you aren't seeing a doctor."

Shrugging, I dig through my purse for my over-the-counter pain medicine as Poppy's fingers start flying across her phone.

"There," she says. "I told Bai you'd be there instead of me."

"Thanks." I pop two pills without a drink. "Now can we go get a hot ham and cheese?"

"Lead the way," she laughs, following me out the door.

—

BRANCH

SWEAT DRIPS INTO MY EYES causing my vision to blur as I hunch over, hands on my knees, and pant.

"I hate fucking shuttle runs," Finn gasps beside me. He's in the same position, struggling to catch his breath.

We make our way to the sidelines of the high school field we've been allowed to use until spring camp starts. Digging into my bag, I find a towel and douse it with water from a chilled water bottle in a cooler. Wiping my face sends a ripple of coolness through my body, and once I can see again, I lay it along the back of my neck.

"You ready to start work?" Finn asks, his face still beet red. "I'm itching to get back on the field with the boys."

"It's what we live for."

"Yeah." He sucks down a bottle of water in one gulp. "I have been enjoying the offseason though."

"You mean you've enjoyed Poppy's pussy." The sound of the words out loud makes me laugh. "It sounds like a porno. Poppy's Pussy."

"I like to pop that pussy," Finn laughs. "But seriously, man. I like her. Like, I might *like her* like her."

"Don't do it, Finn."

"Do what?"

"Start taking this shit seriously."

"We've had our fun," Finn says. "A lot of it. But I just feel different right now, you know? Like maybe the hoes and blows is just too much work."

I look at him like he's crazy. "Have you lost your goddamn mind? They aren't too much work. They're easy. That's the point."

"Maybe it's like ball. Maybe if it's easy, you'll never win the championship. If it's hard—if you're training your ass off and making sacrifices and choosing the work over the weed, you can win. Maybe it's the same."

"I feel like I don't even know you right now," I balk. "You can't be serious."

"Think about it. It might be nice having someone you know will be there when you come home at the end of the day. Someone to talk to. Someone you can wine and dine."

"You can't wine and dine groupies, Finn. It confuses them."

"*Exactly,*" he says like I just made his point for him. "Maybe taking a beautiful girl out to dinner wouldn't be a bad thing. It might feel good to rent a houseboat on Lake Powell and instead of entertaining a bunch of jackasses that don't give a fuck about you, just about your bank account, and spend some time just relaxing and enjoying life."

"Sorry," I say, shoving my things back into my bag. "Enjoying life means women, weed, and work. The only singular thing in that sentence is work."

Finn laughs, but I think it's more *at* me than *with* me. He gets his things together and we start the walk from the fifty-yard line to the gate that leads to the parking lot.

"What are you doing this weekend? Heading up to the cabin?" I ask, hoping he doesn't hear the hope in my voice.

He hasn't mentioned Layla at all in the weeks we've been home. I've brought her up a couple of times as sneakily as I could, but he answered in the fewest number of words he could manage. I did get some insight from Poppy, but her team flag was flying and it didn't have my name on it.

"Nah," he says. "I have a party this weekend."

"Are you supposed to be partying, Mr. Monogamous?"

"Poppy is coming."

"Yup. Don't even know you."

But what I do know without him saying is that if he's going and Poppy's going, odds are pretty fucking spectacular that Layla will be going too.

I don't know what to say to her, especially knowing she has a pretty good idea what went down at Crave. I have no clue how to approach her or if she'll even want to entertain the idea of talking to me. Still, I really, really want to just let her know I didn't fuck that girl at the bar. I don't know what it matters, but it does.

Thankfully, Finn helps me out.

"What are you up to this weekend?" he asks, shoving the metal gates open so we can pass through.

"Not much. Just hanging out, I guess. I do have an interview sometime Saturday. Want to do something after?"

"I have the party, remember."

"Oh."

He side-eyes me. "Wanna go?"

Yes.

"Is it going to be any good?" I say to deflect from the little boy jumping up and down inside me.

"Do I ever go to bad parties?"

"Debatable."

He laughs. "It's at the Standen on Saturday. I'm sure Tiffany Standen will love it if you come."

"Count me in."

Touchdown.

THIRTEEN
LAYLA

"RIGHT THIS WAY."

A tall, thin woman with beautiful jet-black hair leads me down a hall. The walls are adorned with red and black paintings that have flecks of gold glitter on them in what appears to be a random fashion. Something tells me it's not random at all.

I'm taken into a cozy room with seafoam green walls with buttery yellow accents. A grey pillow lays on the end of a long table covered with a fitted white sheet. There are two pictures hanging on the walls of the human body, one from the front and the other from the back.

"Please have a seat on the table and Bai will be in to see you shortly."

"Um," I stammer. "Do I leave my clothes on?"

"Yes," she says sweetly. "For now, Bai will determine your diagnosis. She may treat you today, but often times she gets to know you first."

"Okay."

Once I'm alone, I peek around the room. It's set up to feel relaxing and soothing, but I can't help but feel I'm at some kind of gyno appointment.

My heart is racing, my palms sweaty, when a soft knock raps against the door and a short woman with the shiniest hair I've ever seen walks in. She has a sweet, simple smile and a notepad in her hand.

"You are Ms. Miller?" she asks, extending a hand. "I'm Bai. It's nice to meet you."

"Nice to meet you. Poppy Quinn made the appointment for me."

"Oh, Poppy. She's one of my favorites. I've worked with her for a couple of years now."

"She speaks very highly of you," I tell her, my nerves quieting just a bit.

"I hope she doesn't use that crude language of hers when she does so. That girl needs a bar of soap."

"That she does."

Bai gets settled at the little desk and grabs an ink pen. "Tell me why you're here."

"I have a little kink in my neck. There's a knot," I say, rubbing the top of my spine. "The pain has started to spread down my back and even around into my stomach some today."

"Okay. Got it. Do you know how you arrived at this condition?"

Yes. My head was rammed into a stainless steel refrigerator while a stallion of a man buried himself in me from behind.

"No."

"Okay. Very good." She looks up from her scribblings. "The first thing we will do every appointment is check your pulse and your tongue. In Chinese medicine, we learn so much about your health from these two points. I'm just telling you this beforehand because sometimes it makes people think I've lost my mind."

Laughing, I nod. "I understand."

"Let's start with the tongue. Can you stick it out for me?"

Following her instructions, I watch as she stands and gets closer with a little light. "I'm not telling you what I'm looking for because it would be really confusing, but it looks good. You can close your mouth now."

She jots a few notes on the pad and then comes back to me. "Now your pulse."

She touches me above the left wrist, then on one of my fingers. Her face is passive and I can't tell a thing about what she's feeling. She moves to the right side and does the same series of touches down my arm to my fingers.

Clearing her throat, she sits down again and scratches on the pad. "Okay. I think I have enough here. We can get started today, if you'd like, or we can wait and start next time."

"I'd like to start today, please," I insist. "This hurts."

She smiles. "That's fine. I will need you to disrobe in a moment and lay flat on the table. I do need to be clear that I cannot do certain methods due to your condition."

"My what?"

"Your condition. Acupuncture is one hundred percent safe during pregnancy, but to be cautious, I—"

"Whoa, whoa, whoa," I say, leaping off the table. "Back up. You've mixed up my file with someone else's," I laugh. "I'm not pregnant."

She looks at me like I'm crazy.

"I'm really not," I insist. "I don't even have a boyfriend."

"You should have a physician check to be sure, of course, but the pulse is a very strong indicator in Chinese medicine. I'm sorry you didn't know."

"I can't be pregnant, Bai," I tell her, like I can change her mind and wipe this conversation from ever happening.

I can hear the blood rushing over my ears as I try to calm myself back down.

"If you say so, Ms. Miller. Only you know what can and can't be true. But until I know, I must err on the side of caution."

"You know what?" I say, gathering my purse off the floor. "Let's start this next time. I need to take care of a few things today."

"Good luck," she says softly. "Please check out at the front with Ada and she can set up your next appointment."

"Thank you."

I fling the door open and nearly stomp down the quiet hall. It takes longer than I care to wait for Ada to give me my insurance card back and hand me a receipt. Declining another appointment, I storm out of the office into the hot afternoon air.

Whipping out my phone, I pound my finger into Poppy's name. It rings four times before she picks up. I don't bother letting her greet me.

"That doctor of yours is a quack!"

"What?" she laughs. "What's going on?"

"She's a quack. Bai doesn't know shit about shit."

I rattle on about how acupuncture is fake medicine and how I will never go there again and I might even do a blog post about the dangers of people that pretend to know how things work when really they don't know anything at all. I jabber on and on, all the while trying to force out a little niggle in my brain that asks, "What if?"

My stomach drops as I round the corner. "She's nuts."

"She's not nuts," Poppy whispers. "Hang on." I hear her heels clicking against the floor and the sound of chimes. "I had to come outside you were talking so damn loud. What the hell is going on?"

"You know what she said?"

"Quack, quack?"

"Very funny. No. She *is* a quack. She didn't *say* quack. Ugh," I groan. "Don't distract me."

"Fine. What did she say?"

"She had the audacity to say I'm pregnant, Pop. Can you believe that shit?"

The line goes quiet. My exuberant, chatty friend doesn't say a word.

"Poppy?"

"Are you?"

"No, I'm not pregnant!" A flock of birds launch into a tree above me and I look around to see a group of people staring at me. Rolling my eyes, I storm by them too. "No, I'm not," I say, quieter this time. "Why do I keep explaining this to everyone? You have to have sperm to have a baby."

"Have you slept with anyone?"

"No. Not since Branch."

"Layla . . ."

A full-on shiver that starts at my shoulders and rolls through my body like a Garth Brooks song hits me hard. I stand at the corner of Plane and Veroca and stare off into space.

"Did he use a condom?" she asks.

"Yeah. He did," I say, shaking out of my trance. "So explain that *and* I'm on the pill."

"Weirder things have happened."

"To weird people, maybe. I'm not a weird person."

"You were sick before the cabin, weren't you? Were you taking antibiotics?"

I try to swallow, but my throat constricts at the same time. Bent over, halfway choking and the other half gagging, I nearly drop my phone as I try not to die.

"Layla! Layla, are you okay?"

"Yes," I say past the burn. "Give me a second." It takes longer than a second to get myself upright and fully oxygenated. "I'm here," I croak.

"Dude, you scared me."

"Don't make this about you," I laugh, my voice still hoarse from the coughing fit. Once my laughter has faded and the line is quiet again, I feel the heavy burden of being alone. Despite the sea of people racing by me on the corner of this street in downtown Chicago, I'm *alone*. "I can't be pregnant, can I?"

"I don't know. I tell you what—let me wrap up a project I have open. It might take an hour. Then I'll meet you at your apartment. I'll bring chocolate and tissues and a pregnancy test, then a bottle of champagne for after when it's false."

Despite my need to vomit all over the sidewalk, I smile. "Thanks, Poppy."

"You're welcome."

Fourteen
Layla

LIFTING A SPOON OF VANILLA icing to my mouth, I watch Poppy enter the kitchen. Her phone is to her ear, a plastic grocery bag in one of her hands. She looks at me with brows tugged together, her lips forming a sympathetic curve.

"I'm at Layla's," she says into the phone. "Oh, no. We're just doing girl stuff."

She sits the bag on the counter and drops her keys next to it. "Layla, Finn and Branch say hello."

"Fuck him," I groan.

"That's what got you in this mess," she growls, narrowing her eyes. "Oh, no, Finn. I was talking to your sister. Her, um, her kitchen is a mess. Something she was testing out just turned into a shit storm really quick. That's why I'm here. To help figure out how to clean it up."

"Nice double entendre, asshole," I tell her, not bothering to lower my voice.

"Yes, Finn. I will. I'll call you when I'm done here. Bye." She swipes the phone off and lets it go sailing across the counter. "You ready for the big reveal?"

"This is not a game."

"We should make it fun," she shrugs. "Want to take bets?"

"*No*, I don't want to *take bets*, you lunatic."

She takes a step back and looks me up and down. "This baby is going to be gorgeous. I mean just beautiful."

"There is no baby!" I shout, even stomping my feet a little for effect.

The slight hold I have on my sanity is fraying at an alarming rate and I am almost unable to find any strands left to hold on to. "I'm *not* having a baby."

"Let's take a test and be sure. And then, when you're not, we'll drink the champagne I just paid way too much for at the corner store and celebrate."

"Deal."

She rustles through the bag and pulls out a test that promises to be simple and to provide accurate results sooner than any other brand. She hands it over.

"I can't believe I'm doing this." I march down the hall and into my bathroom and close the door. "I was on the pill," I yell through the wall, ripping open the package. Laying the back of the box on the counter so I know which marking means what, I yank down my pants and sit down.

"Antibiotics!" she shouts back.

"And he wore a condom!"

"Maybe it had a rip?"

"Can I sue them for that?"

"No," she giggles.

Taking one deep, heavy breath that feels like my last as a free, sane woman, I jab the stick between my legs and do my business. With each tinkle, I squeeze my eyes harder, like each second of urine stream is another step closer to a life I don't want. That I can't imagine. That I hope beyond all hope isn't really happening to me.

Branch's handsome face flickers through my mind, and for some unknown reason, I want to kiss him as hard as I want to deck him right in his nine-inch cock.

I clean up, lay the stick on a hand towel, and open the door. Poppy is leaning against the wall.

"Come watch with me. It'll be like the solar eclipse," I tell her. "This will happen once in a lifetime. After this experience, I never want to have a baby."

"I think the eclipse happens more than once," she points out. "And it looks like this won't have to happen again because . . . you're pregnant, Layla."

The end of that is a whisper, but that's not why I don't hear it. I don't hear the words because I can see it on her face—the way her eyes grow, the corners of her lips softening, the ever-so-slight drop in her shoulders.

"Pop . . ." I fall against the wall, my knees threatening to betray my weight. They shake like I'm ready to come, wobble like I've just run five miles which I've never done, but this is what I think would happen if I did.

I can barely stand. I can't think. I can barely even see straight as Poppy lays a hand on my shoulder. Her lips move but I don't hear her. I'm lost in the last words she said to me.

Focusing on her face is harder than it should be and I pick the little freckle just under her left eye and try to see its shape and color. It's a blur. Everything is a blur.

A hand goes to my stomach. I try to imagine what's happening beneath my skin.

I'm pregnant.

I jerk my hand away. Looking at Poppy's face, I feel the tears before I even realize they're falling.

"I can't be pregnant," I whisper, not even sounding like my voice.

"I'm only asking this because I'm your friend, okay? It's Branch's baby, isn't it?"

"Yes."

"There are absolutely no other options. You didn't sleep with Callum and not tell me or drink some wine and just fool around with your neighbor?"

"No. I haven't slept with Callum in, what, four months? Branch is the absolute only person."

She nods, obviously coming to terms with the situation too. "How do you want to proceed? I'll do whatever you say."

"Rewind to that weekend and don't let me go to Linton."

She grins. "I can't do that."

"You said you'd do anything," I sniffle. "What am I going to do?"

My back drags down the wall until I'm sitting on the cool bathroom floor. Poppy plops down beside me sitting crisscross-applesauce and waiting for me to guide the conversation.

"I don't even know him," I lament. "How can I be having a baby by a man I barely even know?"

The tears fall harder, the salty streaks reaching my lips and dripping onto the floor.

"It's going to be all right, Layla."

"I know it's going to be all right. I don't have a choice but for it to be anything but all right," I say, taking the piece of toilet tissue she hands me. "But . . ."

"We'll figure it out."

"I'm the girl I never wanted to be," I say. "Single. Pregnant. Unprepared. So fucking unprepared."

My head falls into my hands, my stomach churning. Just a few days ago—hell, a few hours ago—my biggest problem was Callum texting me. That seems so much more manageable now.

"You aren't any kind of girl unless you're talking about a fun, sexy, best person kind of girl," she says, scooting closer and pulling me into a hug. The contact does it. The river breaks and I sob on her shoulder.

After a long while, when I'm cried out for the time being, she finally pulls away. I mop up my face with the tissue.

"You don't have to make any decisions now," she soothes.

"That's good because I don't have any idea where to start trying to unravel this fucking mess."

"Do you want to tell Finn?"

"Uh, no. Let's not tell Finn. I'd rather him not get involved and kill us all."

Staring at the wall, I feel completely detached from my body. It's almost as if I've been usurped in a coup and now I wait to see where I've been banished.

I drag in a breath, my body shaking as it settles. "This is going to be okay," I tell myself. "This is going to be okay."

"Yes, it is. Let's take it one day at a time and don't get overwhelmed." She twists her lips. "Can I still drink the champagne?"

As I fight not to laugh, she stands and pulls me to my feet.

"I know this is about you," she insists, "but can I be the Godmother? I've always wanted to be a Godmother."

"Oh my God, stop."

She pulls me down the hallway, babbling away about baby names and does what best friends do—lets me lean on her.

FIFTEEN
LAYLA

"I'M GOING TO BE THE lamest party-goer of all time," I lament, holding up two outfits. One is a coral-colored dress that I purchased as soon as I broke up with Callum. It's sexy and fun and flirty . . . and so not becoming of a woman with child.

"You are not." Poppy catches the dress as I toss it to her. "I love this. Are you not wearing it?"

Holding up a semi-fitted blue top that reminds me of the water surrounding a tropical island, I shake my head. "I can't wear that. I bought it to pick up guys. It seems . . . immoral, considering the circumstances."

"You're having a baby, not joining a nunnery."

"This whole thing is so confusing," I sigh. Plopping down on the bed, my freshly curled hair bounces on my shoulders. "The doctor's office gave me an appointment and a link to a website with information overload. It just . . . it still doesn't feel real. How can a baby be inside me?"

"I have such a smartass response to that, but I'll withhold because I see you're stressing." Brushing a lock of hair out of her face, she blows out a breath. "I'm not going to lie and say I get what you're feeling because I don't, thank God. I have no idea what this must be like."

"It's scary."

She wraps an arm around my shoulder and leans her head against mine. We sit on the bed like this for a couple of minutes, my friend just being that—my friend. Sometimes you don't need advice and you don't need promises that it will all be okay. You just need someone beside you saying, "I'm here."

"You know what the scariest part about this is?" I ask.

"No."

"That website has all of these women smiling and glowing and skipping through fields of lavender."

"Really?" she asks, lifting a brow.

"No, but you get the idea," I sigh. "I'm just . . . not. I don't feel like this swamp of love and excitement has hit me yet, and I'm worried it won't."

"Of course you will, but you gotta give yourself some time, Lay. You've only known this for a couple of days."

"But I already feel like a mom failure."

She laughs and stands, jerking the blouse out of my hands and shoving the dress back in them. "You are not a mom failure and you are not wearing . . . this," she snarls, tossing the shirt in the bottom of my closet. "You're wearing the dress and you're gonna be hot and we're gonna go party at Tiffany's and have some fun."

"I don't know . . ."

"I do. Get up, get dressed, and let's get out of here."

After saluting me, which makes me laugh, she leaves me alone to finish getting ready. I wear the dress and a pair of nude heels and even throw on a long necklace with a large, fake blue stone at the end. The color vaguely reminds me of Branch's eyes. Standing still, I handle the stone and wonder what color eyes our baby will have.

"No," I say, when the tears start to come again. "These are tears of fear. You won't cry. You will handle this like the boss you are."

Skipping the smoky eye in case I feel less like a boss later want to avoid a charcoal river down my face, I put on minimal makeup and take myself in when complete. It's not too bad. I can tell I've been crying, but I know me. I don't think anyone else, besides Poppy and maybe Finn, will.

"Don't you look pretty," Poppy says, coming in the room. "I love that dress on you. So much better than the interview blouse."

"I actually did buy that for an interview."

"Yeah. I could tell."

Before I can think twice, I whirl around on my heel. "Have you seen Branch?"

"Yes."

I nod, not sure where to go with this now. I'm not even sure what I want to know or hope to hear, and she doesn't volunteer anything, which both provides both comfort and distress.

"He asked about you again," she says quietly. "Nothing much, just if I had seen you."

"What did you say?"

"I said you got a brand new project that has your hands full for the next nine months or so."

"You did not," I gasp.

"I did. But he's so . . . Branch . . . he didn't get it," she laughs. "It's funny! Come on!"

Glaring at her, I cross my arms over my chest. "It's not funny. I wish you'd stop seeing the humor in it."

"You do not," she groans. "You keep me around for my humor. So, you want to know what else he said?"

Biting my lip, I lift my shoulders up and down like there's a boulder sitting on them.

"You do. The answer is, 'I do, Poppy.' So, he asked if you would be up for having dinner with him if he called you."

My lip pops free as my traitorous heart leaps like a greeting card commercial. "He did?"

"No, I'm making it up."

"I'm gonna kill you."

"*Yes*, he did. He asked me that. I told him maybe he should wait a few days, that you were a little preoccupied and needed a little space. But maybe this is a good sign?"

Staring at the wall, I wonder if he means it. I was certain he'd have moved on by now. No, I'm certain he has. But a dinner is one thing, and being told you're going to be a father is much, much different.

He's the father of my child.

I knew this before, but this is the moment that realization hits me. Hard. I must look worse for wear because Poppy grabs my elbow and bends down to eye-level.

"Are you okay?" she asks.

"Nope."

"Want to sit down? Need water? My instinct is to offer you vodka, but that's not on the menu anymore."

"Branch is the father of my baby, Poppy."

"*Yes . . .*" she says, dropping my elbow.

"How am I going to tell him? I mean, if I could not tell him it would be so much easier, but I can't not tell him, right? I mean, I could not tell him but that's not the right—"

"Breathe," she giggles. "That was like one giant sentence. And, yes, you have to tell him. Not today. Not tomorrow. But you do have to tell him."

My lashes close, blocking out her concerned face and the light that's threatening to give me a headache. "How do you think he'll take it?"

"I've never told a guy I'm having his kid, so I have no idea."

"Do you think he'll think I did it on purpose?"

"Oh, I think the look on your face proves you didn't do this on purpose," she shrugs. "He may not be happy about it, but I'm not sure you are either. And I think you have to stop cursing now," she says, tapping her lips with the tip of her finger. "I think the baby can hear you."

Rolling my eyes, I grab my purse and head to the door. "Well, as long as I'm friends with you, it's going to hear profane language. I may as well keep it consistent."

Poppy's laughter follows me into the hallway. She starts jabbering on about the party and how excited Tiffany is that we're coming. I tune her out.

This might be the last time I get to go out and do fun things for the rest of my life. Dramatic, maybe. But it's also true.

"Pop?"

"Yeah?" she says as we await the elevator.

"Let's have fun tonight, okay?"

She grins. "Yes. Let's."

SIXTEEN
BRANCH

"TIFFANY, THIS IS BRANCH BEST." Finn makes the introduction, his arm around Poppy. "Branch, Tiffany Standen."

Tiffany, the woman of the hour, makes no secret of checking me out. She scoops her eyes down my body, licking her lips on the return trip. Her own body is smashed into a skin-tight white dress and a little tiara with white and pink feathers sits atop her reddish locks.

"Branch Best, it's a pleasure to meet you."

"Happy Birthday," I say, looking over her shoulder as discreetly as I can. A group of women walk in and I scan them quickly and then return to Tiffany when none of them are Layla.

"You could make sure it's a *very* happy one," she breathes.

Finn cackles beside me while I feel Poppy's gaze settling on my features, waiting on my response.

Smiling awkwardly, I take a deep breath. "I think that lady over there is trying to get your attention."

Turning to see a thin woman in a red dress in the corner, she gives her a little wave. "I have to talk to my party planner really quick. I hope we can catch up later."

There's no promise offered of a hook up later from my end. She's fine to look at and I halfway think I've fucked her before, but surely one of us would remember that.

"See ya," she says, waving at me over her shoulder.

She teeters away on heels so tall I wonder how long it'll take her to wind up on that very round ass before the night is over. My guess is broken up when Poppy speaks beside me.

"Finn," she says. "Will you get me a drink? Please."

"Anything in particular?"

"Nothing too hard. It's too early for that."

He smirks. "First time I've ever heard you say that."

She laughs, her hair brushing against her back as she shoos Finn away. Then she turns to me, her face sobering. "I didn't know you knew Tiffany."

"I didn't."

"Then why are you here?"

She knows the fucking answer. She knows I'm trying to run into her *randomly*. But that doesn't matter. What *does* matter is the tone she used to ask the question.

There was no eagerness to it. No excitement. No hint this could be awesome. Nope, none of that. Instead, her eyes are narrow with a touch of something else that leads me to believe this encounter, should it happen, will be anything but awesome.

"Is Layla here with someone else?" I ask.

She takes a second, one too many, to consider this. "Not exactly."

My jaw clenches, my teeth grinding together, as I try to prepare myself to see the girl I can't stop thinking about waltzing in here with another guy. Surely Poppy would've just told me if she was seeing someone else.

"It's not Worthington, is it?"

"No," she huffs. "It's not Callum. It's no one, really. She's . . . Fine. She's alone, Branch."

"Then why say that? You just about got someone hurt."

"Forget it. It was a joke gone bad. Just . . ." She looks at the chandelier hanging above us in the penthouse of the Standen Hotel. "You need to give her some space tonight, okay? She doesn't know you're here and she just needs some . . . space."

"Did I do something to offend her?" I ask, an odd sensation coming over me. "Did I hurt her or say something really stupid?"

"No. Nothing like that."

"Then why are you acting like I should stay away from her, Poppy?"

Very slowly, her chin drops until we're face-to-face. There's no joke on the tip of her tongue, no silly comeback that she always has ready to fire. In the vacancy lies a seriousness that has me forcing a swallow.

She considers her words. "She has some things going on, Branch. I'm sure she'll talk to you, but just be gentle if you see her, please."

Be gentle?

"Just between you and me," I say, "she doesn't like it gentle."

"Branch!"

"Fine. I hear you. Be easy with her. Got it."

Her arms plant firmly across her chest. "You are so not going to heed any of what I said, are you?"

"Nope."

"Damn you."

"I'll be gentle, even though I think that's the pussiest word I've ever heard," I admit. "But if I see her, I'm going to talk to her. If she tells me to go fuck myself for some reason, I'll probably do just that because I've been doing that for the last few weeks every time I think of her."

"Nice visual."

"I have it down to a science. I use the left hand for foreplay and the right to bring it home."

"Oh my God," she laughs, shaking her head.

"You rang?" Finn pops between us and pulls Poppy into his side and hands her a drink. "What are you thinking, Best? See anyone you know?"

"Not yet, but you know me. I make friends everywhere I go."

Finn chuckles. "If that's what you want to call them."

"Speaking of, I'm going to mingle. You two kids behave."

Poppy tries to shoot me a warning glance, but I avoid receiving it. Instead, I spin on my heel and wander about the penthouse that's the stage for the birthday bash.

There are crystals everywhere, dangling off light fixtures and filling vases with big, drippy candles. Music plays through the sound-system, broken up by someone on a mic saying a deejay will be starting soon. I lift a mini-burger off a tray carried around by a man in a white jacket and look for Layla.

People begin to show up in thicker droves, yet the party is much more controlled than I anticipated. I meander through the throngs of people with the burger in my hand, saying hello to various people as I go.

Her giggle stops me dead in my tracks, my eyes glued to an oversized golden mirror on the wall ahead. I listen, my senses on high alert, waiting for the sound to come again.

Watching the reflection, bodies move behind me. The deejay is firing up an early-two-thousands hit when I see her.

A pinkish-orange dress hugs her curves, her hair hanging soft around her shoulders. She looks beautiful with her rosy cheeks and bright eyes. She radiates a simple elegance that I can't look away from.

She catches me watching her, one hand flying to the base of her throat. Her eyes go wide and cause the lady she's speaking with to ask her if she's all right. I see her nod, telling them she's okay, then excusing herself into a crowd to her left. It takes me a whole half a second to follow her, dumping the uneaten burger on a table.

Thanks to her heels and my athletic ability, I catch up with her right as she's heading onto a balcony off a bedroom. The air is warm, thick with the scents of the city with twinkling lights sparkling on the river below.

"Hey," I say, pulling the sliding glass door closed behind me. She stands at the railing, her back to me, and doesn't respond to my greeting. "Are you okay, Layla?"

"I'm fine, Branch. How are you?"

"A little confused."

She nods but still doesn't face me. "The city is so beautiful from here. So peaceful."

I stand next to her so close the fabric of our clothes touch, but our bodies beneath don't. She sucks in a breath as I place one hand beside hers on the black iron rail. "It's quiet," I admit. "It's hard to believe it's Chicago. It reminds me of home."

"What's it like where you're from?"

"Memphis is a city that feels like a town," I tell her softly. "It's nice and quiet for the most part and has that Southern hospitality thing going for it."

"Sounds nice."

"It is."

"Does your family live there?"

Turning my head, I take her in. The breeze rustles her hair, her perfume filling the air making me want to wrap her up and kiss the ever-loving fuck out of her. It's a wild, strange phenomenon to want to simply *kiss* her.

"My family does live there. My parents live in the same house I grew up in," I tell her, not sure why the questions all of a sudden. "I tried to buy them a new one when I signed the first contract, but they're stubborn."

"And proud, I bet."

"My dad has an entire room devoted to me in the house. It's like a shrine or something. It's pretty awkward."

She glances at me and we share a small, simple laugh.

"I imagine your dad is like a grown-up version of you," she says. "Not as bulky, but more handsome in a Sam Elliott kind of way."

"My mom would love that analogy. She has a major crush on him."

"Every girl does, Branch," she giggles. "He's the epitome of getting sexier with age."

"I'll try to remember that," I say, making a face that causes some of the tension in her shoulders to melt away. The faint circles under her eyes grab my attention and a curiosity seats itself in the bottom of my gut. "How have you been?"

And that does it. Her face turns back to the city and I'm met with silence.

It's an automatic response to place my hand over hers, just like it appears to be a reflex of hers to jump when we touch. Her head whips to the side where I'm just waiting to catch her eyes.

"Layla, did I do something to you?"

Her laugh is loud and full-bellied and filled with an anxious edge that has me withdrawing my hand from hers. She's wiping tears from the reaction and catches her breath before even trying to talk.

My stomach flip-flops as I process this response, one I didn't see coming and I don't know how to categorize. Sorting through the memories from the cabin for the millionth time, I can't put my finger on anything I could've said or done that would have been offensive or more stupid than usual.

"I'm glad you find me so funny," I mutter, my gut twisted in a tight knot the same way it is when I'm standing at the line face-to-face with a cornerback.

"It's really not funny." She sucks in a hasty breath. "It's not funny at all."

"You know what," I say, defense mechanisms kicking in, "I apologize for whatever it is. I'll leave you alone. Have a good night, Layla."

I head for the door, not bothering to give her a second to change her mind. I don't even look at her over my shoulder. This is another girl playing games, a girl I just happen to let get under my skin in a moment of weakness.

My hand is on the pull when my name whispers through the air behind me. I freeze, processing the way it sounds like it was uttered on a whim, a last-second decision to call my name even though it's clearly filled with a hesitancy to do it.

"Yeah?" I stay facing the glass, barely able to make out her reflection due to the brightness inside.

I wait, hand still primed to yank open the slider. My annoyance level is far too high, the irritation at myself slipping into anger. My mind is chastising me for even being here, for chasing down this girl who doesn't want to see me, because if she did, she would've reached out. She could've planted a little seed with Poppy. My dumb ass can't take a fucking clue.

The roll of the door just starts to rumble when she finally speaks again. "Wait."

"Layla, we don't have to do this," I sigh, snapping the door shut. "I didn't mean to bother you or put you in some weird position. I just wanted to say hi."

Turning, I take her in. Her posture is defiant, her chin lifted towards the inky black sky.

"Trust me when I say I don't want to do this." Her confidence wobbles. "I need to sit down." She moves quickly across the balcony and slides into a chair next to a small glass table. "You probably should sit down too."

My stomach bottoms out, dropping to my feet, as I drag myself to the chair opposite her. My skin is coated with a cold sweat, every nightmare I've ever contemplated rolling through me like it's three in the morning and I'm lonely.

"What the hell is going on?" I drop into the seat, wiping the sweat off my palms.

"I'm pregnant, Branch."

Falling back into the chair, I blow out a sigh of relief that it wasn't some STD talk. I hate those. The last time that happened a girl tried to extort me for ten thousand dollars until I volunteered to show her my regular screening and that I've never had any sort of venereal disease. Ever.

"What did he say?" I ask.

"Who?"

"Callum."

She slow-blinks. "Callum?"

"You haven't told him yet?" I ask, watching her work through a battery of emotions. My own are a little whirled as I realize my lusting over this woman has probably just had to come to a screeching halt. She has bigger fish to fry than my cock . . . and that's pretty fucking big.

"It'll be all right," I say, as encouraging as I can while setting aside the fact that this is not how I'd hoped this conversation was going to go. "He'll come around. But do you want some advice?"

She slow-blinks again, this time with her mouth hanging open. I take that as a yes.

"Take charge right away. Don't let him start calling the shots or thinking he gets to say shit about your life."

"Branch . . ."

We sit across the table, the moon shining just enough to illuminate her pretty features and I resent the fact that Callum is the one that spent that kind of intimate time with her. Fucker didn't even appreciate it.

A wash of fear trickles across her face. My heart clenches, the do-gooder that's buried so far below the surface I don't see it much chooses this moment to come forward.

"You need help telling Finn? He's gonna be pissed, Layla."

"I know," she squeaks.

"No, I don't think you do," I laugh, just imagining my best friend's response to this little piece of news. "He might drive to Columbus tonight and kick the shit out of him."

"Branch . . ."

"I'll make sure he gets bailed out."

"Branch." This time it's a command, a warning to stop talking and listen. "I need to talk to you."

"We're talking, Sunshine."

Her throat moves with a hard swallow. She leans back in her chair, combing a hand through the side of her hair. "Um, so . . ." She releases a breath. "The baby. Um . . . Branch, the baby isn't Callum's."

"Then whose is it?" I watch her face and realize . . . I'm better off not knowing. With a need to get off of the balcony and into the comfort of a mass of drunk bodies, I start to stand. "You know what, I don't want to know."

"The baby is yours." She blurts the words like it's a burden under the weight of which she's being crushed. That if she just chucks it into the world, gets the offending words out of her mouth, she can breathe.

I stop dead in my tracks.

Replaying the statement, it makes no more sense than it did the first time.

She looks at me like she's watching a man learn his fate after being tried for the most heinous of crimes. It's a mixture of fear at the reaction, but also an acute curiosity.

"What did you just say?" I ask.

"The baby is yours, Branch."

"What the fuck are you talking about?" I scoff, my chair going sailing back and smashing against the glass. "The baby is mine? Your baby is mine? No way."

"I'm pregnant and the only person I've slept with is you."

I laugh because that's all I can do short of exploding everything within reach.

This has to be some kind of sick joke or game or attempt to piss me off for not calling her. That's happened before, but not to this extent. Still, it's possible.

"Layla, really," I say, taking a deep breath and trying to calm down. "If you're pregnant—congratulations, but the baby cannot be mine."

"I know it's hard to believe—"

"Hard to believe? You know what's hard to believe? That it's *you* pulling this shit. I've had a lot of things pinned on me, but, believe it or not, never a kid. I never dreamed it would be you."

The sky looks so dark, so foreboding as I look into it, wondering how the fuck I got here. How did I give this woman enough of a comfort level around me to claim she's pregnant?

As her chair goes skidding against the rails, clamoring as it falls to the tile, I know—this is how it happened. She has that thing about her that's just relatable enough to think she's not like the rest of them. That she sees more than dollar bills and contract numbers. I believed that, and that is what is killing me most right now—I trusted her even when I knew better.

Her golden eyes dance with rage. "You think I'm making this up?"

"I don't doubt you're pregnant, but I have serious doubts it's mine. I used a rubber," I point out, thanking God for that little tidbit. "You're on the pill. Explain to me how the universe pulled off me knocking you up under those circumstances. Hell, if it's even a possibility, do you know how many kids I could have running around out there?"

"I have no idea how many potential offspring you have, Branch, and the fact that I know so little about you worries me too."

"Didn't worry you when you were coming all over my cock."

"And it didn't worry you when you stuck said cock in my vagina and told me how tight I felt wrapped around you before you went and got a condom," she says flatly.

"*Ohhh*. That's where you're saying this happened. In that span of ten seconds I was in you raw?"

She glares at me. "I'm not saying I know when it happened. I'm just saying I know it did."

"This is fucking bullshit."

"You know what's fucking bullshit?" Her arms drop to her side as her tone starts to shift. "That I decided to tell you this because it was the right thing to do, and I almost had myself convinced that we could figure a way to work it out. You know, as I've been sitting around trying not to vomit, crying myself to sleep over not knowing what's going to happen, and how I'm going to handle it all and how you're going to handle it all and what's the best way to tell you and to . . ." She sucks in a breath, her cheeks as flamed as her dress. "Forget I said it. I wish I hadn't."

"Forget you said it?" I laugh angrily. "You just said I knocked you up."

"And that's what it was, wasn't it? You knocked me up. We fucked and now this. That sounds so pretty, doesn't it?" Her features sour. "You think I'm any happier about this than you are? You think I wanted to have a baby by *you*?"

Those words sear into my psyche, the emphasis powering into me. I may as well have taken a hit from the best lineman in the league because my stomach has been walloped hard.

By me? What's that supposed to mean?

"You know what? You can do whatever you want with this information," she says, walking a wide loop around me. "You have my word I'm not saying anything to anyone and I never will. If you don't want to claim this kid, I'll put on the birth certificate that I'm a whore and don't know whose kid it is."

"Layla . . ."

She shoots me the dirtiest look I've ever had someone give me. "If you want to see the baby after it's born, I'd never keep it from you. *I* have a bit of class," she glares, grabbing the door handle. "After a paternity test, *of course*."

With the chilliest final glance she can muster, she yanks open the lever and walks out, leaving me standing in the warm summer night feeling as though I just stepped onto an iceberg.

Fuck.

My.

Life.

<u>SEVENTEEN</u>
LAYLA

"EXCUSE ME," I SAY, PASTING a fake smile on my lips as I bump into a partygoer. My teeth press so hard into one another I can feel the tension in my temples, my jawbones aching from the pressure.

Fighting tears, I scan the penthouse full of people with nothing more on their minds than how much to drink. Jealousy is not something I wrestle with most days, but standing in my too-tight dress in too-high heels and with too much uncertainty wracking my emotions, I'm insanely envious of them all.

The crowds part just enough for me to spot my brother, a good head taller than ninety percent of the attendees, on the far side of the room next to the bar. Again, I go sorting through the faces and will myself to calm down before Finn starts asking questions.

"Hey," he says, stalling his beer bottle mid-air when he sees me coming. "What's wrong?"

"I'm not feeling well." I flip my gaze to Poppy as her eyes grow wide. "I need to go home."

"I'll go with you," she says instantly.

"Stay here and have fun. I'm fine."

"What's wrong, Layla?" my brother asks, the bottle now at his side. "What happened?"

I brush a hand through the air and lie my ass off. "Nothing. I ate a ham sandwich from Yusi's for lunch. Now that I think about it, I think I saw somewhere they had a health code violation last month. I'm probably just having a little food poisoning."

"Which is why I should go with you," Poppy says. "You shouldn't be poisoned alone. You might want someone to call Yusi's and rip them a new asshole and I'm just the person to do it."

"I eat there all the time. I haven't heard that," Finn says.

"Yusi needs his cock removed from his body and shoved down his throat." Maybe it's said with too much gusto, but I've never said something that I mean more.

"Wow. That's harsh," Finn laughs. "Okay. You guys go but take it easy on Yusi. He probably didn't even make the sandwich."

"Oh, he made it . . ." I start, then stop with Finn's brow crooks. "Goodnight, Finn."

Poppy kisses my brother and takes my elbow. She lead-blocks and we make it through the crowd without seeing Branch.

The elevator ride is long and hot and the walk to the parking garage even longer. Each step is like another rung on a ladder with the seat of my car being the top tier. I slide into the passenger's seat and it's instant. The tears come.

Poppy leans over the console and wraps me in her arms, holding me tight. "What did that fucker say to you?"

"Oh, that I'm a whore."

She pulls back, a look of ferocity in her eyes, and grabs the door handle. "I'll be right back."

"No! Pop, stay," I say, jerking on her arm. "He didn't say that. Not outright. Just insinuated that it couldn't be his. That I was either lying or pinning a bastard child on him."

Digging through the glove compartment, I find a handful of napkins and start wiping away the smeared mascara from my cheeks.

"I have to say I'm surprised." Poppy shakes her head. "I thought he'd be more of a man than this."

"I knew he'd be in shock. I mean, look at what I'm dropping on his lap. But he was just so . . . dismissive. Fuck him."

"No. No more fucking him," she cracks. "You've already sucked more from that man than you wanted."

"Really, Poppy?"

"Too soon?"

"Much, much too soon." I toss the napkins on the floorboard, my tears dried up with the anger that's taking the lead. "Will you take me to the store for ice cream before we go home?"

She lifts my purse and grabs the keys and sticks one in the ignition. Moving the car into reverse, she stops and turns to me before letting off the brake.

"Regardless of what he chooses to do about this," she says, "this is an amazing time of your life. I know you didn't expect it now or even want it now, but you're having a baby," she whispers. A slow smile spreads across her thin cheeks. "We're going to give you a few days to let this settle and then we're celebrating you and my little niece or nephew. If Branch opts out of that, his loss."

My head falls to the seatback as I watch her pilot my car through the parking garage. Her words soothe me, and by the time we get out onto the street, I'm drifting off to sleep.

BRANCH

"SORRY. SORRY." MY SIGHT IS blurry as I look at the face in front of me. "I didn't get you wet, did I?"

My arm is extended in front of me, trying to balance the drink that just splashed into the air when I tripped. It continues to slosh, the cool, amber liquid running over my hand.

"What the hell is wrong with you?" Finn comes out of nowhere, despite my best attempt to avoid him.

Truth be told, I should've fucking left. I should've gotten in my car and driven my ass home and gotten away from all this. Despite my inebriated state, this I know. This I regret. But I didn't want to go home alone with too much quiet to think about what Layla said. And the look in her eye. And the words she said after I said my piece. And the way she stormed off.

Bringing the cup to my mouth, I start to suck the rest of it down before Finn snatches it up.

"Hey," I protest, grabbing wildly at the glass. "I wasn't done."

"You were done three drinks ago, buddy."

"Funny. I need three more."

"Let's go."

His palm cupping my shoulder, he guides me towards the door. Women pull on my hand, lure me towards them as we pass, but Finn isn't having it. He just thrusts me on.

"Maybe I want to stay," I say.

"Maybe you need to go to bed before you start looking a lot less like the Branch Best you want the world to remember."

The alcohol finally reaches critical mass and everything goes fuzzy. Warmth hits my toes, the top of my head feeling like it's missing in a great way, and before I know it, I'm in the passenger's seat of Finn's car. As we pull out of the garage, I see Poppy's purse on the floorboard.

"Finn!" I shout.

"What?" He jumps, hitting the brake.

"You forgot Poppy."

"Asshole," he chuckles, accelerating again. "You scared the fuck out of me. I thought I was ready to hit a kid or something."

"Is she in here?" I crane my neck to check the backseat.

"She took Layla home a few hours ago. Something is up with my sister."

Slinking back into the seat, I close my eyes. "Is that right?"

"My guess is Callum, but I don't know. She was ready to cry, all agitated and shit. If that fucker is bothering her, we're taking a road trip and I'm going to dismantle that cocksucker."

I sink further into the leather.

"Layla is too nice for her own good," he continues. "I told her not to trust him, told her guys in this league aren't really marriage material. You know what goes on during away games and hotel nights and at the parties. Shit, remember our first team party night?" he chuckles. "Those guys getting hotel rooms at our hotel for their side pieces and you and I were like, 'What the fuck?' having just met their actual wives the week before."

"Yeah."

"We're professional athletes, man. These guys are used to getting whatever the fuck they want whenever they want. And Callum, he's the worst."

"The Quarterback Effect," I say. "They love calling the shots, the attention, and the glory."

"I'll show him fucking glory," Finn growls, taking a hard right through the streets of downtown.

My breathing is shallow as I imagine how fast it would take for his fist to hit my face if I told him exactly why his sister was upset tonight. I'm guessing three seconds, giving him two for time to process.

My life is so beyond fucked up right now and I don't see a way out. The acid of anxiety hits my liquored-up stomach and I start heaving.

"Don't puke in my car," Finn says, sliding the car over two lanes and into the parking lot of a grocery store with a half-lit sign.

I press open the door and expel my guts, the alcohol burning almost as much as my head. Everything parades through my mind like the clouds on a bright day that zoom by. It's like each thought—Layla, the baby, Finn's reaction, Callum—shoot by, taunting me with their state of undoneness.

Finn hands me a warm water bottle and I don't question it. I just fill my mouth, swish it around, and spit onto the gum-riddled pavement.

"You okay?" he asks as I shut the door.

"No."

He shoots me a curious glance and pulls back out on the road in silence, which is good, because anything I have to say would test out that three-second theory.

EIGHTEEN
LAYLA

EXPOSÉ TOP STORY:
BEST SHOCKER!

W E SEE A lot of Branch Best. (Granted, most of our female readership would argue we don't see quite enough.) Despite the compromising positions we find Number Eleven in, this isn't usually one of them.

Best was seen coming out of the Standen Hotel late last night with Finn Miller. Eye witnesses say Miller was actually holding up his friend and helping him into his SUV.

We can't say there's much Best could do to shock us, but this is very abnormal for him. We've seen him in the throes of a bender and it still didn't look this bad. Not able to stand? There's gossip there and we'll let you know when we figure it out. Stay tuned.

"WHO'S MAKING BREAKFAST?" POPPY TURNS her head to look at me. "You? You're gonna be a mommy. I feel like it would be good training."

"Sometimes I hate you," I laugh, stretching.

"Hate me all you want but I'll take French toast and bacon."

"I'm not making you breakfast."

We lie in my bed, the sun coming through the light blue curtains and filling the room. My body feels like it's been through the wringer and I'm afraid to move.

Morning sickness has been hit or miss, but that's not really my worry. I'm worried how I'll feel mentally once I let the sleep fog roll out and reality fill the void.

Every morning since finding out I was pregnant has been a little rough. Again, not from the nausea, but more from the unknown.

My heart pings with the memory from last night. Remembering his face and the way he looked at me like I was some kind of groupie playing a game is something that might haunt me forever. I'm not sure what I really expected, but I didn't expect to feel like a piece of trash.

"You're going to be fine," Poppy says softly.

I swing my legs off the side of the bed and sit up, feeling my stomach settle. Giving myself a few seconds to gather my thoughts, I'm relieved that I don't feel sad.

I'm pissed.

"I'm going to be better than fine," I say, getting to my feet. "This was unexpected, but, like you said, it's a baby. I'm having a baby." Letting those words wash over my tongue and linger in the air, I absorb them. "I just need a little while to come up with a plan and figure out how I'm going to do this."

"Have you told your parents?"

"Uh, no," I laugh. "I want to have answers to the questions they're going to have before I go in there announcing they're going to be grandparents."

"Do you think they'll be happy?"

"Yes. I'm sure, on some level, they will. But irritated that it's happening this way." The doorbell chimes and I glance at the clock. "Who could that be?"

"Maybe the universe heard my plea and brought me French toast," Poppy says, climbing out of bed. "I'll get the door in case it's Branch. He has an appointment with my right hand."

Laughing, although I'm sure she's not entirely kidding, I change out of my oversized t-shirt and into a pair of shorts and a cami. By the time I walk into the living room, I spy my brother sitting on the sofa.

"What are you doing here?" I ask as I walk by towards the kitchen. "I figured you'd be hungover."

"I didn't drink much," he admits. "Someone had to babysit Branch."

My footsteps falter. "Oh, really?"

"He got shitfaced as hell. He parties as hard as the next guy, but last night was a little overboard." Finn looks at me with a lifted brow. "Did you see him last night?"

"Briefly."

Ignoring further interrogation, I head into the kitchen and pour myself a glass of milk. I'm squeezing in a healthy dose of chocolate syrup when Finn comes in. I see Poppy through the doorway, sitting on the couch and looking nervous.

"What's going on with you?" Finn asks, sitting at the bar.

"Nothing." I take in a long, measured sip of the milk and wait for him to change the subject. He doesn't. "Why do you keep asking me that?"

"Because I'm your brother. Because I know the sound of your voice when you lie."

"I'm not lying."

He's not deterred. Instead, he narrows his eyes. "I'm worried, Lay. Has Callum been bothering you?"

There's so much concern, so much love, shining in his eyes that it breaks the wall I've so carefully erected. It's what I need right now. It's a look of protection, of consideration, of compassion that I didn't get from Branch in any way whatsoever.

My hand shakes as I set the glass down. "I have something to tell you."

"What is it?"

"Before I tell you, you have to promise me you won't go crazy."

"I'm doing no such thing."

Rolling my eyes, I sigh. "Then I'm not telling you."

"I promise I will react proportionately to whatever you say."

"No deal."

"Layla . . ."

Knowing I'm not going to get out of this and hoping beyond hope he takes it well and that maybe that will help my anxiety, I take a deep breath. "Finn, I'm pregnant."

His eyes nearly fall out of his head. "You're what?"

"I'm having a baby in the spring."

He watches me, twisting his lips together. "I'm not going to kill Callum."

"That's good."

"I am going to decimate him."

Avoiding eye contact and scooting to the furthest edge of the bar, I connect the golden sparkles in the granite with my finger. "What if I told you it wasn't Callum's?"

The energy radiating off him changes. Instead of lightening, like I hope, it turns darker. Heavier. More foreboding.

"That would be interesting," he says calmly. Too, too calmly.

"Yeah."

"Whose is it, Layla?"

The lines I'm drawing on the counter start to incorporate the choco-late-colored flecks, the butterscotch, and the cream. I loop more and more of them together knowing damn good and well that within the next few minutes, he's going to have a coronary.

"Lay?"

"Branch's."

I don't even get both syllables out before his fists slam on the counter. "What the fuck did you say?"

"Finn . . ."

"No," he rumbles, glaring at me. "You didn't say my name. Whose baby are you pregnant with, Layla?"

"Branch's."

"That motherfucker."

"Listen," I say, hearing the plea in my tone, "stop. There's nothing that being mad is going to fix."

"Good thing I'm not mad then, isn't it?" he says, his jaw flexing. "I'm so, so far beyond mad. I'm livid."

With movements so calculated it sends chills down my spine, I watch him get to his feet. My palm rests flat against the cool stone as I watch my brother watch me.

"Have you told him?" he asks.

"Yes."

He nods, like his own little lines are connecting. Still, he is not amused. "What did he say?"

I'm not prepared for this question and the extra pause I take is all Finn needs to turn red. He stares me down, pressures me to talk when I don't know the best thing to say.

"He was surprised," I shrug as casually as I can. "I don't need him, Finn. I can raise a baby on my own."

"First, you'll never have to raise a baby on your own. You know that. You have me. Mom. Dad. Poppy. Second, if that son of a bitch doesn't support you, I'll ensure he never has more kids. I'll rip his balls right off his body and feed them to him."

"I don't want that," I sigh. "I don't. I'd rather him just ignore it altogether if he doesn't want a part of it."

"You can't opt out of being a part of your kid's life!"

"He didn't ask for this."

"And you did? And you're defending him?" he scoffs. "What the hell has gotten into you?"

Considering this question, I don't know the answer. What I do know is the little ball of peace that's settled in my soul is welcome to stick around. I also know I mean what I'm saying.

"I'm not defending him, Finn. Not at all. But will you look at me? I'm capable of raising a child on my own if I have to, and I'd rather do that than have someone not want it or make my life hell. It's done. I'm pregnant. Now I have to make the best of it for my child, not for me, and damn it if that doesn't sound like the weirdest thing I've ever said."

Sucking in a breath, I pour over the words that just tumbled from my lips.

"I hate this," he says, his edge missing from his tone.

"Hate what?"

"I hate that he's made you feel like you're on your own."

"I rolled the dice and I came up short. I'm prepared to deal with that."

"Me too." He turns away from the bar and marches into the living room. Pausing at the couch, he bends and has a quiet discussion with Poppy.

I lean against the doorframe and watch them interact. The way she touches his face, the way he smiles softly at her, makes my heart tighten. I can't help but wonder if I'll ever have that.

Finn stands and turns to me. "What's your immediate plan?"

"I'm going to head to the cabin this afternoon. I need some quiet to sort this all out. I can work from there and just . . . breathe."

"I'll call Machlan and have him check on you."

"I'll be fine, Finn."

"I'll make sure of it. Call me when you make it."

"All right."

He kisses Poppy on the cheek and heads to the door.

"Where are you going?" I call out.

"I have some training to do. Call me when you get to the cabin."

And just like that, he's gone.

Branch

I'VE LOOKED BETTER.

My eyes are swollen, the locks of my hair stuck together from sweat, day-old hair gel, and wrestling with my pillow all night. I shouldn't have drunk anything, let alone as much as I did. But I'll cut myself some slack and realize I was a little overwhelmed.

Brushing my teeth, I spit out the toothpaste and rinse it down the drain. My mouth still tastes like puke. And regret.

I fucking hate this.

I'm a great wide receiver, which means I can make decisions on the fly. I have to be able to move with the ever-changing field conditions from play to play. Thinking ahead, anticipating calls and defenses are things I specialize at. How I've managed to take all those skills and *not* use them in my real life is astounding.

Looking in the mirror, I don't like what I see, and it has nothing to do with the eyes or hair or the line running down my cheek from the seam on the couch cushion where I ended the night. It has everything to do with what's beyond that and the panic that's sitting there, mocking me, threatening to bust loose.

The doorbell rings. Maybe it's my hangover, but it sure as hell sounds like it's not just ringing, but blaring. I head down the hall and wince as it rings again. Then a third time.

"I'm fucking coming," I shout, grabbing the deadbolt and snapping it . . . just before I look out the peephole. Finn must hear it click because he shoves the door open, almost knocking me into the wall.

I don't ask why he's here. He doesn't bother to say hello. There's no need for formalities.

I'm not scared of many men. Besides my father, I can't really think of anyone. But Finn has me taking a step or two back and wondering how in the hell I'm going to diffuse this situation.

Then I realize I'm not.

I'm fucked.

"How long have you known?" he growls, his nostrils flaring as he looks down at me.

"Finn—"

"Answer me!" he bellows.

"She told me last night."

He paces a circle, clenching his fists, trying to calm himself down. I've seen him do this in games and in the locker room and even at a party once where a guy threatened the girl he was seeing. I can never remember him doing it quite like *this* though.

My quick-thinking skills are gone and I'm left scrambling to figure out how to put this. I force a swallow. "Finn, honestly, I'm sorry—"

The words are ripped from my mouth by a crisp right hand, whipping across my face—fist closed—and rocking my head back. My face moves out of sync, my jaw working to catch up with the rest of me. I see the left coming and roll underneath it and pop up a few feet to his left and out of punching distance.

Wiping some blood off my chin, I glare at him. "Feel better now?"

"No."

"Go on. Do it again."

He doesn't flinch.

"Do it again. See if it helps. Come on, motherfucker." I stick my chin out, goading him to hit me. My face throbs, already swelling, but I don't give a fuck. I need this. I *want* this. I *want* this pain. "Hit me, Finn."

"Fuck you," he snarls.

I don't see the fist coming. The contact rings me awake, knocks the hangover right out of me. Savagery steels across his face, sinking into my psyche and reminding me of every way I've messed up.

"What were you thinking?" he hisses, his eyes narrowed to tiny little slits. "I ask nothing of you but to stay away from my sister and you can't just stay away from her, you get her pregnant?"

He lurches forward again, but I have my wits about me now and jump out of the way. He crashes into a table with some books and a vase filled with sand from the Wabash River.

Everything crashes to the floor and Finn lies in the middle of it. He falls back to the floor, eyes closed, and doesn't move.

Tugging at my hair, I look to the ceiling and wish I could just make this go away.

"I know you know I didn't mean for this to happen," I say as pacifyingly as possible. "I'd never do this to you . . . or to her."

His eyelids pop open and he looks at me.

"I just . . . We just thought we'd have some fun, you know? I still don't know how this happened."

"Need a biology lesson?" He gets to his feet, brushing dust off his pants. "For fuck's sake, Branch. Did you do this just to spite me?"

"Of course not."

"I took you to my family's home because we were friends. I trusted you," he says, the anger giving way slightly to a look of disappointment. "I thought you were my guy, my buddy, the one I could trust to bring into my world." He considers me again. "You've disrespected my sister and you've betrayed me."

My spirits fall, spiraling from what little height they had left into an abyss I'm not sure I'll ever recover them from. The way he looks at me reminds me of the way Layla looked at me last night, and my stomach builds pressure, threatening to be sick again.

Clearing the bile from my throat, I get my bearings. "Layla is a—"

"—an amazing woman," he cuts me off, "that's so far beyond your league you shouldn't even get to fucking look at her, and I'll blame myself for the rest of my life for introducing the two of you and giving you access to her."

"Damn it, Finn. This isn't your fault."

"No, it's your fault, asshole. This is all your doing with your hedonistic bullshit and greater-than-thou attitude."

"Come on . . ."

He glares at me again, the friend I once knew all but gone from his eyes. "I hope she tells you to fuck off but clearly neither of you listens to me. But I want you to know this: if you're not going to take full responsibility for this baby, get the hell out of her life. Hear me?"

"I hear you."

"I mean it, Branch. She still has a shot at leading a good, normal life but only if you stay the fuck out of it. You can't be half in, half out with your bullshit. You can't be fucking everything that walks and paying lip service to my sister on the side. You hear me?"

"I said I hear you."

He smiles hatefully. "Consider this your last warning. If I ever show up here again, call the police because I'm here to rip you apart."

The door jerks open and he slams it behind him. Pictures on the wall rattle as I bend down and pick up a piece of the shattered vase.

Holding it in my hands, the edges of the rough glass prickling at my skin, I feel the weight of the world sitting square on my shoulders. And as broad as they are, they threaten to collapse.

NINETEEN
LAYLA

ONLY A FEW WEEKS AGO, I lay here face down, bare ass up in the air with Branch smacking my cheeks and thrusting his cock inside me. This afternoon, I sit upright, my sanity up in the air and Branch's words ricocheting through me.

The irony is not lost on me.

Although I've only been at the cabin for a few hours, driving up here as soon as Finn left, already I feel the peace settling in my soul. The water laps against the shoreline, the birds singing from the trees smoothes out some of the franticness that was starting to build up.

The ride here gave me a few hours to think without the distraction of life. There's nothing to do in a car but think, and by the time my car slipped through the gates, I didn't have a ton of answers, but I had options.

I take a bite of a peanut butter cookie and it breaks in half, the bottom part falling onto my tummy. Brushing it off, my hand flutters against my body and an awareness strikes me for what might actually be the first real time.

Cautiously, like my stomach may not be my own, I place my palm against my belly button. It rises and falls as I breathe. Closing my eyes, I try to imagine a tiny baby just inches inside.

Resting my other hand above the first, a warm, tender feeling trickles over me. Nothing else is front and center in my mind, no distractions picking at me from the outside—just me and the sudden feeling of fullness in a way I haven't had before.

"Hey." I say the word aloud and then grin. "I'm not sure if I should talk to you or if you can hear me or anything like that, but if you can . . . I'm your mommy."

A hiccupped breath leaves my lungs as the taste of the word lingers on my lips. It sounds funny and comical but also . . . nice.

"I haven't really made a lot of terrific choices for you so far and I'm sorry for that. I'm just getting the hang of this, you know?"

Opening my eyes, I watch a boat come around the tree-line and remember when Finn and I used to beg our dad to take us out there for hours on end.

"I promise I'll get this mom thing down before you get here. At some point, I'll stop being a chicken and tell your grandmother about this and she'll help." Rubbing a small circle, I wonder how big the baby is. "You're still growing in there and I'm still growing out here. By the time you get here, I'll be ready. I promise."

I get to my feet as the boat turns towards our dock and I see an older women that lives across the lake waving from the bow. She pulls in and gets her boat situated and heads up the walkway towards me.

"Hey, sweetheart," she says, climbing the stairs to the patio. She pulls me into a hug. "How are you, Layla?"

"I'm good, Janet. Want to have a seat?"

We sit down and I offer her a drink but she passes. "I'll be honest. Finn called and asked me to check on you."

"Ugh," I groan, resting my head against the cushion.

"Don't be upset," she says, patting my arm. "I miss having someone care about me like that. Peter's been gone three years now and I miss having someone worry about me. Of course, I have my sister, Kate, but it's not the same."

"You can have Finn," I offer, making her laugh. My hand gingerly rests on my stomach again as I look at Janet. Her face has some age spots since I last saw her, her hair showing a bit of silver now too. "Mrs. Brasher, can I ask you a question?"

"Sure, honey."

"Do you ever regret not having children?"

She smiles sweetly, a simple understanding crossing her face. "Not really. Peter was much older than I when we met, and as you know, he didn't want children. It was something I agreed to before we married. Now, do I wonder what it would be like to have a couple of girls or boys to come visit me? Sure. But do I regret not having that? I can't say I do. Why do you ask?"

"No reason, really," I say, looking at the water. "Just having boy problems, that's all."

"Oh, dear, you'll always have boy problems. I had them until the week Peter died," she laughs. "He was always telling me he'd do something and not do it or not drinking his vitamin drink or leaving candy wrappers on the floor beside his chair. He could be infuriating."

"I think mine are a little more complicated than that."

"Can I give you some unsolicited advice?"

"I wish you would."

She thinks for a long moment, touching the side of her face as she measures her words. "Everything in life is on some unseen, coordinated timing mechanism. Think about it. Everything is circling, staying in perfect harmony every day despite what humankind wants or needs or thinks. The Earth circles the Sun, the Moon circles the Earth, even our heartbeats are timed. Correct?"

"Correct."

"As you go through your life, Layla, remember that. Nothing is random and nothing is coincidence. Everything is running on a schedule, a pattern that we don't see or control. When Peter passed away, I remember wishing he'd have made it to see spring. It was his favorite time of year with the flowers blooming and the waters warming. But spring that year came with the death of many of our friends, the closing of two of his favorite businesses in town, and such horrible politics. I realized then why he was taken from me early. He would've hated that spring."

"I'm sorry he's gone, Mrs. Brasher. He was such a lovely man. I can't see a pink carnation and not think of the bushes that line your driveway."

She smiles with pride. "Thank you. It means a lot that he's remembered fondly." She looks back to the water. "I brought you some dinner. Finn said to make sure you're eating so I made some Salisbury steak and mashed potatoes. Are you hungry?"

My stomach rumbles, my mouth watering at the thought. "I'm

starving, actually. I didn't bring groceries or call Henry to fill the fridge before I came," I say, referring to the handyman that keeps up the cabin while we aren't here.

"Follow me to the boat, if you don't mind, and collect your dinner, sweet girl. I need to get back home to let Mitsy out. She's been so good about not going potty in the house, but I don't want to keep her too long."

We rise and I follow her down the long, narrow path to the water. She hands me a picnic basket and a jug of tea. "Here you go. If you need anything, you call me."

"I'll be fine, Mrs. Brasher. Thank you for this. Honestly."

She pats my hand before untying her boat. "Remember what I said about timing, Layla James. Life is timed to a watch we don't control. Things happen today to set up things later that we can't predict or see or imagine. Don't fight it. Embrace it."

With a little wave, the boat drifts away from the dock. I trek back to the house with my dinner and a little food for thought too.

Twenty
Layla

I SCRAPE THE REST OF the food off my plate and give it a quick rinse. Sticking it in the dishwasher, I pause to look out the window. The sky is a beautiful cascade of purples and oranges as the sun starts to dip on the other side of the lake. It's beautiful and I give a long thought about raising the baby here.

The baby. The words aren't quite as overwhelming as they were a few days ago. I'm still not sure how this is going to work out or how I'll learn to be a mother, but it seems more manageable. Maybe.

"Do you like it here?" I ask aloud, splaying my fingers on my abdomen. "It's quiet. You could play outside with no one to bother you and Mommy could work from the porch and make you lunch like my mommy used to do for me."

There's a serenity about this, so much so that I begin to wonder if it's actually possible. Up until now, raising a baby seemed more like a "Can I do this?" Now it's a "How do I do this?" and that's a totally different thing.

I glance at the refrigerator and think back to Branch. A grin touches my lips immediately, the good memories coming back around, even if they were just for a short time. Our future is going to be tangled, and I find myself hoping we can just get along a fraction as well as we did then.

I go back to the table and sit next to a yellow legal pad and black pen. A few notes are scratched into lists, things I need to work out and prepare and notes from a baby book Poppy brought me.

Looking up as a set of headlights shines through the windows, I stand as they flick off. I walk to the glass and watch Branch trudge towards the door.

A lump materializes in my throat, making it impossible to swallow and just as hard to even breathe. His head is down, his hands tucked into the pockets of his worn jeans as he hits the landing of the stairs. He doesn't look up until he's at the door.

The sound of the knock makes me jump even though I expect it and I stand and stare at the chunk of wood separating him and I. The barrier feels good between us. Like if I can stay inside and keep him out, I can hide in my little cocoon.

Then he knocks again.

I touch the handle like it might burn me, placing one finger on top of the metal knob.

He knocks again. "Layla, open the door."

The command part of that irritates me, but there's a quake in the tone that pulls at a heartstring. One. One heartstring because the rest of them still want to deck him in his handsome face.

"Layla, *please* open the door." There's a long pause. "I know you can hear me and I'm not going anywhere until we talk. So just do us both a favor and open up."

Flinging the door open, I catch sight of his face. His right eye has a purplish-blue circle around it, the underside swollen to the point I'm not sure how well he can even see out of it. The right side of his lip is busted, and it, too, is swollen. He looks at me, his eyes without the cocky glimmer I'm used to seeing in them.

"I didn't open this as a favor to either of us," I tell him. "I opened it to tell you that you need to leave."

"Layla . . ."

"I'm just full of things you don't want to hear, aren't I?" I spew bitterly.

"Will you stop it?"

"Get. Off. My. Porch."

"We need to talk."

Snorting, I go to close the door in his face but his hand stops it mid-push. He doesn't cross the threshold with his feet, but he certainly traipses right over that line with the look he's shooting me.

"I gave you a chance to talk," I say. "And talk you did. I have every word you tossed my way burned into my memory."

"I'm sorry."

"I don't care."

His shoulders fall forward as one arm reaches for the side of his jaw and works it back and forth. He focuses on something on the ground and it reminds me of a little boy that just got in trouble at school.

Like the universe decided to let me get a glimpse into the future, a series of feelings, more than pictures, floods my senses. A little boy's laugh rattles through my ears, the smell of baby soap so real I actually flinch. My heart twists as I can almost see a spray of blond hair and the sweetest little blue eyes—eyes that remind me a lot of the ones looking back at me.

At some point, Branch has lifted his gaze to mine and something passes between us. It's a feeling of confusion, of fear, maybe, mixed with some kind of resolution to have our way, whatever that is.

I chalk it up to the hurricane of emotions swirling inside and the mothering vibe I've been trying to harness and step to the side. Without giving up any of the hostility I have for him, I let him in.

As he passes, he bows his head, and I let out a little huff for good measure. The door pops as it closes and Branch turns to face me.

"What happened to you?" I ask, motioning towards the swelling.

"I ran into something."

"Okay," I say, not giving him the satisfaction of pressing for details. "What do you want? You have five minutes."

"I think we both know this is going to take more than five minutes."

"Then you better get talking and fit in as much as you can."

His cracked lip sticks out a little. "I would start if I knew where to begin."

"This is my point," I say, exhaling sharply. "You don't even have a clue what to say, and I don't have the time or energy to listen to you figure it out. God knows I've had to figure it out on my own."

When he doesn't respond, I give up. I walk away and into the kitchen and hope that when I turn around, he'll be gone. Yet, when I do, he's standing in the doorway.

"Um, how do you feel?" he asks carefully.

"Fine."

He nods, like he's unsure as to whether he has the authority to even ask such questions. "So, you're doing okay?"

"Do you even care?"

"Of course I care," he draws, his brows pulling together. "I'm not a complete asshole, Layla."

I give him a look, one that questions that statement, and he absorbs it completely. His shoulder leans against the wall and he scoops up a deep, weighted breath. "I'm trying to do what's right here."

"I don't want you to do *what's right*. I don't want you coming all the way down here, which, by the way, was totally unnecessary, and asking me how I am like I'm some kind of rabid monkey. I'm a grown woman, Branch. I'm intelligent. I'm capable. I can handle all of this and I *will* handle all of this. If it's too much for you to deal with, I get it. I'm not asking you to."

I fight the wetness welling up in my eyes, determined to not let him see me cry. He sees the break and starts to move off the doorframe but stops when I take a step back.

"This whole thing just threw me for a loop," he says. "I just, uh, I need you to have a little patience."

"Oh, because this is about you, right?" I scoff, turning my back to him.

The need for a hug overwhelms me, the need for someone to tell me this is going to be okay. I don't even try to dismiss the part of my brain that screams for him to come to me and just be here, tell me he'll be here, because it's too loud to ignore.

As the tears I've been struggling to keep at bay begin their journey down my cheeks, I let myself just feel the emotions as they come my way. My back vibrates as the tears fall harder and despite knowing he's in the same room as me, I still feel so alone.

"Can I get you something?" he asks quietly. "A drink or a towel or something?"

"No," I sniffle, sucking up snot that's dripped to my lip.

"Look, Layla, I'm trying to figure out what to do. I'm not . . . this kind of a guy."

I spin around to face him with my puppy eyes and dark circles and tear-stained cheeks. If I weren't going to get as big as a house in the next nine months and have chipmunk cheeks and an even rounder ass, I'd be embarrassed for him to see me like this. But now? It's the least of my worries.

"Bet you're regretting all of this, huh?" I ask, sniffling again.

He looks at the ceiling and sighs. "I had one of the best weekends of my life. It's almost comical how many times I've thought about how easy it was to be with you and how much we laughed and how . . . how I could just put my guard down. Guess I put it down a little too far, huh?"

"Well, you know I was just waiting for it to drop far enough so I could trick you into having a baby." I stop myself. "I mean, it might not even be yours, so we should really watch how we say this, huh?"

"Layla . . ."

His words from last night, the disdain on his face when I told him the news, propel into me. When I look at him again, I don't see the handsome, sexy guy I hoped to see again. I see the guy who thinks the worst of me.

"Your five minutes are up," I say, willing my bottom lip not to tremble.

"We haven't worked anything out."

"You can have your attorney send me a—"

"Layla. Stop," he pleads.

"I want you to leave. I need to be alone," I lie, needing the opposite so much more. "I have a lot to figure out, and I came up here to do that, and I can't do it with you looking at me accusingly."

"I need you to cut me some slack."

"Cut *you* some slack?" I almost shout. "You act like I'm repulsive for having the nerve to get pregnant by you. You do realize I didn't choose this, right? You do realize this wouldn't *be* my choice, right? Because as amazing as you think you are and as good of a time as we had together, if I had known this is the man you really are, I wouldn't have gotten anywhere near you."

I breeze by him and tug the door open. The fire in my eyes must shock him because he steps slowly to the front door. "Get out, Branch."

He stops inches away from me and squares his broad, thick shoulders to mine. There's a defiance in his narrowed gaze. "I'm sorry."

"You've said that a couple of times."

"I mean it."

I put my hand on my hip and smile. "What are you sorry for?"

There's no response, just a look that probably gets him out of most things he doesn't want to say or do in his life.

I pull the door until it can't get any more open. "And that's why you're leaving. Now."

He storms by me, his shoes hitting the porch. The door bangs shut, putting that precious barrier between us once again. Although, this time, I hate it.

Twenty-One
Branch

THE SKY IS DARK, THE stars not even that bright as I stand and look over the lawn and into the water. I've dreamed of this place and replayed the things we did here—me, Finn, Poppy, and Layla James—over and over. Standing here again, the magic isn't as palpable.

With no energy to walk all the way to my car, I slump into a patio chair. If she sees me and wants to come out and yell at me some more, she can. Hell, I might even like it. God knows I deserve it.

The little seed of regret that I woke up with this morning was originally about being careless. I kept thinking of how I really messed up and what this meant for my life and how I wasn't built for this kind of thing . . . and don't want it. But now? It's so much more than that.

I touch the pout of my lip and can feel the crack across the middle. There's some flaked up blood that comes off on my finger and I flick it into the darkness.

My body aches, my mind is dead, and it's worse than it is even after a game. Fucking Finn.

"Oh, God," I groan, filling my lungs with oxygen as I realize I can't do what I was going to do—call him for advice.

This emptiness, a complete feeling of having no rudder in this storm, is the most unsettling thing I've ever encountered. There's no one to turn to, no one that I care about that will tell me I didn't completely fuck up this situation because . . . I have. I so absolutely have.

A light upstairs sends a glow across the patio, but my chair is in the shadows. It's on for a few minutes and I wonder what she's doing.

I imagine her washing her pretty face and pulling back her hair and putting on the little jumpsuit she wore when I was here before. She's probably crawling into bed with a magazine of some sort. Then the light goes off.

The darkness feels isolating and I start to feel sorry for myself. How am I, Branch "Lucky" Best, sitting on a fucking porch in the middle of nowhere with a woman inside who hates my guts?

Resting my head against the cushion, I let my muscles relax. It's only then, when I quiet my head, that I hear it.

My eyes shoot open and I sit up straight, craning my neck from side to side to figure out what it is.

My stomach drops, crashing spectacularly into hell, when I hear her muffled sobs coming from above me. Leaping to my feet, I turn to the windows, but they're dark. The closer I get to the house, her cries get just a touch louder.

Choking back a lump the size of Texas, I listen to her. Her tears wash away so much bullshit and my own fucked up ego and the situation looks so much different than it did a few minutes ago.

Here I sit, bitching and moaning about how awful this is for me, when it's her that must be terrified. I could ignore the whole thing, cut her a check at the end of the month, and be done with it if I wanted. She has to live with this. Have her body changed, her life altered, because she's a damn good person.

Despite the crazy things I've done, I've never really felt bad for any of it. Women know what they're getting into with me.

She didn't do anything. She didn't ask for this. And she doesn't deserve it either.

I head to the front door and try the handle, but it's locked. Each window on the ground floor is latched tight too. I spring over the railing and jog to the back, to a little door that leads into a mudroom from the lake. Flicking the lever, it's locked.

"Shit."

Looking up, I see a little balcony off a room that I think is Finn's. There are four wooden posts that hold it in the air and I grab one and give it a good shake. It's solid.

"Here goes nothing."

I grip the wood with both hands and ascend the pole in the same way we do a rope in training. The rough material digs into my hands as I try to keep my sweaty palms from slipping and dropping me on my ass.

The dark night doesn't help, and I have a hard time seeing what's ahead of me, but I reach the floor above a little quicker than I anticipate.

Working my hands to grab the edge of the balcony, I pull my weight up, groaning so hard I swear I bust a blood vessel in my face, then I collapse over the handrail and onto the planks.

Sucking in breath after breath, I lay on my back for a second to make sure I'm not dead. I bring one hand inches from my face and feel the warmth of blood trickling down my palm.

"Great," I groan, getting to my feet. With a press of the lever on the door, I sigh in relief as it swings free.

The room is dark, but I can see through to the hallway. A little light is plugged in out there and I feel my way through until I'm in the hall. The room I stayed in is two doors on my left and Layla's is three on my right.

My heart thunders as I realize she could shoot me or scream bloody murder and I don't know what to do to not completely freak her out over my breaking and entering. But when I hear her sobs coming from her room, I forget about all that and knock gently on the door.

"Layla, it's me."

I hear a rustle of blankets and the cries stop.

"It's Branch. I'm going to open the door, okay? Don't shoot me."

I give her a moment to tell me no, but she doesn't. Carefully, slowly, I move the door into her room. My hand drops to my side when I see her thanks to the glow of a candle from a desk a few feet away.

She's lying on her bed, blankets pulled tight around her. Tears trickle down her cheeks as she watches me come into her room.

She looks so small in the bed, so frightened like a storm is coming that might take her life. Only . . . I am the storm in her opinion and that pummels me.

There are so many things I want to say—things I didn't even come up here *to* say. Things I didn't even realize I felt. Things that feel absolutely necessary to get out at this moment, yet I can't. The look of misery on her face stops me and all that matters right now is *her*.

The girl from that weekend, the one I couldn't stop thinking about, the one whose laugh made me feel alive and spontaneous fed something that was dormant inside me for a long time, is hurt because of me. Because I'm an asshole.

I wait for her to tell me to fuck off as I pad across the carpeted floor of her bedroom and expect her to slap me across the face as I kneel at the side of her bed. Assuming she's going to rip into me, I lay my left arm around her narrow hips and slide her to the edge with a frazzled breath. There's no way I don't believe she won't tell me what a dickhead I am as I pull her into my chest.

But none of that happens.

Her cries are hushed against the fabric of my shirt, the same fabric she knots up in her hands. She shakes as she empties her soul into the cotton blend and presses her knuckles firmly into my chest, biting at my skin.

Squeezing my eyes shut, I hold her tight. Saying anything seems wrong and probably would be wrong because this is all new to me. This is territory I'd have to ask Finn about, and he won't speak to me.

Little by little, her hands ease on my shirt and her stifled sounds become quieter until she's completely still and quiet in my arms.

I scoot her back from the edge and tuck the blankets around her once more. She snuggles into the sheets. Rocking back on my heels, she lies motionless before me. She's so goddamn sweet, so simply perfect that I remember just a few days ago I was angling every which way just to see her again.

"You are a fool," I whisper to myself as I get to my feet.

Knowing I shouldn't, but being the rule breaker that I am, I bend forward and plant a single kiss to her cheek. "I *am* sorry," I whisper against her skin. "We'll figure this out. I promise."

With a final look at her tucked in bed, I leave her room and let myself out the front door into the night.

TWENTY-TWO
LAYLA

SQUINTING AT THE BRIGHTNESS OF the sun, I yawn and then rub my eyes to try to wake up. My face feels puffy and I pause, remembering Branch getting inside somehow last night.

The softness of his touch, the tenderness in his arms as he held me against his sturdy chest, is so fresh in my mind. He didn't have to do that . . . but he did.

After a quick scan of my room, the only thing I see is that I'm alone and the only thing I hear is the outright pounding of my heart.

It almost feels like I dreamed it, like I needed comfort so much I made it up in my mind, but I smell his cologne on my hands and I know he was here.

Maybe he still is.

Yanking back the blankets, I climb out and head to the window. His car is parked next to mine, lined up in a row like it's supposed to be there.

"Fuck," I mutter, not sure how I feel about that or what it means or where he is or what *that* means. "Why does this have to be so complicated?"

Switching from my long nightshirt into a cute and easy denim romper, I race to the bathroom and wash up and get my hair into some semblance of tidiness.

I peek into the room he stayed in before and it's undisturbed. Door to door, I glance into each bedroom, bathroom, and even closet to find them all empty of life.

The energy coursing through my veins has my head buzzing. I sweep the living room as I go by but it's empty. So is the kitchen. There are no traces of Branch in the entire house.

The front door is unlocked when I try the handle and I tug it open. Stepping onto the patio, I freeze in my tracks.

My heart pulls in my chest, a smile breaking across my cheeks as I spy him.

Branch is sitting on a chaise lounge up against the house, an Illinois Legends hat sitting over his face. His big, bulky arms are folded across his chest and one sneaker-clad foot is crossed over the other.

I want to pretend he stayed for me and that he didn't just sit down and pass out from the stress of the last couple of days plus the trip up here. But dashed hopes are a hateful thing that I try to avoid if I can and how do I have any grounds to hope he cares at all about me? It will be easier if he doesn't anyway.

Even so, I can't deny the relief that he didn't just walk away last night like he could've so easily done and that he did even more by coming into my room and just being *present*. That means a lot. If I'm going to roast him for all of his mistakes, I need to give him a little teeny-tiny bit of credit for the good moves too.

Scooting his legs over to make room for my bottom, I take him in one last time before I lift his hat off his face. He makes a sour grimace, groaning as the morning sun shines in his eyes. Once he gets them open enough to see me, he's awake.

"Good morning," I say, each word calculated.

"Good morning." His voice is gravelly, rougher than I've ever heard it. He clears his throat. "You mad?"

"At you?"

"Of course at me."

His face tells the tale of a long, hard night. I know the look. I wear it often these days too. The judgmental glare, the lines of anger that have been around his mouth are gone, and in their place is an aura of concern.

"What happened to your face? For real?" I ask, reaching out and touching the corner of his eye.

He flinches. "It doesn't matter."

"You have blood caked in your lashes. It must've bled while you slept." He looks up at me through those very same lashes like he's not sure what to make of me.

I sigh, frustrated at what I'm about to say. "Come on."

I stand and wait on him to follow. He doesn't. He just sits in the chair with a bewildered look on his face.

"What?" I ask. "You need a hot shower and I need coffee. Decaf. God, I hate decaf."

"Why are you drinking decaf if you hate it?"

"Because caffeine in the amounts I need to feel decent aren't good for my baby."

As soon as I say it, I realize it's his baby too. I also realize he picks up on my word choice, but chooses not to say anything about it. Instead, he cocks his head to the side.

"Are you mad at me?" he asks.

"Will you stop acting like a child?" I ask.

He stands, pulling his hat over his head to cover the messy blond locks sticking up every which way. "Fine. Lead the way."

I head to the house and hear his footsteps behind me. He shuts the door, the sound echoing through the house, as I enter the kitchen and rummage around in the refrigerator.

"Are you hungry?" he asks.

"Never ask a pregnant woman that."

"*Okayyyy.* So . . . what are you hungry for?"

"A hot ham and cheese, if it matters, and I don't have either thing."

The doorbell rings and Branch and I look at each other. Without saying a word, I walk by him and see Henry on the other side carrying a large cardboard box.

"Well, good morning," I say, taking the proffered carton. "How'd you know I was here?"

"Mrs. Brasher called from down the road. Said you came up alone and could probably use some groceries."

"Oh, Henry," I say, leaning on my tiptoes and kissing his cheeks. "You're so sweet. Rachel is a lucky woman."

"I'll tell her you said so," he chuckles. "If you need anything else, you call me. My number is pinned on the corkboard in the laundry room."

"I will. Thanks again, Henry."

"Is everything all right, Layla girl? I saw another car out front and Mrs. Brasher said you were alone . . ."

"I'm fine," I assure him. "If I need anything, you'll get a call."

"I'd better. Have a good day, darlin'."

Heading back to the kitchen, I plop the box on the counter. Pulling the items out one-by-one, I look up at Branch. "Guess we have things for breakfast."

He smiles at the implied offer and I kick myself for saying it so easily. "You have food delivery out here?"

"No. That was Henry."

"Who's Henry?"

"He takes care of the cabin when we aren't here. Mows the grass, maintains our dock, does little fix-it projects here and there. Basic stuff."

"I see." He leans against the chair, watching me unpack the box. "Can I help you with something? I can't cook worth shit, but I can pour juice like a champ."

"Why don't you get a shower?" I offer. "I'll put something together while you're gone."

"I can help you. You don't have to cook for me."

"I know. It's really just a way to get you out of here faster."

He doesn't seem to believe me and heads up the stairs with a smug grin on his face. I flip him off as soon as he's out of sight, the little bout of immature rebellion cathartic.

Scrambling a pan of eggs and cooking sausage patties keeps me busy for the next twenty minutes. The rafters above me squeal as Branch gets in and out of the shower, a little reminder that a conversation is still going to be had and just thinking about it makes me almost drop the patties onto the floor.

"That smells good," he says, coming around the corner.

I look up from the table and almost drop the glass of juice in my hand. He's shirtless, a pair of Finn's black joggers on his legs, and a white towel running over his hair.

"Have a seat," I say, turning away to keep myself focused. I busy myself grabbing my vitamins from my purse before heading back to the table and taking a seat at the opposite end.

He smells crisp and clean, and despite the black eye, he looks divine.

"Did you sleep okay?" he asks, picking up his fork.

"Yes. Did you?"

"I slept like shit. That chair isn't made for a night's sleep."

"Could've gone home," I shrug.

His fork clamors against the table, the sound making me jump. He holds my gaze hostage, a plethora of emotions warring in his eyes. As he swallows, his Adam's apple bobbing, he seems to have made a decision and that scares me.

I hold my breath, anticipating his words.

"Look, Layla, I want to apologize."

"You already have."

He rolls his eyes and leans back in his chair, clearly perturbed. "No, I haven't."

"This will be easier for both of us if we find a middle ground to be friendly," I say. "It'll be good to have a rapport, but our chilling out has made this a little awkward."

"No, me being an asshole did. I've given you a bunch of half-assed apologies that haven't meant jack shit. You know it and I know it."

This is not what I was expecting. I drop my utensil too and place my hands in my lap. Something tells me this one is different, but I want him to have to say it.

"What are you sorry for, Branch? Why is this half-assed apology any different than the others you've half-assed?"

Although my questions are legitimate and I don't feel sorry for asking, I do have a kink in my throat at the look of sorrow etched on his face.

I hate it. I'd give anything in the world to have him sitting across from me laughing, telling me some cocky story or some filthy thing he wants to do to me. Hell, I'd even take teasing about the sex therapy card.

"I'm sorry for a lot of things," he says, his tone clear. "I'm sorry for not being more careful. I'm sorry for betraying your brother. I'm sorry for being such a fuck-up in the first place that Finn would rather kill me than see you end up tied to me."

My mouth opens, words primed on my lips, but he stops me with a single look.

"This black eye came from Finn," he says. "And I'm lucky he didn't pop the other one too."

"Finn did that?"

"Yeah. He did. And I can't blame him. If you were my sister, I'd hate to think you were fucking around with me."

"He shouldn't have done that. It's not going to help anything," I gulp. "I'm sorry, Branch."

His laugh catches me off-guard. "Would it be weird to say that it felt good?"

"Um, yeah. That would be very weird."

"Well, it did. It kind of snapped me back to reality a little. Or a lot," he says, looking around the room. "I did pull a complete dick move on him."

"No, you pulled the dick on me and then turned into one."

He half-grins. "That's what caused this situation."

"That you turned into a dick? Or that you dicked me? Either way, and regardless how complicit I was in the second dicking, I'm still blaming it on you."

"I wasn't referring to either, actually," he chuckles. "I was referring to your sense of humor."

Searching for a comeback, I find nothing.

"That's a lie. I think it was your ass first, then the sense of humor," he cracks.

"Branch, shut up," I say, not able to hide a laugh of my own.

"You know what I'm really sorry for?" he asks, undeterred. "I'm sorry for acting like a bitch."

There's no chance I have a response for that, and I'm not sure he expects one. Over our plates of sausage and eggs that are growing colder by the minute, the chill that settled between us since I told him I was pregnant begins to warm.

"I can't blame you if you want me to hit the road and just send child support payments, Layla. I don't know how to be a dad or even be responsible for myself sometimes. I just keep seeing you hating me down the line and this situation turning ugly." His eyes darken, his lips forming a thin line. "Listening to you cry last night made me feel like a complete and utter piece of shit."

My breathing halts, my body unable to process functions necessary for life and Branch's words at the same time. A bubble swells in my stomach, the one that usually predicates tears or a nervous giggle or some other reaction to whatever stimuli is in front of me.

"Branch, you aren't a piece of shit," I gulp, relieved that I actually believe that.

"I am. I was. And for *that*, I'm sorry. You deserve better than what I've been."

"You're right," I say, my voice low. "I do deserve better than what you've been. I have all of these monumental things to think about and I was scared to even tell you and then you said the things you did and . . . that's hard to forget."

He hangs his head.

"I don't blame you for feeling the way you do, but I do hate that you reacted the way you did and made me feel like this was some big plot to take over your life or something."

"Layla—"

"But," I say, cutting him off, "I know this is a shock. It's nothing you wanted, especially from me, a girl you slept with once. I can't blame you for not being excited or even neutral about it and maybe *I'm* wrong and should apologize for putting expectations on you."

His head shakes back-and-forth as he lifts his chin. "For what it matters, I didn't want this. But it's not fair to say I didn't want this *especially with you*. I just didn't have this on my five-year plan. Hell, maybe not my ten-year."

"I didn't either."

I pick up my fork and push the eggs around my plate.

"I play professional ball, Layla. Nothing in my life is predictable or even solid. My contract could get traded and I could be on a plane across the country on a whim. That's part of the reason why I haven't wanted to start a family or settle down. Why would I? Why would I just add another thing on my plate that I can't control?"

"I understand," I whisper.

He tugs at his hair, clearly stressed and that stresses me.

"It's more than that," he groans. "I see this eat people up and spit them out. My instincts scream to keep you far, far away from this madness."

"I can take care of myself, Branch."

"This isn't casual fucking anymore," he points out. "You can't just decide you can't take it and walk. You're tied to me now. You've just bought into this world that you shouldn't be in and now I'm responsible for it."

We sit across from each other, the air in the room heavy. My shoulders sag with the weight of his words. He looks at me after a long while, studying my face. The somberness drifts from his eyes and is replaced with the tenderness that makes me weak.

"For what it's worth," he says quietly, "if this was going to happen, I'm happy it was with you. At least we kind of like each other, right?"

"Yeah, my ass and my sense of humor," I deadpan. "I'm sorry to say both of those are going to get worse as the days go on."

"That shouldn't be something I laugh at . . ." His voice trails off, replaced by a chuckle.

I narrow my eyes. "You're right. You shouldn't. Because you know what they say?"

"No, what do they say?"

"The daddy's gain weight too."

It's like a fireman's hose douses us with bone-chilling cold water. All levity is gone, whatever easiness we've managed to sneak into this conversation is out the window.

"I'm going to be a dad," he says, more to himself than anything. "That sounds so . . . Wow." Blowing out a breath, he leans back in his chair. "This is kind of terrifying."

"I don't expect anything from you. I want you to know that."

"That makes me feel like a complete loser."

"I don't mean it like that," I say, sitting back in my own chair. "I don't mean I don't *need* anything from you . . ."

He lifts a brow. "What do you want from me?"

Glancing around the room—at anything but him—I try to form a response. It's such a loaded question, one that I can't seem to take the bullets out of.

In a perfect world, I'd want so much from Branch. I'd dream of those things. This world is so far from perfect that I can't even go out on that limb. The entire tree might break.

"What do you want from me, Layla?"

"I don't need anything from you," I say, forcing a swallow.

"That's fine. But what do you *want*?"

Confused as to why he just won't let this go, my emotions build higher and higher and I shove my plate away. "I can't want anything from you."

He pushes back from the table and licks his lips. Taking a deep breath, he blows it out slowly. "What can I do to make this easier for you? What's my job, my role? Give me directions and be clear so I don't fuck it up."

"Be nice," I say, shrugging my shoulders. "That's the main thing."

"I can be nice, but as far as the rest . . . I'm not gonna lie—it feels like I was forced into a game with no playbook."

"I think that's pretty normal," I laugh. "If not, I'm as screwed as you."

My hand falls on my belly, a new habit of mine, and Branch's gaze follows the movement. When he looks back at my face, his expression is totally different.

"Come on," he says, standing.

"Where to?"

"You told me to be nice and you also told me you wanted a ham and cheese."

"But I made breakfast."

"And now it's cold because some asshole had to spend fifteen minutes rambling apologies." With his bottom lip between his teeth, he carefully extends a hand. "Let's go get you a sandwich."

TWENTY-THREE
LAYLA

"HI, LAYLA!" RUBY, THE LITTLE old lady that works in Linton's min-iscule library waves at me from the top step. "How have you been?"

"Good, thank you. How about you?"

She rambles on about her arthritis and the turnout for the preschool arts and crafts program and how it's been low and she wants to turn it around. She goes on and on. I try to nod as best I can and seem interested and not like I'm listening to Branch standing behind me whispering that she looks like the old lady from some cartoon he used to watch as a child.

"I'm glad to hear it," I say when I can find a moment to cut in. "We need to get going, Ruby. Take care."

"You too. Good to see ya." And with a wave, she disappears inside the library.

Branch and I turn the corner and start up Main Street. On each corner is a big pot fashioned to look like a basket filled with flowers. There's a little plaque on the front of each one with the name of the citizen that volunteers their time maintaining that particular arrangement.

American flags hang off the streetlights, fluttering in the warm af-ternoon sun over the street. Mix in the smells of Carlson's Bakery and the sounds of the children two streets over at the town pool and it's the perfect summer day.

"What's that smell?" Branch asks, wrinkling his nose. "It smells like heaven."

"That's the coffee cake at Carlson's. They use butterscotch pudding in the cake and it's seriously divine."

"Want to get some?"

"I just had a hot ham and cheese sandwich, a pickle spear, and a side of home fries. Do you think I need coffee cake?"

He considers this as we walk along. "Will it make you happy?"

"Yeah, but I don't need it."

"My job isn't to decide what you need. It's to make you happy."

Blushing, I kick a pebble and watch it roll into the gutter. "I think I said it's for you to be nice."

"Doesn't me being nice make you happy?" he asks.

"Yes. Mostly. But it also makes it harder," I admit, looking at him out of the corner of my eye. "Could you be likeable yet irritating? Can you find that balance?"

He laughs, leading me to Beecher Street. It's a little side street that houses a few businesses and lots of little homes built in the early nineteen hundreds. The houses have hanging ferns dangling from porches and yapping dogs in the yards. It's adorable.

Beecher Street rises as we reach the middle and sitting on top of the crest is a railroad track. On the other side is the only doctor's office in town, the post office, and Crave.

As we near the bar, Branch shoves his hands in his pockets. "I want to tell you something."

"Okay."

"I guess it's half tell you, half ask you."

"Okay," I laugh.

"When you left the cabin that weekend," he starts slowly, "you saw something online about me, didn't you?"

The image of him with that girl on his lap, one I'd mostly forgotten since the appointment with Bai, pops in my brain. My stomach churns.

"I thought so," he mumbles.

"It doesn't matter," I point out. "You and I were nothing then. We're nothing now," I add for good measure.

"Then why did you leave?"

"Let me ask *you* a question."

He doesn't answer, but gives me a look like he's not sure he wants to go this route. I go on anyway.

"What if the night you and Finn went to Crave, Poppy and I had gone out and I had slept with someone? And then you and I still hooked up the next day like we did. How would you feel about that the next morning?"

"Well," he draws out. "I've actually been in that position more times than I care to admit."

Curling my lip, I try not to show my total disgust.

"I'll be honest, it didn't generally bother me because I didn't expect to see that girl again anyway," he admits.

"Well, all right then."

"What do you think happens on road trips, Layla? Hell, there are guys on my team that have little set-ups for each city in our league. There's a girl in every zip code we routinely go to just waiting for that direct message."

"That. Is. Disgusting."

He laughs. "That. Is. Life. On. The. Road. Sure, there are guys out there who avoid it. There are a few—very few—that have something at home strong enough to keep their dick dry. The rest just do what they can to not give their wife enough ammo to void the pre-nup."

I shiver before I realize it, imagining living a life like that. Constantly worried. Constantly second-guessing. Constantly having your self-esteem whittled away. Just thinking about a life marred with insecurity and self-doubt makes me anxious.

"Callum didn't make it out to be that bad," I admit. "Lord, now I only imagine how dry his dick was *not* while we were together."

Branch laughs. "I'm sure it wasn't. But now you know why the league divorce rate is over eighty percent."

"Are you kidding me?"

"Afraid not. Doesn't seem fair, does it? To anyone. It's fucked up on so many levels."

We stop in front of a little bench at the end of a dead end street that faces the water's edge. Branch sits and I follow suit.

"That's why I won't get married. Not at least until I retire." He looks at me out of the corner of his eye, gauging my response. "I don't want that on my conscience, and I don't feel like it's a good thing to do to someone, especially if you think you like them enough to consider such a thing."

He strokes his chin. "There's this guy on the team. He was married, had the cutest little boy, right? They used to have me over for barbecues and whatever. He had a great set-up. Then he got swept away in all the press when we won the championship. Next thing I know, he's got his side piece an apartment close to mine and she's picked up dick because he's not paying attention to home. They're both ruined. It's awful."

"I don't even know what to say to that."

"It seems ridiculous with my reputation, I know, but it *is* responsible to not be responsible. I make no promises, no commitments, and no one gets seriously hurt because it's not serious."

I don't give him a lot to go on. I just watch him blankly, processing everything he's told me and well aware that he didn't answer my original question. Like he reads my mind, he grins.

"Your original proposed situation had you and Poppy going out and *you* fucking around with someone, not a random girl doing it," he says softly. "When I think about it in that light . . . I'd have been pissed."

"Why?"

He considers this. "A competition thing, I guess. It would've bothered me to think someone else had you and you were comparing us or maybe you were thinking of him and not me."

"Exactly," I say, giving him a shy smile. "But I wouldn't say I was pissed."

"What were you then?"

"I was embarrassed, I think."

"By what?" he blurts, a laugh in his voice. "What could you possibly have been embarrassed about?"

"That I was a number," I say, slipping a laugh in my voice too. "Same reason as you, I guess, I'm just a little less confident about it."

"For what it's worth and it may be worth nothing, but I didn't fuck that girl that night."

I don't want to be relieved, but there's no denying the sigh that escapes my lips. "So you didn't do anything with her?"

"I didn't say that, but I didn't sleep with her. I'm not going to lie to you, even if it's not what you want to hear. I also didn't sleep with Selma Puress. Just throwing that out there in case you saw a picture online."

Looking straight ahead, I just nod.

"I know what that sounds like, but I didn't realize I'd be explaining myself later."

"Why are you?" I look at him, my brows pulled together. "Why are you telling me this, Branch?"

He shrugs and looks at the water. "I don't know. Maybe it felt like it mattered."

"Do you think I want to hear that? I mean, I can't get mad at you and you certainly weren't wrong, but that doesn't mean I want to hear some girl had her lips around your cock hours before you stuck it in me."

"Gee, just put it out there bluntly, why don't you?" he grins.

"Why mince words?"

He looks at the sky, a softness on his rugged features. "Maybe," he breathes, "maybe it bothered me to consider you thought I just wrote you off like another girl."

"But didn't you?"

"Depends how you look at it. Did I think I'd be back here? Hell, no. But I knew from the moment you got out of that car and shook my hand that I was going to have a hard time putting you in a box, you know?"

"I hate boxes, if you'll remember," I say, referring back to our un-packing conversation.

He laughs. "This is what I mean. The more time I spent with you, the more I wanted to spend even more. Even that first night, the night we went to Crave, if I could've gotten Finn to let me stay behind with you, I would've."

His words are sweet and maybe even what I want to hear. Still, it's just another one of those things that will make it even more painful when I'm home with the baby and he's sleeping with half of Detroit or wherever they are.

"This conversation seems a little too deep for late morning," I say, getting up and starting down the sidewalk. He follows a step behind, giving me the space he can tell I need.

His words at any other point in my life would've left a huge grin on my face and maybe even had me riding his cock if the timing was right. But with it following up the words that he'll never be serious, never settle down, until he's out of the league? That makes it a little less sweet being that I'm pregnant with his child.

Whatever I had vaguely hoped in the back of my mind is now erased and the stark reality of the world I live in is blindingly bright. All I can hope for is for Branch to love his child and for us to co-parent to some extent.

We reach his car and he opens my door. "Want to get some coffee cake?" he asks.

"Is this your plan? Feed me to keep me happy?"

I sink into the plush leather seats that he helped adjust until it was at the perfect position for me before we left.

"I've noticed that you're more manageable with a plate of food in front of you," he winks.

"Branch?"

"Yeah, Sunshine?"

I take in the way the sun reflects on his hair and the way his eyes look even bluer than normal when he's wearing a white shirt.

"I'm going to need two slices—one for now and one for the middle of the night."

His laughter trickles through the car as he shuts the door.

TWENTY-FOUR
BRANCH

THE TELEVISION GLOWS ON THE wall in front of us, hanging on a stone fireplace. Below it is a mantle with pictures from the Miller family at various stages of their lives. Pictures of Finn and Layla on boats as babies, them on the sand as toddlers, even at past Water Festivals. It's a restful ambiance that I could appreciate if I could stop looking at her.

Layla sits on a sofa a few feet away, a book in her lap.

After our early lunch in town and walk through the streets, we stopped at the lake on our way back to the cabin and sat on the sand. We didn't talk much, but sort of each processed what had already been said.

Just sitting next to her, being in her air space, makes me feel . . . well, it makes me feel like I want to stay here. I find myself waiting to hear her laugh or for her to say something I can play off and start a conversation. It's weird. I'm not the converse-with-women type of guy unless it means their tongue is against my cock while I tell them how hard to suck it.

Not with her though. That confuses me.

"Did you see that?" she giggles.

Shaking out of my daze, I look up. "I didn't. What happened?"

She sighs. "You've been somewhere else mentally a lot tonight."

"Yeah, well, I guess I have a lot on my mind."

She nods, like she's reminded that the weight of the world is on her shoulders. Picking up her book, her grin is gone.

"Hey," I say, waiting until she looks at me again. When she finally does, I realize I have no follow-up. "Um, what are you reading?" I stammer.

"A book about pregnancy." She holds the paperback up and shows me the cover. It's a patchwork of pastel colors with rattles and bottles and these pins with little pink bows on top. "This is my first rodeo, you know."

"What are you learning?"

"To not watch labor and delivery images and not to read the stories," she laughs. "If they showed you this before you had sex, it would effective birth control."

"Guess we're a little too late for that, huh?"

"I guess so." Something washes across her face as she sets the book beside her. "I haven't said this yet, but thank you for coming up here. I didn't expect you to and—"

"Stop."

She squirms in her seat as I grab the remote and flip the television off.

"Don't thank me for doing the right thing," I say.

"I just want you to know I appreciate it."

"I appreciate you not punching me in my good eye," I chuckle. "As unexpected as it is, we're having a baby. That means we are going to be on the same team for a while. And if you want to sit in the stands with me to cheer him on when he takes over the ol' eleven jersey for the Legends, it'll be a few years longer."

"It's a girl," she says off-handedly, turning her nose a little into the air.

"It's a boy," I tell her.

"How would you know? You don't know anything about this."

"Maybe not, but I can predict the future."

"Oh, really?"

"Yup. He's going to have blond hair like me and golden eyes like you. He'll have your wit and my athletic ability."

"Hey, now," she says, wagging a finger my way. "My brother is Finn Miller. I have some damn good athletic genes too."

"Meh."

She throws a pillow at me. I catch it mid-air and toss it back at her. Because she had turned away, it hits the side of her face.

Her laughter fills the air, the worry lines on her face from today all but gone. That is, until she moves her neck to the side and flinches.

"What's the matter?" I ask.

"Oh, nothing. I hurt my neck a few weeks ago and it's hurt ever since."

"What did you do to it?"

"I don't know."

I catch the blush of her cheeks and her hesitation to look me straight in the eye. "Layla . . ."

"Stop, Branch."

"What happened?" I say in a sing-song voice. "Sounds like a good story."

Her lips quiver as she finds her resolve. When she faces me, the little vixen I've seen before is back. "Well," she says, "I was with this guy, right? And he had me up on all fours on this patio chair at our lake house and—"

"Better stop there."

"But I was just getting to the good part."

"Oh, Sunshine. I remember the good part."

We exchange a knowing smile before she moves her head and winces again.

"Turn around," I tell her, moving off the chair and onto the sofa beside her.

"Why?"

"Just turn around," I chuckle. "Don't you trust me?"

"Um . . ."

Shaking my head, I lay a hand on her shoulder and gently encourage her to turn away from me. Finally, she gives in, shifting until she's sitting facing the wall.

My heart beats in my throat, a steady strum as I lean in and breathe in a scent that's pure Layla—a sweet smell of pineapples and the warmth of vanilla. I think I could get high on it if I breathed it in for long. It's a risk I'd be willing to take.

Bundling her hair in one hand, I try to figure out what to do with it. She reaches back, a brown elastic in her hand.

"Let me pull it up," she says.

Instead, I remove the tie from her fingers. She stills as I work the bunched strands up higher on her head and then twist the elastic around it a few times until it stays.

I've done a lot things with women. A lot of things so crazy I wouldn't admit to them, a lot of things done both publicly and privately. But this simple exchange feels the most intimate out of all of them and I'm not even touching her.

She sits patiently, waiting for me to do whatever it is I'm going to do. Her profile is perfect with her long, thick lashes, button nose, and soft, smooth lines.

For the first time in a few days, she's just Layla. She's the same woman I met a while back and enjoyed the hell out of in so many ways. She's the smart and gorgeous and easygoing girl that doesn't give a shit I'm a wide-out on the Legends or on the cover of three magazines this month. She's . . . her.

My hands lay softly on her shoulders. Under my palms, they sink instead of tensing as I feared, her head falling to the side. My thumbs press against the back of her neck, her skin warm and supple against my own.

"Where does it hurt?" I say gently, working her dainty shoulders in my hands.

"Mostly in the back and on this side." She motions to her left, her fingertips brushing mine. Instead of pulling them away, she leaves them touching for a long moment.

I work on the spot she indicated, spending time on areas that she signals feels good. As I watch her reaction to me and feel my pulse find a steady rhythm, my anxiety starts to wane, a hint of a smile tickling my lips.

"I went to that birthday party just to see you," I say, pressing my thumbs against an area just below her neck.

"You did?"

"Yeah. I wanted to call you before that, but didn't really know how to work around your brother, and Poppy kept saying you were really busy."

She bends her neck farther, giving me more access. "Well, I didn't really want to see you. It seemed pointless. And then I was scared to see you."

Her admission, although understandable, twists something deep inside my chest. Imagining her so vulnerable and alone because of some reaction I might have, and did have, makes me want to kick myself.

"I wanted to spend more time with you," I admit, ignoring everything else. "I just wanted to toss a football around with you or eat some candy and tell stories."

She blows out a breath, grimacing a little as I rub out a knot. "I think we could've had fun together if so many things were different."

With a final press, I drop my hands. "If I would've called, you would've answered?"

Her chin dips just a touch. "Even though I knew it was a terrible idea for every practical reason, I would've. I don't think I could've refused."

"What do you think it would've been like?"

"Everything it can't be now."

"Why?"

I know the answer, I just want her to remind me. Maybe I even need her to remind me because being with her makes all those reasons get blurry.

"Now it can't be the easy, fun, sexy time it would've been before. Our relationship now is built on a baby, not orgasms."

"I'd say it was built on the orgasms, but maybe built up by the baby."

"However you want to look at it," she says, cracking a smile. "We're at a point that most people reach when they're in love and we aren't. That dooms us, I think. When things get hard or confusing or we're totally sleep-deprived, we don't have that connection to keep us working together and liking each other. Our foundation is as shaky as the orgasms that brought us together."

"Great, yet terrible, analogy."

She sighs. "Our only hope is to try to build a friendship over these next few months and figure out a good system to co-parent. That's the responsible thing, right?"

"Definitely."

Maybe.

LAYLA

THE SILVERWARE JINGLES IN THE drawer as I rummage for a fork. With only the stove light on, it's a little dim to be milling about. I could totally turn the chandelier on, but I like the ambiance of the low light in the middle of the night when I'm foraging for a snack.

Settling on a utensil, I open the container from the bakery. The kitchen fills with the smell of sweet cinnamon and as I dig into it, a sound filters in from the staircase. In a minute's time, Branch pads into the room, his hair sticking up, yawning.

"What time is it?" he asks.

"Two a.m.," I say, sticking a forkful of coffeecake into my mouth. "Why?"

"Just wondering."

I'm stopped when he takes the fork and shovels more cake in my mouth. Laughing, I chew it up and swallow.

"That wasn't very nice," I point out.

"You talk too much." He takes his own bite of the cake. "Damn. This is good."

"Told you. You should've bought your own slice." I take the fork out of his hand and scoop up another piece. "Why are you up?"

"I don't know. It's so quiet here. So dark. I love falling asleep to it like this, but if I wake up, I have a hard time going back to sleep. Is that weird?"

"Probably."

"I saw this show once where this guy would sneak in houses and, while people were asleep, he'd—"

"Stop!" I giggle, shoving him backward.

We still, our eyes locking, as my hand touches his chest. I force a swallow, my entire body tingling from the contact.

He shakes his head as he gets two glasses out of the cabinet. "Want a glass of milk?"

"Sure."

I watch as he pours us both a drink, his back muscles rippling even under the not-so-bright light. I imagine him waking up in the middle of the night to change a diaper or feed a baby and my heart swells, then falls because I won't see that.

"What are you thinking?" he asks with a quirked brow, handing me a glass.

"Nothing."

"Bullshit. You have this weird look on your face."

"I was watching you pour the milk and realized we'll be making lots of milk runs coming up in the middle of the night. We'll have to trade notes," I say, choking back a lump, "so we make sure we stay on the same schedule and stuff."

His lips twist together. "I might have to get a nanny. I've been thinking about it. I have to be at the complex at five in the morning. I'm gone all weekend every weekend through the season."

"I can keep the baby. I mean, you could come see it when you can."

"I don't want to be that guy," he sighs. "I don't want to be the dad who sees his kid twice a week."

I try to force a smile, but fail. "I've been thinking about moving up here."

"Here? It's three hours from Chicago."

"Hey, you told me not to let Callum start calling the shots," I point out.

"I'm not Callum."

I can't help but laugh. "I know. I'm just thinking about it, mostly to take my mind off Finn calling tonight. I told him you were here, and I don't really know how well that went over."

"He thinks I'm the worst choice you could've made."

"Except I really didn't choose you."

"You didn't, probably because you were smart enough not to. I hate that I'm the one in between you. You have this awesome dynamic and then I come in and fuck it up. I can't just mess up your life, I have to do his too." He shakes his head. "I'm on a roll."

"We'll get it figured out before the baby comes."

"What if I'm a shitty Dad?"

"What if I don't know how to be a mom? What if we disagree on everything and you do one thing at your house and I do another at mine and the kid is all screwed up?"

He laughs, almost reaching for me, but he stops himself short. "As long as we agree on what's important, we'll do fine."

"So, like, religion and non-GMO's?"

He makes a face. "I was thinking like the Legends, the Tennessee Arrows baseball team, and Beau McCrae's music."

"Oh, Beau McCrae," I say, fanning my face.

"Second thought—no McCrae."

"I'm going to have to disagree on the Arrows too," I say, loving the easy smile on his face.

"Ha. No. There's no compromise there."

"I used to love them until Lincoln Landry retired. Now I pull for the Lions."

"No way. My son will *not* be a Lions fan."

"Your *daughter* will do what her mother says."

"You're right about that," he says, leaning against the cabinet. "My child, regardless of sex, will do what their mother says."

My heart tugs at the look of sincerity in his eye. His lips upturn, an easy, sleep smile that I find myself hoping to see one day with a baby in his arms.

Shaking my head, I refocus. "I don't know what to do about Finn."

He lingers against the cabinet, quirking a brow. "I have to head back to the city tomorrow. I have an interview and a few appointments I have to get out of the way before the pre-season starts. Will you be okay here?"

"I'm leaving too, I think." I toss the fork in the sink. "I have to get back into the real world and start making some plans."

"Like what?"

"A lot of things . . ."

Not bothering to explain, I brush past him and head to my room. I hear him behind me, but he doesn't say anything.

Pausing at my door, I feel him behind me.

"Night, Branch."

"Night, Sunshine."

TWENTY-FIVE
BRANCH

I PULL MY CAR INTO the driveway and kill the ignition. The last few hours have given me time to consider how to approach this subject and how to try to mend the fence that might just be irreparably broken.

A sprinkler kicks on as I make my way up the walkway, and I make a dash to the porch before getting doused. With a deep breath, I push the doorbell.

The little *pop, pop, pop* of the sprinkler head as it mists the entire yard frays my nerves. As footsteps become apparent on the other side of the dark wood decked out with a stained glass window, I steel myself.

"What the fuck are you doing here?" Finn glares at me from the other side of the threshold.

"I want to talk to you."

"Didn't I tell you if you showed up here I'd call the police?"

"No," I correct him. "You told me if you showed up to my house that I should call the police. You said nothing about me coming here."

"Go home."

"Finn, who is it?" Poppy appears at his side, her arm going to his bicep. She looks at me with a much warmer level of acceptance than her boyfriend. "Hey, Branch."

"Hi, Pop."

Finn isn't amused by her cordiality or my willingness to act comfortable on his porch after being ordered to leave. His knuckles turn white as he grips the door and starts to swing it shut.

"Oh, is this how it is?" I ask, knowing I'm playing with fire. "You just write everyone off because you don't like our choices. Good call, Finn."

The door shoves away and he stands in the middle of the doorway. Poppy shifts to see around him.

"You want to know how it is?" he asks carefully. "This is how it is: you are not my friend. You have no idea what loyalty is or the respect that goes with a friendship. You took your little motto of doing whatever you damn well please and elbowed your way into my personal space. My sister's fucking womb, you asshole."

He takes a step back and narrows his eyes.

"If anyone in this world knows me, it's you," I tell him. "You've been at my side for the good, bad, and even the ugly ones."

He almost smiles. Almost.

"But because you know me, you should know this: I fuck up. I make mistakes that are sometimes bigger than anyone thought possible. It's my trademark. But so is my ability to make good on promises."

"What are you getting at?"

"What I'm saying is I'll take responsibility for that."

"Um, I think Layla was more than gung-ho," Poppy chimes in, a move that gets her a glare from Finn too. She just shrugs.

"It doesn't matter," I say, looking at her. "I am Finn's friend. I'm the one that should've seen the boundary and not crossed it. But I didn't and that's on me. I want you to know," I say, my gaze crossing back to Finn, "that I'll do whatever I can to make sure I'm there for her."

"What?" he snorts. "What's that even mean?"

"I'll let her take the lead and tell me what she needs and then make sure I do that. I don't know what else to do."

"I think that's a great plan," Poppy admits.

"You think that's a great plan?" Finn snorts, looking down at her. "That Layla gets to figure it all out while he sits back with a checkbook? That she has to go through a pregnancy and have a baby she's responsible for twenty-four seven while he's out fucking a whore in every city on our schedule?"

Poppy raises a brow, a hand going to her hip. "I think I don't like the tone you're using with me."

"Oh, you wanna fight now?" he asks her.

"No, I don't wanna fight with you, but I sure as hell am not going to be talked to like I'm an idiot. I have faith that Lay and Branch can figure this out between themselves."

"So you're taking his side?"

"No. I'm taking Layla's side." Poppy strides through the living room and grabs her purse. She shoves her way past us and heads to her car. "You both need to have a little faith in our girl. And until you," she says, glaring at Finn, "can get your head out of your ass, don't come for mine."

Her tires squeal as she takes off down the road. When I turn back to Finn, he's still looking at the street.

"I'm sorry," I tell him. "I came over here to apologize. You're a great guy, a good friend, and a hell of a brother. I don't want to get between the two of you."

"You already did that."

"I'm trying to fix that. I'm trying to make things better for her. I can't do that and not be a part of her life, not talk to her at all. Don't you see the position you're putting me in?"

"Nah, you put yourself in this position," he says, grabbing the door. "Go home, Branch. We're done here."

The door shuts, the Legends flag on the door bouncing, as I turn and head back to my car.

***

LAYLA

"SO YOU AREN'T EVEN KNOCKING now?" I laugh as Poppy waltzes into my kitchen unannounced.

"I have a key. Why knock?" She sets her purse on a barstool then heads to the refrigerator and pulls out a bottle of wine. "You can't drink this anymore, so you don't mind if do, right?"

"Sure . . ." I watch her remove the cork and lift the bottle straight to her lips. "Bad day?"

There's no rush as she takes a few long, lingering drinks of the white wine. All I get as an answer is a slight nod of her head as she chugs the alcohol.

"Oh, I can't wait to hear this," I giggle.

Making a face and wiping her lips with the pretty kitchen towel on the stove—the one not meant for actual use—she sighs. "Finn and Branch just had a standoff."

"Oh, God," I groan. "What happened?"

"I was at Finn's, sitting on his pool table while he . . . never mind," she blushes. "And the doorbell rang. So he . . . stops doing what he was doing and goes to answer it. It was Branch."

She sets the bottle down and burps.

"Poppy. Really?"

"Don't judge."

"I withhold the right to bring this back up later," I say, arching a brow. "But I'm too curious about what happened."

"Right, so, Branch is at the door looking as suave as usual. Seriously, girl. Whew!"

I look at the ceiling and pray for patience.

"Anyway, he's standing there, doing his best to ignore Finn's hatefulness and Finn is just letting him know what a fuck-up he is."

My head tips back farther.

"Finn's going on and on, telling Branch to leave, that he doesn't know anything about friendship while Branch is letting him have his say but telling him he's going to prove that he's a good guy and just made a mistake."

"So I'm just a mistake now," I say, feeling my spirits sink.

"See," she says, climbing onto a stool beside me, "I don't think that's what he meant. I think he meant sort of messing with you under Finn's nose was a mistake, but not that he was all that sorry for actually, you know, messing with you."

I rest my head against her shoulder and she leans her head on mine. We sit in the quiet for a minute.

"I think you spilled wine on your shirt," I say without bothering to look.

"I did, but just a drop."

"My senses, especially smell, are on overdrive right now. It's so weird."

Sighing, I sit up and look at my friend. "How did it end with the two of them?"

"I don't know. I left."

"To give them space?"

"Nope. Because I pointed out to Finn that what Branch was saying made sense and he needed to give the two of you some room to figure it out. And Finn, being the dumbass he can be, got an attitude. So I left."

Grinning as I imagine her laying into my brother, I laugh. "I bet that was something to see."

"I'm always something to see. Anyway, enough of the bromance chronicles. Tell me about what happened in Linton with Branch."

I go into a quick version of the important details, not wanting to get into it. It feels too intimate to share with anyone, even my best friend.

Poppy watches me tell the story and, in a very un-Pop like way, doesn't rush me. She sits in her chair, her arms at her sides, and lets me talk for a good ten minutes.

When I'm finished, she leans on the counter. "Sounds like a good time."

"It wasn't bad. We ended up getting along and working a few things out," I admit. "And I kind of hate that it wasn't a mess."

"Why would you hate that?"

I shrug. "I appreciate that we can get along, but it hurts to be in this situation. It's like the more good memories, the more it stings."

"Maybe it will develop into something," she offers. "He was pretty clear to Finn that he wants to be there for you and the baby."

"I know he will. I believe that. But . . . damn it. Why couldn't I be having a baby with someone that I could build something with for me too?"

"You never know."

"No, I do know," I say, scooting off the stool and feeling my heart drop right with my feet. "He made it clear he wants to be there for the baby and for me as its mother. Done. He even went so far as to tell me what the road was like and how many girls are at their disposal and how that's not fair to the women who marry the players in their league."

She stands and leans against the cabinet. "That tells me he's aware."

"Aware of what?"

"Of life. Of reality. That's a good thing, Lay." She laces her fingers together. "He doesn't want to hurt you. Obviously. Wouldn't you rather him be honest like this than just go through the motions and then 'go through the motions' with road bitches?"

"I guess."

"You don't guess," she scoffs. "You know. This means he's more mature than I think any of us thought. He's pondered these things. That's more than most guys do until it's too late."

"True. But you know what? We're missing the point."

"Which is . . ."

"Which is," I say, grabbing a bottle of water from the fridge, "that I don't even want that life. I don't want to be with a guy I can't trust. I don't want to worry about what he's doing and who he's doing and what will be said in the rag mags. I want to be cuddled up on the sofa next to him, our baby on our laps, watching the news and eating ice cream."

She sighs. "Can you imagine him with a baby? God, my ovaries."

"He was standing in the kitchen last night, pouring us a glass of milk. All I could think about was how sexy he would look making a bottle, you know? Then it occurred to me I'd probably never see that." I rest my forehead on the cool counter. "This is so confusing."

Her hand finds the back of my head. "You just relax and take care of my little goddaughter. I'm going to get us some sandwiches and we are going to eat and watch television and forget about boys."

"This is why I love ya, Poppy."

"I know."

TWENTY-SIX
LAYLA

RING!

My head shoots off the island counter, the bar stool wobbling beneath me so hard I think I'm going to fall. I clamor down, rubbing my eyes, trying to figure out where I am.

The phone continues to ring as I get my bearings, the sky outside the kitchen window dark. Glancing at the clock, it's just past ten. The last I knew it was eight-thirty when I sat down to work on an advertising contract.

Ring!

"Shit," I grumble, grabbing my lit-up phone and pulling it to my ear. "Hello?"

"Hey." His voice is quiet, warm like a fleece blanket on a cold winter night. "Were you asleep?"

"Yeah. I fell asleep in the kitchen. Must've been tired."

"Are you getting enough sleep? Eating enough?" he chuckles. "We know you're eating enough."

"Go to hell," I laugh, yawning. "I was up late last night. Guess I can't be doing that anymore."

"What were you doing?"

"A little of this, a little of that."

"Huh." He takes a deep breath, blowing out slowly. "I just wanted to check on you. See how you were doing. I haven't talked to you since yesterday afternoon."

His sincerity is on the surface, not at all hidden. The tenor of his voice gentler than I have heard. There's an intimacy to it that causes me to fall back into the cabinet.

"I'm good. Hanging in there, you know?" I say. "How are you?"

"Just finished a workout and dinner."

"What did you have?"

"I threw some chicken breasts in the oven. Nothing fancy."

"I'm impressed. I don't even bake chicken breasts. I just buy them in the deli," I laugh.

"You need to eat red meat more than chicken. The iron is good for you and the baby."

My jaw drops. "What?"

"I . . . um . . . I was asking the nutritionist today that we work with at the Legends facility. She said to make sure you're eating lots of iron and folate and calcium. There's a delivery service where you can order plans especially for pregnant women and—"

"Branch. I'm good," I say softly. "I know what to do."

"I just want to help."

His words hit my heart, but it's the way he says it that slays me. Tears flicker in my eyes, making the lights look like kaleidoscopes. "I really appreciate that."

"I hope you don't get mad," he says, a hitch in his voice, "but I ordered you five boxes a week. They'll be delivered. If you don't like what they send, you can go online and customize them. But I thought, you know, maybe it would make things a little easier for you."

"That's super sweet," I whisper.

There's a pause in the conversation, not exactly an awkward moment, but one we haven't traversed yet. It's born more out of respect and consideration than a failure to know what to say.

"I go to the doctor the day after tomorrow," I tell him. "If you want to go, you can, but you totally don't have to. I'll let you know whatever they say."

"What time is it?"

"Four."

"I'd like to go, if you don't mind."

My cheeks break into a grin. Heading down the hallway, I flop onto my bed, one hand on my stomach. "Want to meet me there?"

"Could I pick you up?" he asks. "Maybe we could grab dinner or something? I don't know. It just feels like something we should do together, right? Or am I wrong?"

"I'd like that."

"Good." He clears his throat. "So, did you ever get your boxes unpacked?"

Looking around my room, I see the stacks of cardboard. Some are empty, some are full, and I have no energy to care. "No. They're still looking at me. Some of them, anyway. I've decided you might be right and I'll just trash them."

He laughs. "We can have a bonfire together. Just burn it all to the ground."

"Sounds better than unpacking at the moment," I yawn. "A lot of it is just extra stuff for the guest room—baby's room, I guess, now—and things that I have nowhere to put."

"I'm going to have to get one of these rooms ready for a baby. How do I do that?"

"I don't know," I admit. "A crib. A changing table, maybe, if you'll use it. I don't think a baby really needs that much. A lot of people just get excited and want to buy it all."

"What camp do you fall in—buy it or don't buy it?"

"My heart says buy it but my budget says don't," I admit. "I figure between the two of us, we'll have a good balance. I'll keep the baby frugal and you can spoil it."

"A guy in the locker room today was showing this video of his kid in one of those cars that look like real cars, right? They're battery operated and they really drive them around. Have you seen these things?"

"Yes," I say, grinning at his excitement.

"Our kid is going to have a fucking fleet of those things."

We laugh, Branch's a little self-conscious and that makes my heart swell.

"Just try to save it for a birthday or Christmas," I suggest. "Don't just get things because it's a Tuesday."

"I'll try. No promises." He takes a deep breath. "I've been thinking about what it will be like when the baby comes. There's so much you don't think about until you think about it."

I lay the back of my hand across my forehead as I listen to him speak.

"You'll be a great mom, Sunshine."

"Thanks," I say around the lump in my throat. "Our baby will be lucky to have you as her dad."

There's a giant pause. "Thank you," he whispers.

"For what?"

"I don't know. For believing that I can do this. For not writing me off from day one or sticking it to me when I was a dick when you told me. You've definitely proved you're the better person, but it's not like we didn't know that already." He blows out a breath. "I need to go so you can go to sleep. But I just want to say one more thing."

"What?"

"I don't want you to be scared to call me."

The lump grows bigger, merging with the swelling of my heart, and I can't speak.

"I have a lot going on," he says slowly, "and as the season gets started, it's gonna get crazy. I don't want you to hesitate to tell me if you need something or think I'd want to know something, okay?"

"I'll be fine."

"The other players' wives don't tell them shit until the season is over. They only want to focus on football from August to February. I wanna know if something is wrong or you go to the doctor. I might not be able to go and you might have to leave a message, but it . . . it matters to me, Sunshine."

"Thanks," I croak.

"Go to sleep," he orders. "You'll get your first food box tomorrow."

"Branch?"

"Yeah?"

"Thank you."

"No problem."

He's gone before I can say anything else, but it's just as well. The tears that come, this time from a good place, fall fast and hard. Curling up on my blanket with no energy to even get beneath, I fall quickly into a deep, peaceful sleep.

TWENTY-SEVEN
BRANCH

I SLAM MY LOCKER SHUT, the sound barely heard over my teammates catching up after practice. It's so loud I've considered bringing noise-cancelling headphones with me just so I can hear myself think.

Despite my workout efforts over the summer, my body still aches like a motherfucker. Every part of me contests every movement I make, each muscle fiber begging me to stop. Although we've practiced every day for the last week, the soreness just gets worse.

I kind of love it.

It reminds me that I'm alive, that I'm doing what I love, that my body, while not a young stud anymore, is still capable of competing with them. Six years in the league is long enough to take a beating that makes every penny I make fully earned.

"What'd you do this offseason, Best?" Chauncey slips on his shirt and grins. "You always have the craziest stories, man."

"I just played it cool, you know? Did a little of this, a little of that . . ."

Knocked up Finn's sister . . .

"Look at you being all discreet," he says, closing his locker. "Nah, I got you. You're keeping a low profile."

"You could say that. What were you up to?"

"Hangin' around the house, painting the baby's bedroom, doing some fishin'. Just basic shit, ya know?"

"Life with a wife," I kid.

"Hell, no," he says, bursting out laughing. "My girlfriend had me painting. My wife don't give a shit about paint. She'd just hire someone to come in and do it. Ain't her money, you know?"

I try to smile, to come up with a joke like I'd usually do, about his girlfriend and his wife taking all his damn money if he doesn't watch it, but I come up empty. There just doesn't seem to be a lot funny about it.

I instantly think of Layla and what color she'd choose for our baby's room and if this is something she's even thought about.

"You okay, Lucky?"

"Yeah, yeah, I'm fine." I grab my bag and heave it up on my shoulder as we head towards the door.

"What do you think Coach's surprise is on Monday? 'Bring your best selves,'" Chauncey says, mimicking Coach. "If he fucking brings out that Godzilla drill, I might feign a pulled hamstring and sit it out."

"I bet it is. That or Hammer Time. He hasn't killed us with that yet."

"Don't even talk about that," he laughs. "I hate that thing. Fucking Miller beat everyone last year. Remember that?" He looks around the locker room. "Speaking of, where's Finn?"

"I don't know."

"I wanted to say hey, get back into the flow of things, but he disappears every day as soon as the reporters leave." We stand at the bank of elevators, Chauncey needing to take the right one, me the left. "Tell Miller to find me tomorrow."

"I will."

The ding is my opening and I nod to my teammate. Getting into the elevator, I hit the "close" button before anyone can join me.

The ride down to the parking garage is quick, and I'm in my car before I have to talk to anyone else. Practice was good, but the high is over and I feel antsy.

Sitting at the gate, waiting for security to let me through, I play a game of chicken with myself.

I can go home and call Layla, or I can do what I really want to do: see her.

She sounds so tired on the phone, I wonder if she's getting any rest. I was checking out a few web articles about pregnancy and some women want to sleep half the day or more. How can she do that if she's working and living alone?

Not only that, I miss her. I've told myself I don't, but I do. The Branch that's with her is different from the Branch on the field or the Branch in public. He's calmer. Happier. The Branch from before I got into the league. I kinda like him.

I kinda like her.

Glancing at the passenger's seat, the coffee cake I picked up this morning at the bakery still sitting there, I make up my mind.

The guard releases the gate and I make a last-second decision. I go right when I should probably go left.

———

I PRESS THE DOORBELL, CLUTCHING the coffee cake, and wait. The hallway is small, more confined than comfortable, with cheap brown carpeting and cold white walls etched with deep, random scratches.

Her laugh sounds through the door, followed by a deep male voice, before she undoes the lock. Her eyes go wide when she sees me. "Branch," she breathes, gulping.

"Am I interrupting something?" I grind my teeth together, looking over her shoulder. A tall, dark-haired man stands near the sofa, smiling brightly at me. "Who the fuck is that?"

She opens the door and I walk in, squeezing the plastic tin so hard it crackles.

"Branch, this is Max Quinn," Layla says. "Max, this is Branch."

"Nice to meet ya." Max sticks his hand out, his Southern drawl deeper than mine. "I've heard a lot about ya. Congratulations on the baby."

Tossing a glance at Layla out of the corner of my eye, I shake Max's hand. "Thanks. And who are you?"

"I'm Poppy's cousin. My buddy, Cane, and I are up here with our wives for a wedding. Poppy left her sunglasses over here and I was in this part of town, so I offered to grab 'em."

I attempt to control the exhale of breath, but Max notices and grins.

"You're gonna be fine," he almost whispers. "Just relax a little. And ease up on the cake, son, or you're gonna have a mess on your hands."

He grips my shoulder as he walks by me, telling Layla goodbye. I don't get involved with them, just work on settling the adrenaline that had me ready to come to blows with Max.

As I listen to her giggle and tell him to come back and visit, it dawns on me this is a real thing. Probably not a one-time deal. How many times will I walk into her home to get the baby and another man will be in there?

The plastic pops again.

What if it's her husband and he tells me I can't see my kid? Or didn't give him a Popsicle and made him cry?

Fuck that guy. I'm gonna kill him and he doesn't even exist.

I'm losing my damn mind.

"Here," she says, taking the coffee cake from me. "There's no sense in abusing a poor dessert."

Releasing the container, it's dented and the cream cheese icing is stuck to the top. "Sorry," I offer sheepishly.

"What's wrong?" she asks, carrying the cake to the kitchen.

"Why do you think something is wrong?"

"Well, you're here, for one. And for two, you look like you're ready to brawl."

I shrug because I'm not completely sure. Instead of answering, I watch her grab a plate and fork.

Her legs look toned in a pair of white shorts, her yellow top tight against her chest. Her hair is messy in a half-up, half-down thing and her eyes shine even more golden next to her shirt.

Watching her, I can't help but acknowledge the tightness in my chest. She's beautiful and sexy and sweet and sincere. But it's how she makes me feel that's crazy.

I don't want to just undress her and lick every part of her body. I want to kiss her, take my time and adore her. I want to take her to a stupid movie or get her coffee cake in the middle of the night.

But why? What's the point?

"You gonna offer me a piece?" I ask.

"Maybe." She shoves a forkful in her mouth. "God, this is so good."

"I love hearing you say that."

She rolls her eyes, but cuts me a piece anyway. "Here. That's all you get."

"Stingy."

She smiles and goes back to her cake. I take a bite and look around.

Her apartment is small with white walls and muted, feminine touches. The couch is a simple grey with so many pillows I don't know how she even sits on it. There are images of beaches and skylines and simple artistic drawings adorning the walls, helping to make them not look so dull.

It's a one-eighty from my house with its large, barren rooms and black and white canvas. I thought modern and sparse was my jam, but I'm not entirely sure now.

"What do you think?" she asks. "I loved the light in here. That's why I chose this apartment."

"It's nice. It's what I thought your apartment would look like, actually. Pretty. Tasteful."

"I hope you thought it would be cleaner," she laughs. "I hate cleaning. Hate it. I'm not good at domestic crap. Callum used to say . . ." She stops when she sees my reaction. "It doesn't matter what he used to say."

"No, it doesn't."

"So," she says in an attempt to change the subject, "want a drink? Pop? Tea? Decaf?"

"Water?" I ask.

"I've drank my weight in water today," she says, swiping a bottle from the refrigerator. "I read that drinking more water keeping swelling down. Does that make any sense to you?"

"The therapist we use at work says the same thing. It seems counterintuitive, but the owner only hires the best, so I'm assuming she knows her shit."

I take a long, cool drink and use the time to try to settle my nerves. Being in her home feels different than I thought it would. The cabin felt more like neutral ground. This is completely her domain and I wonder what she would look like in my kitchen.

"How was your first week back?" she asks, getting an orange out of the basket beneath the microwave. "Did it feel like home?"

"Yeah, it did. It was good to get out there with the guys." She tosses me the fruit. "What's this for?"

"You should eat it. It's good for muscle fatigue."

Layla walks by me and heads back into the living room. I follow, unsure if I'm supposed to bring the water and fruit with me or not. I set them on the counter to be safe.

I hate that I don't know the rules here, that I don't know all her little idiosyncrasies. As we sit on the sofa, I look around.

"What color do you want to paint the baby's room?" I ask, thinking back to the conversation I had with Chauncey.

"What a random question."

"I know," I say, feeling a little silly. "I was just curious, that's all."

"Well, I thought a pretty light grey would be nice, if the room is bright. If it's not, then maybe a pale yellow to make it a little cheerier. Both are pretty neutral colors."

"If the room is bright? You don't know which you'll use as the nursery?"

She bites the inside of her cheek and shakes her head. "I'll be moving before she arrives, so I'll wait and see."

My stomach bottoms out, hits the floor, before lodging itself in my throat. "You're still thinking about moving?"

"I have to, I think. I'll stay around Chicago," she says softly. "I just can't afford the rent here with a baby."

This time, it's my heart that hits me over the head. I follow her gaze to the floor, feeling like a complete dipshit for not considering that. Babies are expensive, or so everyone says. She's a fucking blogger. She can't make much.

As I look back up at her, my chest tightens and I realize I don't want her to be too far from me. The thought of not being able to drop by like I did tonight after work or have dinner delivered to her when she says she's tired like I did on Wednesday really bothers me. *Really* bothers me.

"It's fine," she says, shifting on the sofa. "Really. I wanted to move anyway."

"I thought you loved it here? You were just telling me how you like to look out the window and watch the people."

"I do, but not that much. It won't be that big of a deal. Besides, I might move in with Poppy since she and Finn are still on the outs."

"They still aren't talking?"

"Nope. She refuses until he apologizes to her," she laughs. "She's so stubborn. Finn met his match with her."

Warring over what to do, what to offer, what to say, I fiddle with the hem of my shorts. "You know I'll help you with rent—"

"No."

My gaze flips to hers. "I can give you what I make a year if you want to make an estimate about child support. You know I'm Branch Best, right?"

"I don't give a fuck who you are."

Her words are cast off with an angry tone, intended to cut a little with the sharp edges. Instead, a light has been switched on inside me and I can't help but laugh.

"I'm not kidding," she warns.

"I know you're not."

She bends her neck and grimaces.

"Your neck still hurt?"

"A little. Not as bad."

"Face the wall," I say, guiding her around with my hands. She does as I instruct and moans as I start to work the tense muscles in her shoulders. "How does that feel?"

"Amazing."

She moves her body so I can get a better angle. I push and pull, kneading and pressing, working her little shoulders around in my hands. Every now and then she sighs or moves in a way that throws a scent of pineapples my way.

It takes everything I have to stay focused on the task at hand and not the task between my legs, as I touch her gorgeous body.

Her back arches as she stretches over her head, her ass scooting back against the couch towards me just enough to catch the spark that's always ready to go off around her into full blaze. The burn is slow, the embers starting to smolder, as she sits upright again.

"Thank you," she says, her voice breathless.

"Any time."

She looks at me over her shoulder, her eyes radiating the same heat that's coursing through my body. There's a hunger there, a desire that's unmistakable.

"Layla?"

She sucks in a breath of the air that's changing between us more every second. Her lashes flutter, her lips part. Without thinking, my fingertips fall down her spine.

"I'm not sure," I say, "if I'm not supposed to say this now, but goddamn it if you aren't fucking beautiful."

I lift the hem of her shirt just enough to touch the small of her back. She sucks in another breath at the same time as I do, her body flexing against my hand. Both hands grip her waist, the curve of her hip causing me to almost lose my mind.

"Careful, Branch," she warns breathlessly.

My hands shake, fingers tremble, as I fight with myself about what to do. I want her. Maybe I even need her. But if I do this, it's gonna blur the fuck out of even more lines that I'm having a hard time seeing as it is.

"If you tell me to stop, I'll stop," I say, letting my finger dip into her soft skin.

"I didn't say stop. I said—"

Leaning up, I capture her mouth with mine. It's like an explosion on Independence Day, every firework going off in quick succession.

She moans into my mouth, the sweet taste of her breath causing me to shudder. I bite her lower hip, holding it between my teeth, as I work her shorts down her delectable body.

Arms are flailing, legs moving, as she gets rid of the fabric separating her from me. Off goes her bra and her panties, her mouth moving ferociously against mine.

"Damn it," I groan. She sucks my tongue into her mouth, nipping at it with her teeth in a way that makes my cock ready to blow.

My pants fall to the floor along with my boxers and my t-shirt goes sailing, landing on the shade of a lamp. The light rattles around on the table. She giggles, never breaking the kiss.

I roam her body with my hands, cupping the globes of her ass, running up the arch of her sides, until her breasts are sitting in my hands.

The weight of them, the gentle weight of each, causes a groan to rumble from the depth of my desire to be buried inside this gorgeous woman.

Leaning back on the sofa, I wrap my arms around her and pull her down with me. As her rounded body lies on top of mine, my palm resting against the back of her head, she kisses me like there's nothing else to do.

The tempo slows, the licks of her tongue coming in longer, thicker strokes. Our lips burn from the onslaught, but not enough to make either of us stop.

As she moves her knees up along my sides, the heat from her pussy hovers over my thickened length. Her wetness leaves a trail down my shaft as she slips her body up.

Gripping both sides of her face, I press my lips against hers in the hardest, most forceful way I can—in a way that causes my chest to pull.

Both palms plant on my chest, she pushes away and sits upright. Her nipples are peaked, her hair spilling around her shoulders. Then she gives me my favorite thing of all: her smile.

LAYLA

"I THINK A CONDOM IS pointless, don't you?" I move my hips against him, watching him grit his teeth. "I mean, I was tested again at the doctor. You?"

He squeezes my hips and his eyes close. "I'm clean."

Planting my hands on either side of his head, I grip the armrest. Tilting my hips until the head of his cock is positioned at my opening, I toy with him for a minute. "You are so hard, Branch."

"If you don't sit down on me soon, I'm going to hold you down and pound the shit out of you."

My laugh makes him open his eyes. He shoots me a slow, sly smile. "God, I love that."

"What?" I say, still hovered over him. Every few seconds, he raises his hips, but I pull back far enough so he doesn't part me.

"Your laugh. It's so untainted by anything. You're laughing because you're laughing, not because you think something I said was funny or drawing attention to yourself."

"I think I have your attention without laughing, handsome."

"That you do." He rises up from his waist and sucks one nipple into his mouth. Propping himself up with one hand, he uses the other to squeeze my breast as he works the beaded nub with his tongue.

"Ah," I moan, my head falling back.

He scoots us closer to the arm rest so that he's braced by the sofa. One of my knees digs between the seat and the back, the other leg dangles off the side of the couch. He's hard, so worked up that his temple is throbbing.

Digging my hands into his thick hair, I press his face harder to my chest. He switches breasts, his hand taking the place of his mouth on the first, kneading it so carefully that I think I'm going to come.

I lift off of him just enough that I can palm his length under me. My body positioned just over the tip, I let my weight fall, crashing down on his shaft.

"God," I moan, sucking in a hard breath. He bites down on my nipple, tugging it as he groans. We still for a moment, giving me a second to adjust to his size.

My body feels completely full, stretched to an almost painful point, but as he begins to move, I know I haven't even taken it all.

One hand on each of his shoulders, I rock. With each motion, each subtle flick of his hips below me, a shot of fire scorches me from the inside out.

"You feel amazing," he says, giving my tits a final squeeze and running his hands down to my hips again. "Your body is perfect."

I close my eyes and soak up the sensations rioting through me. It's a wonderful, chaotic feeling to have every nerve ending firing at the same time.

His cock hits the wall of my pussy as I lift and drop onto him in deliberate strokes. As if he knows what I need, he splays a hand just below my belly button and when his thumb presses on my clit, I bite down on my lip.

"Branch," I warn through gritted teeth. "I need to stop or I'm going to come all over your cock."

I open my eyes to see a wickedness in his that does nothing but propel me towards an orgasm. He looks at me like he could devour me, his bright blue eyes gleaming with lust.

"Just hearing you say that has me dripping inside you." He holds the bottom of my ass and raises me up and down, urging me to take quicker strokes. "Are you ready to come, baby?"

Each movement hits the target, the need to climax so strong I can't even hold my eyes open. I feel his gaze on me, watching my breasts bounce in his face, watching my mouth slack open as I draw closer and closer to the end. Any sense of self-awareness has long left the building as the sound of our bodies, slick with desire, rings through the living room.

"Branch!" I call out, letting him press deeper, farther into my body. "Oh God."

My jaw aches as I bite down, the eruption starting at the base of my stomach and flowing out until every bit of my body is engulfed in the bliss of climax. A flurry of colors sparkles through my vision, and I'm only faintly aware that he's calling my name. I only barely hear the groan of his warning, the feel of his hands biting into my skin, the thrust of his hips, or the heat of his body expelling into mine.

Any ability I had to keep moving is long gone, and I sit on top of him, as he rides out his own orgasm.

We sit, both panting, our bodies glistening with sweat. At the same moment, we open our eyes. It takes a second for us to smile, for him to reach up and wipe the hair stuck to the side of my face away.

"I know you're not supposed to say a woman is wrong," he teases, "but I think I did just prove you wrong."

"How do you figure?"

"This proves, despite whatever else, we can still have fun together."

I smack him on the chest and climb off, making a beeline for the bathroom. "I've never said we couldn't have fun. I just said we need to be careful."

"That wasn't fun for you?" he shouts after me, a laugh in his voice.

"No. It was awful," I yell back. Before I can reach the bathroom, I hear his steps coming behind me and squeal as he picks me up and cradles me in his arms.

Looking up at his face, I see something besides the lust. Besides the need. Besides the physical attraction we have to one another. I see something else entirely and it's that look, that feeling, that worries me.

"If that wasn't fun, it's only fair you give me another try," he says, carrying me down the hallway.

"What do you propose? Blackjack? Rummy? Maybe chess?" I tease.

He kicks open my bedroom door and lays me on the bed. Standing over me, he grins. "Something more like Twister, but you can call it what you want."

My knees fall to the side as he climbs on top of me. He surprises me by lying next to me.

"I've always liked Twister," I say.

"Seems fitting," he says, bringing his lips closer. "You know how to twist a man up."

Before I can ask for an explanation, he kisses me again and I lose myself to him.

TWENTY-EIGHT
BRANCH

"THE DOCTOR WILL BE RIGHT in." The nurse picks up the file and gives me a sultry look as she walks out the door.

"I like her," Layla says, folding her hands on her lap.

"Don't."

"Why?"

"She'd fuck me in a second if I told her to."

She makes a face. "How do you know?"

"Trust me."

She picks at the white paper covering her bottom half. "This is so awkward."

"Do you want me to leave?" I ask. "I can go out to the waiting room, if you'd like."

Her head rolls to the side as she lies on the table and looks at me. She seems to be caught up in whatever she's warring with in her pretty little head.

She's done that a lot since last night. I guess I have too. We had sex three times before we finally had our fill of each other. It's so easy being with her, so natural. Unlike with most women, being with her is not a show of what I can do or watching a woman perform for me. I want to make her feel good, hope she knows how beautiful she is, and relish the fact that this woman wants to be with me.

Glancing around the room, I'm shocked at how calm I am. This place should freak me the fuck out, but it doesn't. It's almost exciting being *here* with *her*.

"I want you to stay," she says finally. "It's your baby too."

We wait in the quiet for the doctor to arrive. I pick up a magazine and leaf through it, not paying much attention to the words, only to Layla out of the corner of my eye. A few minutes later, the door presses open slowly and a man comes in. He's older, in his sixties, with white hair and a kind smile. He shakes my hand. "You must be Mr. Miller?"

"No," I say, standing. "I'm Branch Best."

He quirks a brow. "The Branch Best?"

"The one and only. This," I say, clearing my throat, "is Layla Miller."

The doctor introduces himself to her and takes a seat on a little wheeled stool. They go through basic medical information, family history, and a list of health questions that Layla answers without hesitation. I listen, realizing how much I don't know about this woman.

"You are the father, is that correct?" Dr. Howard looks at me.

"Yes."

He scribbles again and then stands. Pulling up Layla's shirt, he places a stethoscope to her abdomen. Her eyes pull away from his hands and over to me, holding my gaze.

"You okay?" I ask quietly.

She nods, turning back to the doctor as he speaks.

"Do you want to hear the heartbeat?" he asks.

Layla nods, her eyes wide, as he puts a little machine up to her belly. I reach for her hand, holding it in mine. A little tear dots the corner of her eye.

Holding my breath, I listen to the crackle of the machine as the doctor moves it around. And, finally, there it is. The steady beat of a heart.

It's unmistakable—*woosh-woosh-woosh*—that sounds through the room is a heartbeat. Our baby's heartbeat.

Tears stream down Layla's face as she clutches my hand. I lock them together, entwining our fingers and squeezing hers back. We watch each other as the sound gently strums through the room like a lullaby.

With each beat, something rustles deep inside me. An overwhelming sense of responsibility, a fierce need to protect the little boy nestled inside her.

She blinks, the tears falling faster, and I realize it's not just the baby

I want to protect. It's her too.

I watch her grin, then laugh, then look at me in amazement.

"Do you hear that?" she asks, sniffling. "It's so loud."

"He's going to be a wide receiver," I manage to say. "Listen to that. He's a beast already."

The doctor laughs, wiping the gel off the machine and from Layla's stomach. "It sounds good and healthy. You can sit up now."

I jump to my feet, helping her get situated. My efforts are rewarded with a smile.

"Everything looks and sounds good," he says, picking up her chart. "Congratulations. You two are very lucky."

I slide my gaze to the woman still holding my hand.

Maybe I am. Maybe I really am.

—

LAYLA

THE KEYS CLANG AGAINST THE table. My purse hits the floor, my shoes slide off my feet, and I hit the couch with a thud.

"You okay?" Branch laughs, sitting at the end of the sofa. He pulls my feet into his hands and rubs them. "Doctor's office and drive-thru is all you can handle in one day, huh?"

"I'm so sleepy," I say, my eyelids drooping closed. "I feel like a toddler that's missed my nap."

His hands swamp my feet, easily bending them at his will. It feels so good as he presses his thumb into the arch and releases all the stress that's held there.

"Thank you for going with me today," I say. "I appreciate it."

"Thanks for letting me." He works my feet back and forth, his leg starting to tap beneath me. "Can I talk to you about something, Sunshine?"

"Of course."

Holding my breath, I feel his hands slow down until they're eventually resting on top of my feet. I have no idea what he's going to say and it makes me want to vomit.

Hearing the baby's heartbeat was the most amazing thing I've ever done. It was a connection to the inside of me I had to go to the outside to get. Having Branch there, watching his reaction, was the sweetest part of all.

His eyes lit up like he was mesmerized, his hand clenching mine for all it was worth. I couldn't tell if he was scared or shocked or overjoyed, and he didn't mention it on the way home. He didn't speak much at all. I pretended to sleep and he just drove, and with every mile that went by, I felt a little more unnerved.

He takes a deep breath. "What if . . . what if we were wrong?"

My heart skips two beats. "If you were wrong about anything, I wouldn't be surprised. But me? I'm never wrong," I joke, hoping to calm my nerves. It doesn't work.

"I think you were this time."

I open my eyes to see him watching me closely. It's my favorite look on him, the one that's as soft as it is tough. There's a glimmer in his eye. The way he licks his lips makes me wonder if he's nervous too.

"What's wrong, Branch?"

"What if . . ." he shuffles in his seat. "We keep talking about things like it's me and you. What if it isn't me and you? What if there's no me and you?"

Trying to sit up, I'm stopped by him clamping down on my feet. My heart stills as I look at him.

"What if it isn't me and you, Sunshine?"

"I don't understand," I gulp, a hand falling to my stomach. He watches it rest against my navel before he looks back at me.

"What if it's . . . *us*?" he whispers.

"Branch . . ."

I'm glad he doesn't speak because I couldn't hear him over the roar in my ears anyway. My heart is beating so damn hard I'm lightheaded.

Wetness pricks my eyes but it doesn't fall. Shock prevents that. I just look at him and try to gather what he really means from his face, but the look of sincerity doesn't change.

His hand comes down gently on top of mine, applying a small dose of pressure to my stomach. My heart nearly bursts in my chest, the lump in my throat refusing to allow any words by. Instead, I just take in the worry lines on his forehead and the clear blue in his eyes.

"I've been thinking it for a while now about you and me and what we might've been and what we could be," he says. "Then I heard the baby today. God, wasn't that amazing?"

All I can do is nod and hold my breath, waiting for him to continue.

He reaches out and tips my chin towards him so I have no other choice but to look him in the eye. "I have reservations about whether I should do this or not, but looking at you lying by me, thinking about that motherfucker in here . . ."

"Max?"

"Whatever his name was," he sighs. "This thing with you isn't going to go away. As a matter of fact, it's getting worse."

"This thing with me?" I say, my voice crackling.

"It started the day I saw you. It got worse when I saw the sex therapy card, almost fell out of control at the festival, and spun so far past me when we were together that night that I knew there was no turning back. I just didn't want to fuck you all up, but I already had, in another way."

I try to speak, but only a whimper comes out as salty liquid streams down my face. He pulls me into a hug, laying me across his lap, and holding me so hard I can barely breathe.

Wrapping my hands in his shirt, I press my cheek against his heart. It's beating loud and strong, just like our baby's was just a little while ago. The thought makes me smile through the tears.

"I don't know what this means," he admits. "I know there are still things we have to work out and I can't figure out how to protect you from my life. I just know I want to be here every day to check on you, for you to know I have your back, to make sure our baby gets Popsicles."

"What?" I laugh, wiping away tears.

"Nothing."

Pulling away, I look into his sweet, blue eyes. "We had very real reasons to not be together and those aren't going to go away."

He pulls me all the way into his lap so I'm facing him. "I know that and we'd be stupid to pretend they aren't real. But . . . I think we're stupid to also pretend that you and I are strangers. When I look at you, I don't see a random girl. I see a girl I want to get to know and see what happens."

"Doesn't this set it up to end even worse?"

"Maybe," he shrugs. "But until I know you and I aren't doomed one hundred percent, I'm probably going to kill anyone that comes around. I almost ended Max."

"Max is no chump," I giggle.

"I'd have pieced him out," he teases. "But stop changing the subject. Let's give this one try. One good, solid effort, and if I think I'm fucking it up or if you think I am or if it becomes too much, we stop right then. Done. No more."

"Okay," I whisper, grinning like a loon.

He digs under the neckline of his t-shirt and removes the necklace his grandmother gave him. He holds it in his hand and looks at it for a long moment before placing it around my neck.

"I want you to wear this," he says softly, positioning it carefully so the cross sits in the center of my chest. "There's no reason why and it's really dumb but I want to know it's there."

"It's not dumb," I say, placing my hand over his and pressing it against my body. "It's sweet."

He smirks. "Who knew I could be sweet?"

"I had an inkling," I shrug.

"Did you really?"

"Mmhmm. You come in with this cocky swagger, but I could see through you."

"That's impressive," he says, moving so that I'm lying on my back. He hovers over me, his smirk growing wider.

Reaching between his legs, I cup his hardening length. "That's impressive too."

"You know what's double impressive?" He lays kisses along my neck, to the base of my ear, and over to my mouth.

"What's that?"

"Showing you how impressively sweet I can be with my impressive cock."

I giggle, but the sounds are swept up by his kisses. When he pulls away and rests his forehead against mine, I grin. "I'm willing to give you an opportunity to put your money where your mouth is."

"Don't you mean my mouth where the honey is?"

"Oh my God," I laugh, my body shaking. "That was awful."

Before I know what's happening, my dress is bunched at my waist and he's between my legs. A wicked look in his eye, he stares at me through his lashes. "This, Sunshine, will be good. I promise."

His head dips between my legs and I'm reminded just how good he can be.

TWENTY-NINE
BRANCH

"WHAT THE FUCK ARE THEY doing here?" I ask.

Chauncey and I watch as the Columbus Tigers come onto the field. The offense takes over the opposing end zone and starts to run basic plays while we watch.

"Is this Coach's surprise?" Chauncey looks at me. "He's a sadist."

Finding number seven, Callum throws a pass that spirals perfectly into the hands of a receiver. Callum raises a hand in the air before turning and finding *me*. He stares at me for a long minute, going so far as to take off his helmet to make it clear who he's looking at.

I wave.

My entire body shivers as a shot of testosterone mixed with adrenaline shoots though me. "It's gonna be a long day, Chauncey," I say, heading back to our huddle.

Coach is in the center of our offense with a clipboard. "Okay, boys. We're trying something different today. This will demonstrate how necessary it is for you to be willing to change it up and go with the flow, all right? I want all backs and receivers to join the Tigers' offense. All linemen and Frutter," he says, nodding to our quarterback, "down with the Tigers' defense."

Finn is across from me. Our eyes meet for a split second before he looks away.

Coach ends the huddle and we all start off to our assigned positions. I hang back a little and step in time with Finn.

"Hey," I say, looking up at him.

"What?"

"How are you?"

"Good."

"Great. That's great," I say, sarcasm thick in my voice. "When are you going to stop this?"

"Never."

Blowing out a breath, I take my assignment from the Tigers coach and line up on the outside. Finn lines up on the far side of the field. I'm too irritated with him to listen to the play Callum calls.

The play starts, the defense rushing. I break around the side only to turn around and have the ball smashing against the side of my helmet about a good four steps too early.

The ball falls to the grass, the play stopped, as I look up at the sound of my name.

"Gotta keep your head up, Best, if you want to catch it," Callum taunts, glaring at me through his facemask.

"Get the ball where it's supposed to be and I will."

We line up again. The play starts, and this time I don't even get a step off the line before the ball pelts me in the side.

This is something I could normally laugh off because he obviously looks like the idiot. But it's Callum. He's calling me out, and I'm not about to back down.

Unlatching my chin strap, I yank off my helmet. My cleats dig into the field as I march my way through the linemen and to Callum.

His helmet is off by the time I reach him, his pupils narrow.

"What the fuck?" I shout, the vein in my temple pulsing. "You got a problem, Worthington?"

"Just a receiver that can't catch a ball."

I grin, one I know he'll read into. "Oh, I can catch. I think you can't keep it within reach."

We're nose-to-nose, sweat dripping down our faces. Neither of us will look away. I barely register Finn's hand on my chest guiding me backwards. I swat it down.

"You got something you wanna say?" I ask the quarterback. "Say it, motherfucker."

"Easy, Best," the Tigers' coach says, but I ignore him.

"How do my seconds taste?" Callum grins. "God, she's good, isn't she—"

My hand connects to his face, right against the cheekbone. He drops his helmet with a thud. Recoiling, he rears back, but my fist smashes him again, this time in the mouth.

Every cell in my body wants to rip him apart. I lunge forward, seeing red, but feel hands on me, pushing me back. Callum gets farther away as a body physically comes between us.

"I'll fucking kill you!" I yell over top of the Tigers' coach separating us. "You hear me, cocksucker? I'll kill you."

Callum laughs, his eyes slits in his face. "Go home and fuck that little whore. Tell her I said 'hi.'"

In slow motion, Finn's hand comes over top of the coach and rocks Callum. Callum trips over his own feet, crashing into the grass.

All hell breaks loose and I try to break free and get to him again, but am pulled backwards. Our team lines up in front of me and Finn so we can't even see Callum anymore.

We're sucking in air, adrenaline still high and strong. I angle to see Worthington, but it's no use.

"What the fuck are you two thinking?" Coach is in our face out of nowhere, ready to blow a gasket. "What could have possibly happened in two fucking plays to cause that? Huh?"

"He deserved it, Coach," I say, still seething. "But if you put me back out there, I'll kill him. Just letting you know."

"You're out of here today. You too, Miller." He turns his attention, and disappointment, to Finn. "I almost expect this out of Best, but you? Pick your friends more carefully."

"Best is a fuck-up, sir, but he was right this time." Finn takes off his helmet, his hands pulling at the face guard.

"Gee, thanks," I say, shaking my head. "Can you cut me some fucking slack?"

"You impregnated my sister," Finn growls. "You want to do this here, Branch?"

"I don't want to do this anywhere. I want you to stop being a dick."

"Both of you!" Coach booms. "To the locker room and get off team property until tomorrow morning. You better come back with a better attitude, got it?"

"Yes, sir," I mutter, bumping Finn in the shoulder as I walk by.

I watch for Callum all the way to the locker room, but don't see him. My helmet goes sailing across the room, hitting a folding chair. The sound blasts against the lockers.

Falling onto the chair with my name on it in front of my locker, I put my head in my hands. My head pounds, my jaws aching from clenching my teeth so long.

Finn comes in, shoving his shit on the ground and dropping into his chair. He's across the room from me.

It's perfectly quiet, only the sound of our breathing breaking the peace. Once I've caught my breath and my blood pressure is somewhat stabilized, I look up. Finn does at the same time.

He tries to glare at me, but he fails miserably. At the same time, we start laughing. It begins as a slow chuckle and ends up with an all-out cackle.

"God, I want to kill him," Finn laughs, catching his breath. "That was a decent right hand you had there."

"Fuck him. Fuck that motherfucker."

"What did he say to you?"

"Want to go to jail?" I ask him, raising a brow. "Because if I tell you, you will. I'm the one getting that pleasure and when I do, someone needs to bail my ass out."

This silences my friend. He hangs his head. "I'm not sorry I hit you," Finn says. "But I'm sorry I did it as hard as I did."

"Nah," I say, standing up and taking off my shoulder pads. "If you hadn't given it all you had, I'd have called you a pussy."

"That wasn't all I had."

"The hell it wasn't," I taunt, grabbing my stuff for the showers. "But I get it. And I respect it."

He takes a deep breath and walks across the room, stopping a few feet in front of me. Extending a hand, I take it and we shake.

"Layla said you went with her to the doctor," he says.

"I did. It was amazing. I know what that sounds like, but I don't have any other way to explain it," I shrug. "I did that, you know? It's . . . incredible."

"I think it's nice you think it's incredible and I'm really glad you went with her."

"I told you I was going to be there for her." I force a swallow. "In all honesty, when I said that originally, I really meant the baby more than her. But now . . . I mean it. I want to be there for her, Finn. And I hope you understand what I mean by that."

He returns my smile. "Just be good to her, okay? Because if you don't, I'll show you just how much power I have in both hands."

Laughing, I head to the showers. "You aren't doing this just to get Poppy's pussy back, are you?"

"Not totally . . ."

We laugh again and there isn't any more to say. Things are getting back on track, even if my hand might be broken.

———

"LUCKY! WE HAVE A COUPLE of questions."

A reporter for *Exposé* is waiting by my car. I wonder vaguely how she got in the facility as security is pretty good at weeding out the media except in designated areas.

"I'm not really in the chatting mood," I say, hitting the unlock button.

"We were sure you'd want to set the record straight." The woman looks at me with a smug grin. "But if not . . ."

My blood cools in my veins, the hair on the back of my neck standing up. "Set it straight about what?"

"We know about your fight with Worthington, and Miller, for that matter—"

"Already?" I ask, opening the back door and tossing my bag in. "How does that shit get out so fast?"

"We have our ways."

"I guess." Closing the door, I lean against it. "So what am I commenting on?"

She's too excited to talk about this. I've been around enough to know if a reporter is giddy, that spells bad news for me.

"I really need to get going. I have something I need to do." Turning, my hand is on the handle when she speaks.

"We hope you work everything out. You've always been so good about talking to us, so to see someone do this to you . . ."

She wins.

"What are you talking about?" I ask.

"We were just told that Miller's sister is pinning a baby on you."

"What?" I bark. "Who the fuck told you that?"

"So it's not true?"

"No, it's not fucking true. No one is *pinning a baby* on me." Annoyed, I jerk open the driver's door.

"Callum said that's what the fight was about on the field," she says sweetly. "That she's pinning the baby on both of you, not sure whose it is, and that's what caused tempers to boil on the field today."

I watch her click the recorder in her hand through the reflection in the glass as my breathing gets shallow, my pulse strumming. I'm too shocked to even respond. My brain simply won't compute this.

All I can see is Layla's face and wonder what this will do to her. It's not true. There's no fucking doubt about that. But she's going to be humiliated to think people—Callum—are saying this.

"It has to be hard for Miller to be in the middle of this," she says. "I mean, you were his best friend. That has to be difficult, right?"

"What did Callum actually say?" I ask. "What were his exact words?"

She whips out her phone and logs onto the *Exposé* website. Front and center is a video with Callum front and center.

She presses play.

"It was really no big deal," Callum says, wiping his brow. "Just a little heated personalities over a girl in common." He listens to someone off camera and shrugs. "Yeah, I mean I was with her for a long time, up until a month or two ago. We were having a break, working things out, and then she apparently sleeps with Best. I had no idea, obviously, until today. I thought the baby was mine—at least, that's what she told me. I guess we'll wait and see."

"That's bullshit," I say, shoving her phone out of my face as I clamor to get to Layla.

"Is that your statement?"

Scowling, I climb in my car and stick the key in the ignition. "Yeah. That's my statement."

Barely getting the door closed, I peel out of the parking spot.

THIRTY
LAYLA

"HEY," I SAY, IMMEDIATELY STEPPING to the side. My nerves shoot to high alert as I take in the stress lines on Branch's face.

He marches by me, his forehead marred in an alarming way. His lips form a thin, angry line as he turns to face me.

"Branch, what's wrong?"

"Have you seen *Exposé*?"

"No," I gulp. "Why?"

I need to grab on to something to steady myself, but I'm too scared to even move. Frozen in place, I watch him slide his phone out of his pocket and cue something. He hands it to me.

My lungs fail to operate as I see not Branch, but Callum, on the screen. With a shaky finger, I press the triangle to play the video.

With every laugh, every line spoken, my emotions grow deeper. More confused. More infected with the poison of his actions.

I should deny this, I should be outraged, I should look at Branch and see what he's thinking. But I can't. I'm stuck in this state of disbelief that I can't even look up from the phone.

My mind keeps reeling that Callum is purposefully painting this picture of me. To the world. To everyone. To Branch.

Tearing my eyes away from the phone as the next video begins to play, I look into his handsome face.

"Branch . . ."

Some of the fury in his face is gone, but in its place is nothing better. There's a distance there, a wall similar to the one I saw the day I met him.

"This isn't true," I insist. "You surely don't believe this."

His response takes too long. It gives just enough time for all of my fears to break the shock of what just happened and send me into a nearly full-blown panic.

"This is bullshit," I say, my hands trembling. "This is complete bullshit."

"That's what I said."

That quells a touch of my anxiety, but not nearly enough. "You don't believe this, do you?"

Images I'd allowed myself to consider—holidays at the cabin, sitting in the stands and watching him play with our child, him holding the baby on his lap while they're both asleep—trickle through my brain, teasing me with the future.

Even if those things could be my reality, so would *this*. Headlines. Gossip. Me and my child being fair game.

"No, I don't believe it," he says. Blowing out a breath, he sticks his hands in his pockets. "I'm right not to believe it, right?"

"What? Are you seriously asking me that?"

He looks to the ceiling.

"If there's any part of you at all that believes that asshole, then I wouldn't want you anyway."

His head drops slowly, his gaze landing on mine. The Branch I know, the one I might even love, looks back at me.

"You know I don't believe any of this shit. It's not a question. I know you and you shouldn't want me." He laughs to himself, hanging his head.

"It's not you I don't want. It's *this*. I don't want this."

"I don't want to give you this, and I'm not just talking this ridiculous gossip," he says. "I see it in your eyes. It's the start of the hatred, the ruination of your world. You were right. You deserve so much better than this."

"Branch . . ." I say, tears rolling off my lips.

"You don't think things like this are going to keep happening? They're saying you're a whore, Sunshine. That you don't know whose baby this is."

The vein in the side of his temple pulses like he's ready to blow a gasket.

"What will it be next?" he asks. "What will they have me doing next?

What situation will I be next to in a hotel in some other city and all of a sudden, because of the life I've led, I'm lumped in with those things? What will you think then?"

I don't answer because I don't know how. He's right. As much as it feels like a punch in the gut, he's right.

"Maybe this is a warning shot for you to not fuck up your life with me," he says quietly. "My life is a weapon half-cocked. It's a game of Russian Roulette with me."

"Do you really think that?"

"It was you that thought it. Now I see it. I can't control anything in my life and you want to control it all. You want a plan, to know what's happening when, and I have a life that changes by the minute sometimes. And I can't really keep you separate from that because . . . eighty percent."

His face is blurred through the tears filling my eyes. My hand goes to the little cross at the end of his necklace that's tucked under my shirt. Even if I could find the words to argue with him, there's no point. You can't argue the truth.

"I can't do this to you," he says, brushing his thumb along my jaw. I lean against his hand, feeling the warmth touch my cheek. "Especially when this is the one thing you don't want and the one thing that should never happen to a girl like you."

"So, what are you going to do?" I ask meekly through the tears, shocked that I'm holding it together this well. That works just fine until I see the blues of his eyes cloud too. That does it. The dam breaks and my cheeks are soaked.

In one swift move, he pulls me into his chest. Smelling like soap and cedar, he presses my face so hard into him that I couldn't pull away if I wanted to. I wrap my arms around his waist, feeling him against me.

"I will always be here for you. And," he gulps, his voice wobbling slightly, "I'm proud to have a baby with you. But I can't do this to you, force you to live this life I chose. You and our child deserve way better than this fucked up life."

Despite the tenor of our conversation, even with the splintering of my heart, I've never felt more safe in my life. I've never felt more considered. More *loved*.

Callum would've never walked away from me for my own good. Everything in his world centers around him, even if it means trying to ruin my life for fun.

"I'm sorry they're making you out to look like an idiot," I whisper, feeling the warmth of his skin under my palms.

"I don't give a fuck."

"But they're saying—"

"I don't care." He pulls away and looks me in the eye. "I know you. I know this baby is mine. I just can't do this to you, Sunshine."

"You aren't. *He* is," I assert.

"This time. Next time, God knows what it will be. But I guarantee you there will be a next time in the tabloids, of nasty things said because I'm *Branch Best.*"

He says it like it's a bad thing, almost spitting the words out like they're poison.

Brushing a strand of hair out of my face, he places a kiss to the center of my lips. "I'm a call away. Always."

His hand drops to my stomach and it sits there for a long moment. As his eyes blur again, he looks down and walks out.

⸺

"WHERE THE HELL ARE YOUUU . . ." Poppy's voice falls as she finds me on my bed. "Layla! What's wrong?"

Bags drop to the floor, the plastic rustling as it lands just before my mattress sinks as she lands near me. She shoves me over and hovers over my face. "Are you okay?"

The light is too bright. Her voice too loud. The smell of the garlic she had for lunch too strong.

"I'm gonna puke," I groan, trying to sit up.

Everything hurts, from my heart to my head, as I work my way against the pillows. The sky is almost dark outside the windows and I wonder how long I've been lying here.

As I try to do the math, all I can see is Branch's sweet face and the tears come again. This round, they feel like little knives in the side of my temple, stabbing me over and over again.

"Layla. Talk to me." Poppy takes my hands and holds them on my lap. "What happened? You wouldn't answer the phone so I came by to check . . ."

"Have you seen *Exposé?*" I croak, my throat so damn dry due to all the moisture in my body leaving via tears.

She flashes me a look. Swiping my phone off the nightstand, she types in the passcode and brings up the website. I give her a few seconds to make it all the way through. I know when she's done because the phone drops to the bed.

"Oh my God," she says, her mouth wide. "Layla."

"I know." Grabbing a pillow, I smudge it around my face in hopes that some of the wetness will stop. "It's a mess."

"Branch doesn't believe this, right?"

"No."

"Thank God," she says, falling back on the bed. "I knew he was smart."

"So smart he left me."

The words are hiccupped, tears filling each opening, and my heart starts the process of breaking again.

"I don't know why I'm so upset. I knew this would happen eventually. But," I shrug, "it's what I get for going against my gut."

"What did he say?"

"He said he won't put the baby and I through this shit. He was so sweet . . ." Pressing my face against the pillow, I cry until I can't cry anymore. My chest burns, my face twinges with the strains from crying all evening. "Why? Why couldn't he be a dick?"

My phone glows, the ringer turned off, and Poppy picks it up. The fire in her eyes when she looks at me has me plucking it from her hand before she can do any damage.

I see the name on the screen. "You have the audacity to call me?" I almost shout into the phone. "How dare you, you sick fuck?"

Callum's laugh belts through the line. "I'm good, thank you. How are you?"

"I'm much better than you because I'm not a miserable, disgusting human being."

"So you aren't that upset? I mean, thank fuck it's not my kid, but I thought Best deserved it after that little stunt he pulled, answering your fucking phone."

"How did you even know I was pregnant?" I seethe, my hands shaking with the anger rolling through me.

"Someone snapped your picture coming out of the doctor's office. It's online, sweetheart."

"Don't call me that," I snap. *"I hate you."*

"I bet you do. I bet your boy does too." He laughs again, an unaffected, carefree laugh. "I'll remember that when you come back to me with his bastard child, wanting me to take you back."

"I wouldn't take you back if someone gave me the entire world to do it."

Like it's in slow motion, Branch's face spirals through my mind. A need seated deep inside me to hold him, hug him, *love him* burns as hot as a wildfire.

"As a matter of fact," I swallow, "someone practically gave me the entire world not to."

"Ah, isn't that sweet? I love how you just pretend you don't love me."

The smile that touches my lips is genuine. "I didn't love you," I say simply. "I didn't know what love was when I was with you."

Poppy's eyes grow wide, her hand resting on my leg. She gives me a thumbs-up.

"Callum, go to hell."

My phone goes sailing across the bed and I fall back into the pillows again.

"What now?" Poppy asks. "I mean, I have a plan if you want it because I looked those grapes up and—"

"Stop." I flash her a look and try not to grin. "There's no plan to be made."

"What do you mean? You want him. You just said you loved him without saying it. Of course there's a plan to be made!"

I shake my head. "This doesn't change anything, Pop. Now he just knows what I already knew: our lives are not compatible."

Tears well up again. "I had hoped maybe . . . Um, maybe we could figure a way around it and we . . ."

She leans forward and hugs me, letting me cry on her shoulder.

"I love him, Poppy. I think I actually fell in love with Branch Best and now it's too late."

THIRTY-ONE
BRANCH

"THIS IS WHAT I GET." I say the words aloud, as if somehow hearing them will make me accept them. "You've gone your whole adult life knowing this would happen, yet you still got caught up."

My legs dangle off the countertop as I sit in the kitchen, smack dab in the middle of the island. Every now and then, the soles of my feet kick against the wooden cabinets and remind me I'm *still* sitting here. In the same place. For a couple of hours now. My ass is starting to hurt.

I've never sat and watched the sun move across the sky until tonight. It's pretty cool. The colors change from blue to purple and pink and even a fiery orange for a moment. Shadows change, birds stop flying—it's pretty incredible. You can also get kind of philosophical watching that shit.

Pondering where my life would sit if I were comparing it to a setting sun, I have to go with the tail end of the colored phase. Layla is, without a doubt, the brightest, most organic thing that's ever happened to me. She's lit my life with the most basic things, the most ordinary things, just like the colors a few moments ago reflecting off the kitchen windows. It's things like candy apples and stupid jokes and private grins that I've never found anywhere else and can't imagine ever sharing with anyone else either.

I've always thought if I ever found love, it would come in some big lightning strike. That some massive crack of thunder would happen and light would shine down from the heavens with a little arrow saying, "This is the one for you."

Now I know, it doesn't work that way.

Finding love happens at Water Festivals with sugar rushes. It happens in little deli shops over ham and cheese sandwiches. It happens on beaches with stories about grandmas and really listening to each other and making an attempt to understand the other person.

It's choosing to be together because you don't have to be. It's walking away when you can't be together for their own good, no matter how much it kills you.

This is heartache. This is the thing those Beau McCrae songs are talking about, the ones I love the beats to and got stuck in my head but had no way of identifying with the lyrics.

I get it. I get it all, and it hurts like a motherfucker.

A knock pounds on the door as I lift a bottle of Jameson to my lips. "Come in," I shout, taking a long swallow of the liquor.

The door opens and shuts, and I don't even bother to turn around to see who it is.

"You aren't even locking your doors now? What the hell happened while I was pissed at you?" Finn's voice rings through the room. His footsteps grow closer as I take another drink.

"I figured I'd leave it unlocked. Maybe someone will make my day."

"That sounds like a Clint Eastwood reference."

I shrug.

He strolls into the kitchen. His posture is tight, his eyes curious as he takes me in. "What the fuck happened to you?"

"Just life, man. Just life."

"I saw the *Exposé* thing, if that's what you're talking about. Callum is a dead motherfucker."

"I was sitting here plotting his demise."

A smile begins to form on his lips, but doesn't quite stretch. "How'd Layla take it? She won't answer my calls."

"She won't take mine either." I take another swig, the burn a nice distraction from the rest of the pain.

He leans against the sink, arms crossed in front of him. "You don't believe that, right?"

"Nope."

"Then what's the problem?"

The door opens again, and this time, I look back. Poppy storms in, taking in Finn and I. "Hey, it was open. You don't want me coming in, close the damn door."

"Pop—" Finn starts, standing straight up.

"And you," she says, pointing a finger at him, "can shut the fuck up."

"You two *still* aren't talking?" I say, looking from one to the other.

"He hasn't apologized."

"Poppy . . ." Finn all but whines. He's desperate, and if he's fighting it, it's a sad, sad attempt. "Let's talk."

"I'm here to talk to Branch."

"Can we talk after?"

"That is totally up to whether you want to be a man or not," she shrugs, blowing him off. She turns to me. "What the hell are you doing?"

"I don't know what you're talking about."

"I just left Layla's," she says, a hand on her hip. "And she said you left her."

"You did fucking what?" Finn booms.

"Here we go again." Poppy blows out a breath. "I'm going to give you a field goal for being hugely gentlemanly about this, something Finn could take a lesson from. But I'm taking away a touchdown because you're *stupid*."

"You left my sister?" Finn asks again, trying to catch up. "I'm not following along."

"Then stop interrupting and listen," Poppy advises.

"I was here first. You technically interrupted me," he fires back.

"Both of you," I say, slamming the Jameson on the counter. "Stop it. Fuck it out later, but I can't listen to it."

My head falls into my hands. Poppy rests her palm against my back, a gesture that's well-meaning but feels wrong.

"I can't do this to her," I say, my words muffled. "We've talked about this before, Finn. This is why you and I fucked around. This is why we didn't try to go the normal route with life because it's not possible in this industry. Damn it."

"I think you're wrong," Poppy offers. "I think you're using an excuse because you're afraid."

"Afraid?" I laugh. "I'm afraid I'll never find someone like her again. I'm terrified I'll mess this up with her and it'll hurt our child. But afraid of loving her? As wild as it sounds, I'm not."

"Then go for it," she insists. "Stop being a baby."

"And soil her life with mine? Look at what's happened. The kid isn't even born yet and the media has presented it to be a bastard child," I say, gritting my teeth. "I'll be the same shit, different day tomorrow."

Looking up, I see Finn watching Poppy. There's a quiet confusion in his features. "Maybe you have to take some risks."

He's talking about me, but not to me. Those words were aimed right over my head to the little raven-haired sass that's removing her hand from my back.

"Maybe things wouldn't have worked out before," Finn continues. "Sometimes we have to sort of get to the right spot, with the right person, to see the alternate routes that we couldn't see before."

Finn cocks his head to the side. "You left her because you wanted to protect her?"

"Yeah."

"Then I'm taking away a touchdown and a safety for being a pussy."

"What?" I say, scooting off the counter. "This will ruin her."

"No, you not being with her will ruin her. All this shit? Did you forget how strong she is?" He looks at Poppy again. "I forgot, until someone reminded me."

"That's super sweet," Poppy teases, "but I'm gonna need an apology."

"I'm sorry, baby."

She squeals, running towards him and wrapping her legs around his waist. "That took you long enough."

"You're so damn hard-headed."

"Hey!" I say, shaking my head. "Can this be about me for like ten seconds? I don't know what to do."

"Strong women create new challenges and we're gonna have to draw some new plays, Branch," Finn says.

"That's your plan? That's all you got? This is your sister, one you've already punched me in the face—twice—over and you tell me to draw new plays? Can you at least, like, tell me to leave her alone or something?"

LUCKY NUMBER ELEVEN 215

Finn kisses Poppy, and then, only reluctantly, does he pull his gaze away to me. "I always do what's best for Layla."

"I know."

He grins. "So go get her, asshole."

"But . . ."

"If you'd walk away from her to make her happy, that tells me you'd literally do anything to keep a smile on her face. So you go and do that while I use your guest bedroom to get reacquainted with my girl."

As they walk out of the room, Poppy throws her head back and looks at me upside-down. "Make it good. Go get her and don't give her another option but to say yes."

To say yes . . .

I grab my keys and head to my car. The key in the ignition, I head out of my subdivision and onto the highway. Nowhere to go, no one to see, I just need space and fresh air before I do something really stupid.

Like the universe is playing some kind of game, everywhere I look, I see happy couples. Couples with children. Families skipping down the sidewalk. They're everywhere, like it's some kind of family day out.

As I stop at a light, I notice a little girl. She's holding her father's hand. Hair as blonde as the sun is pulled into two little pigtails with pink ribbons on each side. She looks up and smiles like she knows me, like she's trying to tell me something. It's eerie as hell.

The light changes to green and I hit the accelerator hard, my heart strumming wildly in my chest.

Part of my predicament is clear: I can't half-ass it with Layla. It's all or nothing, one way or the other. It needs to be nothing because that makes sense. It's logical. It's safe. But as I turn the corner, my tires screeching against asphalt in a totally not-safe fashion, I realize my mistake.

Sometimes that play that wins the game isn't the safe one. It's not the pass over the middle that will definitely get you ten yards. It's the Hail Mary at the end that you toss up with nothing but a prayer.

THIRTY-TWO
LAYLA

EXPOSÉ TOP STORY:
BEST A BABY DADDY?

W E CAUGHT UP with embattled Branch Best last night at the Hopetown Mall. The charismatic (and sexy as hell) wide receiver had a little something to say about recent headlines surrounding him.

Turns out Branch is going to be a father with Finn Miller's sister, Layla James. According to Branch, Callum's statement was nothing more than an attempt to make Layla look bad in a bout of jealousy. Branch insists this is a non-issue.

When asked if this means he's off the market, our favorite hottie said, and we quote, "I'm going to be the best father I can be in every way."

We don't know what that means, exactly, but we can't wait for our ovaries to explode with pictures of him with a baby.

TOYING WITH THE NECKLACE AROUND my neck, I peer into the refrigerator. There's nothing in there that looks good. Of course, the box of food delivered earlier today from Branch's delivery service is in there, but I moved it to the back and created a wall with milk, juice, bacon, and a very creatively positioned tub of Greek yogurt so I don't have to see it.

Sure, it would've been easier to throw it away. But I can't do that either. I like having it in there. I'll probably even eat it later. But every time I see it right now it makes me sad.

I've been sad for two days now, ever since he left. He's called a few times and I've sent them to voicemail because there's nothing to say. Anything he does say will make me cry and I'm not going to cry. I'm going to find Layla James, the one pre-Branch, pre-baby, pre- . . . love. I'm going to stop with this weak girl nonsense.

The necklace twirls in my fingers as I look at the Exposé article again. He looks so calm in the photo, wearing a light blue shirt that makes his eyes look unreal. Still, there's something missing in them. The light, the sparkle, the mischief is gone, and it kills me.

I miss him. I miss him and his jokes, touches, and caring glances so much it physically hurts. It's only not having him around that makes me realize how much having him around means to me. How wonderful it makes me feel. How awful it is right now.

Grabbing my purse off the sofa, I head to the front door. I have to eat and I need fresh air, so I take out my phone to call Poppy to meet me for lunch. I pull open the door and almost run into someone.

"Oh!" I say, taking a step back. "I'm sorry."

She's tall, with long, red hair that's pulled back into a chic chignon. Her dress is black and long with two gold necklaces hanging fashionably between her breasts. "No worries. Probably my fault. I'm standing on your doorstep, right?" she laughs.

"Um, sure. Can I help you?"

"Forgive me," she gushes, moving a clipboard to her left hand. "I'm Daisy Markus. Are you Layla Miller?"

"I am."

"Oh, good," she says. "I've been trying to get ahold of you since yesterday. Do you mind if I come in? I really need to talk to you."

With a puzzled laugh, I block the door. "I apologize, but I have no idea who you are or why you'd be trying to get ahold of me."

"Oh, I assumed you knew." She takes a piece of paper from the clipboard with a flourish and hands it to me. "You've been listed as the main point of contact for the Best project."

"The what?"

Skimming the paper, I step back into the apartment and Daisy follows with a wide smile.

My name is there, right where she said it would be, with Branch's above it. There are measurements and dollar amounts and paint chips in both grey and yellow paper clipped to the top.

The paper rattles as I drop it to my side and look at her.

My mouth is lined with cotton, my breathing shallow. I pull the paper up and look at it again.

"We have a four-month window to get this complete," she says, "and with the extensive updates, we need to get started."

"I'm sorry," I laugh, trying to make sense of all this. "What's going on?"

"Mr. Best hired my firm to redesign his home. He said everything would be changed to your specifications and billed to him. He's given you complete creative control with every avenue except one."

"What's that?" I ask, choking back tears.

"The nursery." Her voice softens as she hands me a tissue. "He asked that he gets to pick between the grey and the yellow. I think that's so sweet."

My legs give out and I fall to the sofa, and despite the terrible manners, I cry in front of this woman. I don't even offer her a seat, but I figure she gets the point because she sits across from me anyway.

"He also asked, strangely, for candy-apple red sheets in the master," she notes.

My head snaps to hers, and instantly, I laugh. It's a full-bellied, this-isn't-as-funny-as-I'm-making-it-out-to-be-but-it-feels-so-damn-good kind of laugh.

She must think I'm a lunatic because she laughs too, more of a what-the-hell-have-I-gotten-myself-into kind of chuckle.

Why would he do this? Why would he put me in charge of something like this? I feel like I can't breathe, like things are coming at me too fast and I can't keep up.

I press his number on my phone, but it goes straight to voicemail.

Just hearing his voice on the message makes me smile.

"I have no idea what's happening," I say. "I can't accept this task without talking to someone first."

She stands, a sweet grin on her face. "There's an incredibly handsome man standing outside your door."

"What?"

"Branch is in the hall. He said he wasn't sure if you'd throw me out, but he really hoped you'd want to see him."

She's still talking as I fly by her and jerk open the door. Sure enough, he's leaning against the wall, one foot crossed over the other.

"You let her in. That has to be a good sign, right?" he winces.

"What is all this?" I ask, forcing my legs not to move my body to him. I want to touch him, kiss him, breathe him in, but I can't. Not yet.

He tries to explain, but all I can do is look at him and hear my thousand questions in my own head.

"Did you hear any of that?" he laughs, pressing off the wall.

"No."

He chuckles, reaching for my hand. "Daisy, if all goes right, she'll call you tomorrow."

"Give her my number, please." She turns her attention to me. "It was nice meeting you, Layla."

"You too."

"And whatever he's done, give him another chance. He's so cute," she winks.

We step inside and Branch locks the doors. "Your brother and Poppy have this new thing where they just walk into people's houses. It's really uncomfortable."

I watch him fiddle with the lock. It broke last week and it's hard to snap. When he finally gets it, he turns to me. "God, I've missed you."

"I've missed you too."

"I'm not doing this again," he tells me, walking into the place like he owns it. He goes to the fridge and does an inventory. "Have you been eating?"

I stand in the same spot, brows pulled together. "What?"

"Have. You. Been. Eating?" He casts me an annoyed glance before going back to moving things around in my fridge. "What did you have for breakfast today?"

"I haven't."

The door snaps closed. "Really, Layla?"

"I'm sad."

"Get your shit."

"What?" I ask again, a hand on my hip. "You're coming in my house and ordering me around after you just left me days ago? Slow down there, buddy."

He grumbles, but must sense how serious I am and doesn't object. Instead, he marches to the couch and sits. "Fine. Fire away. Let's get this ironed out so we're both clear as to where we stand."

"I think we're clear now."

"I think we're clear, just one of us is still fighting it. And that one of us isn't me," he grins.

My hand trembles as I reach for the armrest of the chair by the island. Sinking into it, I try to keep my voice even. "We were on the same page a couple of days ago."

"Then I wised up." He laces his fingers together and looks patiently at me. "Go. What do you want to hash out? Let's hear it."

"Why are you here?"

"To get you to move in with me."

Thankfully, I'm already sitting or I think I'd have fallen over. "Move in with you? Branch. Really?"

"This thing between us has always been there and will always be there. I think I realized it when I heard the baby's heartbeat," he says softly. "But I knew it so strongly when Callum said that shit that I got scared. It was the first time I've ever felt that kind of loyalty to a woman. I knew that wasn't true. I didn't even think twice and that was a little unnerving."

"I can imagine. You've been quite the player."

"I have been. No doubt. I've been the best, actually."

Rolling my eyes, I sigh. "Only you would take pride in that."

"Now," he insists, "I'm taking pride in being your man. If you'll have me."

My eyes fill with tears as I watch his face wash with sincerity. "What about away games? And the media?"

"Fine. Let's say we stay apart from each other because of the fucking media. Is that the golden ticket? Is that going to get them to stop printing ridiculous stories and listening to assholes spewing garbage?"

I just look at him.

"We're together, whether you want to realize that or not. Our lives will always be entwined, our stories overlapping in one way or the other. What I do will affect you and what you do will affect me."

He shrugs. "Staying apart isn't going to fix anything. You're still going to wonder about road trips and I'm still going to want to break what's-his-face for being here."

"Max?" I giggle.

"Yeah. Max. I hate him." He steps back and grumbles. "Our problems aren't going away and neither are our fears. But I'd much rather deal with them together, where we can communicate and know what's happening and have each other, than not."

"What about the eighty percent?"

"There's still twenty percent who make it. The smart twenty, the twenty who have something so good at home they don't want to risk it. And you, Sunshine, are so worth it."

I feel my walls giving in, his charm wearing me down. My brain says to be careful. My heart says to jump in head first. My gut, though, has a different reaction.

It's my gut that says to give it a try, that it might not work but it's worth seeing.

He's always been honest with me, even when it was hard. When he's been wrong, he's apologized. And when he faced ridicule in the media about the baby, he trusted me.

As I look at his handsome face and the way his foot taps against the floor and he chews his bottom lip, I listen to my gut. Because my gut's always right.

"What if it doesn't work?" I ask.

"Then we can say we tried. I don't know how to manage it all, but I want a family with you," he whispers. "A real one. The holidays at the cabin and Christmas cards and a dog named Snickers."

"Snickers?"

"Or Caramello. Whatever," he whispers, reaching for my hand.

I place my palm in his and he pulls me to my feet.

"I want us in the same house," he says, walking towards me, "figuring everything out together, eating coffee cake at midnight."

"Promise?"

"I promise to love you and the baby and do everything I can for you."

"No, I meant about the coffee cake."

He picks me up, making me laugh, as he swings my legs over his arms. "You are going to be the death of me."

EPILOGUE
LAYLA

NINE MONTHS LATER

THE FLOOR CREAKS AS I tiptoe down the staircase. Sunny has been asleep for a half an hour and there's no way in hell I'm waking her up.

She's a beautiful little girl with blonde hair like me and the bluest eyes like her daddy. She came into the world as calm as a dove. The nurses tickled her feet to make her cry so her lungs would dry out after the C-Section.

Her biggest issue so far, besides her refusal to breast feed, is her daddy. He holds her nearly every moment she's awake when he's home. He sanitizes every bottle and nipple she might come into contact with and she already has two battery-operated vehicles waiting for her in the garage that she can use when she masters things like sitting up and walking.

It's the sweetest thing I've ever witnessed. As good as he is to her, he's just as good to me.

Things with him are easy. Yes, they require work, but it's not hard to love Branch Best. He's kind and thoughtful and brings me flowers and ice cream and leaves me notes on the dry erase board on the fridge when he leaves for work every morning.

He's everything I never dreamed he'd be. Plus more.

After getting Sunny back to sleep, I laid her in her bed and took a bath. Branch has to work in the morning, so he'll be up in just a few hours. I want to make sure his juices are restocked in the fridge so he has a cold one to drink before he leaves.

Turning the corner, I stop.

My first instinct is to be annoyed, but that drifts away at the pure love before me.

Branch stands in the kitchen with just his boxers on, Sunny nestled in the crook of his arm, as he heats up a bottle. He's whispering something to her, the soft tone of his voice making me melt. He has a way of doing that. A lot.

"Hey," I say, padding into the room. "I hate to interrupt this love fest, but why isn't she in bed?"

"She wanted to get up with Daddy."

"Oh, she did, did she? Doesn't she know Daddy needs some rest before practice tomorrow?" I say, leaning in for a kiss.

"She does. But she wanted to be awake when Mommy came down for coffee cake."

Laughing, my cheeks pink. "How did she know Mommy would do that?"

"Because Daddy told her." He leans in, pulling Sunny away. "I didn't tell her what's going to happen to Mommy when she goes back to bed though."

He touches my lips with his, the softness of his mouth making me moan. That just encourages him. His tongue parts my lips and slips through my mouth with a laziness that has my thighs clenching together.

"Is that a hint of what's to come?" I ask, catching my breath.

"Yes, my lady. You're going to come."

With a grin that's a permanent fixture lately, I grab a fork. Under his smirk, I lift the lid to the coffee cake.

"You were right," I sigh, pulling it in front of me. "I'm so going to—OMG. Branch?"

The fork hits the floor, the little ping startling Sunny. Branch ignores me and soothes her until she settles against him once more.

My heart is racing, my gaze going from the dessert and back to him again. Surely, I'm seeing this wrong. I have to be.

"Branch?" I gulp. "What is this?"

His eyes glued to mine, he reaches in the middle of the cream cheese icing and plucks the diamond ring out.

"I wasn't sure how to do this," he says, an edge of anxiety in his tone. "I didn't know where to put it so I'd be sure you found it and I didn't have time with my schedule to take you anywhere. Plus, Sunny really wanted to be around for this."

"Did she?" I say, blinking back tears.

"She did." He kisses her forehead while watching me. "You've given me everything in life that means anything. I don't just mean Sunny, but of course she's the main thing. You've given me a reason to get up, a reason to go to bed, a reason to come home."

He takes my finger and slips the ring over it, the icing smearing down my hand.

"I can't control where I play or how long I play, but that's okay. I can control what's important . . . and that's this team right here." He gets down on one knee, our daughter still cuddled against his wide chest. "I promise to love you and cherish you and to try to get hotter as I get older like Sam Elliott."

I laugh through the tears that well in my eyes.

"Layla James, will you make me the luckiest man in the world and be my wife?"

There's no nerves, no wobble, no panic. There's nothing but complete and absolute certainty that this is what I want and where I need to be.

I take his face in my hands, feeling the coarseness from his stubble against my hands. "Yes. You know I will."

He stands, pulling me into his other side. He kisses my cheek, fixing little pecks reverently until he hits my mouth.

The fire, the passion, that initially brought us together, is hotter than ever. He pulls away, resting his forehead against mine.

"I promise to be patient," I tell him, "and to try not to worry about everything. I'll give you the benefit of the doubt and be the best damn cheerleader you've ever seen."

"I know you will." He kisses me again, lacing our fingers together. "I'm putting love bug to bed and then I'm making love to you in ours. Deal?"

I nod, watching him head out of the kitchen.

"Hey, Branch?" I say.

"Yeah?"

"I didn't think you believed in luck?"

He gives me a little grin. "I don't deserve this and there's no way I worked for it. So, I don't know. Maybe I do."

EXPOSÉ TOP STORY:
WE'RE NOT CRYING. YOU'RE CRYING.

O UR FAVORITE COUPLE, *Branch Best and Layla Miller, tied the knot this past weekend in tiny Linton, Illinois. Sources say Layla carried their daughter, Sunny, down the aisle at her family's lake house.*

Finn Miller was the best man and sources say he may or may not have swam nude in the lake afterwards. We're still waiting on pictures. (God, let there be pictures.)

We would like to wish Mr. and Mrs. Best a big, heartfelt congratulations. May this be your lucky ever after.

The End

LUCKY NUMBER ELEVEN is just one of six scandalous romances from Best Selling Authors.

Read all about it in Expose, the gossip column to sink your teeth into.

Each story in the Expose Collection is a STANDALONE. See them all here: *http://bit.ly/ExposeLanding*

ABOUT THE AUTHOR

USA TODAY AND AMAZON TOP 10 Bestselling author Adriana Locke lives and breathes books. After years of slightly obsessive relationships with the flawed bad boys created by other authors, Adriana has created her own.

She resides in the Midwest with her husband, sons, and two dogs. She spends a large amount of time playing with her kids, drinking coffee, and cooking. You can find her outside if the weather's nice and there's always a piece of candy in her pocket.

Contact Adriana

Adriana can be found on all social media platforms. Look for her on the ones you frequent most!

Her website is the place to go for up-to-date information, deleted scenes, and more. Check it out at *www.adrianalocke.com*. Don't forget to sign up for her newsletter, sent monthly, filled with news, pictures, fun and giveaways.

If you use Facebook or Goodreads, there's good news! Adriana has reader groups in both places. Join Books by Adriana Locke (Facebook) and All Locked Up (Goodreads) and chat with the author daily about all things bookish.

ACKNOWLEDGEMENTS

FIRST, I'D LIKE TO THANK my Creator for life, love, and listening.

Life is a funny thing. We're constantly trying to balance what we want to do with what we need to do. Rarely are those things the same. I'd like to thank my family for understanding that and for being so patient while I manage both sides of the coin.

Sending big hugs to Mom, Peggy, and Rob for their support and enthusiasm of my work. You are loved.

Another book with my amazing team. Kari (Kari March Designs), Lisa (Adept Edits), Christine (Type A Formatting), Kylie (Give Me Books) and Red Coat PR—thank you for working with me. You are the best in the business.

Huge thanks to my assistant, Tiffany. Thank you for keeping me organized and in check.

Susan and Jen are still with me all this time. I don't know what I did to have you two as friends, but I'm forever grateful.

My betas rock. You know who you are. Thank you for your loyalty and energy and time. You made this book so much better.

Oh, Carleen. There aren't words, my friend. (Even though you can't squee.) I'm convinced we share the same brain in so many ways. Thank you for . . . everything.

Kara saved my life. Thank you so much for stepping in and helping a girl out. I appreciate you!

Thank you to Ebbie for managing the FitBit Challenge in Books by Adriana Locke, Jade for helping to manage All Locked Up on Goodreads, and Deva for spearheading our Locke Fantasy Football League. You guys are sincerely the best!

We made it, Mandi Beck. (Now to send Lisa something nice.)

Thank you, readers, for taking a chance on Lucky Number Eleven. I know how many choices you have. Thank you for choosing this.

Dear bloggers, what would we do without you? You are so appreciated.

And last but not least, thank you to Dawson, who helped inspire a line in this book.

Dear Reader,

I hope you've enjoy LUCKY NUMBER ELEVEN. It's been a labor of love—football and books. Two of my favorite things!

If you would, please consider leaving a short review when finished. It would be greatly appreciated.

Coming up next is an angst-filled standalone titled More Than I Could, as well as the start to a brand new family series, The Gibson Boys. If you'd like an email from me when it's live, feel free to let me know here: http://bit.ly/AmazonAlertAddy

Thank you very much for reading through to The End. I appreciate you.

~Adriana